Contract Bride

Ayn Amorelli

ISBN 978-1-936556-01-4

Published 2006 Republished 2015
Published by Black Velvet Seductions Publishing

Contract Bride Copyright 2006 Ayn Amorelli
Cover design Copyright 2015 R. J. Savage

Published 2015
Printed by Black Velvet Seductions Publishing
A division of Savage Publications

Visit us at:
www.blackvelvetseductions.com

Chapter One

"What type of girl are you looking for, old buddy?" asked George, neatly stacking numerous invoices for his topless maid agency at his large gray metal desk. "Maybe I can help."

"You're going to think I'm nuts," Bob murmured, crossing his legs Indian style, as he took a sip of tepid coffee from his paper cup. Hell, maybe he was crazy. But he was also desperate.

Spreading the twenty color photographs of nude blondes, brunettes, and redheads on the floor around him, Bob adjusted his wire-rim glasses as he studied them. All the girls were seductively posed, standing with one shapely hip jutting out and one knee slightly bent. They ranged in age from the mid-twenties to the mid-thirties, and all were pretty and sexy with big, firm, thrusting breasts, shiny nipples, small waists and slender hips. Hell, he got hard just looking at them. If he could afford it, he would try every one. But not only didn't he have the cash, he was short on time. He'd been racking his brain ever since his late aunt's lawyers had called him a week ago. He'd finally devised a plan that just, as insane as it was, might work.

"So? That's never stopped you before. I know whatever it is, is damn important for you to get out this early on a Saturday. So spill it. What gives?"

"You've got to keep what I tell you confidential."

"Oh, shit!" moaned George, stiffening. "I hate cloak and dagger stuff. I'm sorry I asked now."

"Too late. I've got to tell someone."

"Damn!" muttered George.

"But you've got to—"

"I know. I've got to keep it confidential. So what is it? You in trouble with the Feds...or is it drugs? Is that it?"

"Nothing as exotic as that," Bob whispered, glancing around

suspiciously, "but it wouldn't do for what I'm about to tell you to get out. If the wrong people heard about it, they might misunderstand."

"Hold it! Can I go to jail if I know what it is you're up to?" George asked, pushing aside the pile of invoices, as he studied his old friend.

"To be honest, I'm not sure. I don't think so, but then I'm not a lawyer and I haven't got time for you to consult one. I've got a little legal matter that has to be settled by the end of the year. But in order to do that I need to get started implementing my plan right away."

"How little?"

"How little what?"

George ground his teeth. "How little is the legal matter? Are we talking about a 'you'll go to prison if you're wrong' legal matter, or a 'jail-time' legal matter?" "Neither. I'm....oh, shit!" grumbled Bob, taking a swig of his stale coffee; stalling for time, trying to figure out how to best tell his friend without sounding insane. "What I need is a woman who's sexy and attractive enough for me to screw as much as necessary to knock her up right away. She *has* to deliver by the end of the year. But she can't be cheap-looking. She has to look and act enough like a lady to be my wife and the mother of my child. She has to be able to pass the inspection of some old geezer legal types."

George looked blankly at him. "You're pulling my leg, right?" He laughed loudly, shaking his head. "Got to hand it to you, though. You had me going there for a while. I thought for sure you were serious."

"Do I look like I'm pulling a prank? I've never been more serious about anything in my life. A lot of money is riding on this. I've got to find a nice-looking girl who's willing to marry me temporarily, have my kid by the end of the year, and give me a divorce after the kid's born."

"Let me see if I've got this right. You've got to have a kid, correct? One who's born this year?"

"I need a wife too, George. I've got to look like I'm a stable family man."

"Because?"

"I'm in my late aunt's will. I don't get the dough unless I meet her terms."

"How much dough are we talking about here?"

"Does it matter?"

"Hell, yes. If we're talking below a hundred, you can take care of the matter yourself. But if we're talking about an amount large enough for you to generously pay your friend several hundred for his help, then I'll do what I can."

Sipping his coffee, Bob kept his face bland. There was no way in hell he'd tell George about the whole twenty million bucks. As much as he liked the guy, George had a strong tendency to be greedy. He'd never passed up the opportunity to make a fast buck, even off his friends. "Let me put it this way, I'd be willing to pay you a generous finder's fee if you can steer me toward a woman who meets my requirements."

"How generous?"

"One, maybe two, three hundred."

"Too bad. My definition of generous is seven hundred."

"That's highway robbery. I'll give you five."

"Six."

"Either you know someone or you don't, and all I need is her name. Five. That's my final offer."

"Five-fifty?"

Bob shrugged. "Doable. But for that, you'll have to help me set something up with her. I'm not going to pay you until I decide she's the one, and she accepts my offer."

George studied him speculatively. "That's fair," he grinned maliciously, suppressing his welling laughter. "I accept cashier's checks or cash."

"What?"

"You heard me. Cashier's checks or cash."

Bob went rigid. "Are you out of your mind? I'm your friend, dammit! You think I'd stiff you with a bum check? Hell, man, you know where I live! I'm not stupid."

"I didn't say you were. But I never take chances with money."

Bob muttered a curse under his breath, then held out his hand. "Deal."

"What does this fantasy woman of yours have to look like?"

"She has to be sexy and attractive, of course. And the way I see it, she'll have to be someone who needs money badly enough to go along with my plan. But she can't look needy. She's got to be a sharp dresser with a flair for style. She has to speak well and think fast on her feet. But...you know how easily I get bored. Hell, that's one of the reasons why I'm still single. I've never found anyone who could satisfy me long enough to consider having a long-term relationship, so—"

"Just like your old man, huh?" interrupted George. The minute the words were out, he regretted them. He watched Bob's face turn stark white and his green eyes gaze off in the distance, filled with so much pain it hurt to look at him. Nervously, George cleared his throat.

But Bob didn't seem to notice and, instead, nodded slowly. "He had a new girl every week." He sighed raggedly, his voice raw with emotion. "It was fortunate for him he was so good looking. Girls weren't interested in him for money."

George mentally kicked himself for bringing up the subject he knew his friend was the most sensitive about. Bob had scars from that period, still, even though his parents were dead...just as dead as the look now in Bob's sad eyes. It was small wonder Bob's father had affairs, though. He'd been married to a bat straight out of hell. And worse, he'd had to stay, because he worked for his damn father-in-law, who'd made him sign an iron-clad contract.

"I think Dad loved Mom on some level," Bob muttered, as if talking to himself, forgetting where he was for the moment, and that George was listening. "At least he claimed he did, once. I remember their fights three, four times a week with Mom throwing things. Over time, her aim improved and she sent him to the hospital."

Listening to Bob's words, feeling his anguish, George had a strong urge to throw up. He'd never felt this uncomfortable before in his life. He had to restrain the need to rush out of there, before he himself was swamped in the palpable waves of Bob's pain. Nervously, he coughed, very uncomfortable.

But Bob wasn't through. "I promised Dad I'd never marry. You didn't know that, did you?" He continued quickly, just as George opened his mouth. "No one did, except Mom. He sighed heavily. "Thank God he isn't alive to see what I have to do today."

"Yeah," George agreed, rubbing his temples, feeling a pounding headache coming on. He looked everywhere but at Bob, hoping he was saying the right thing. "Um...I think there's a way I *can* help you." he said, summoning up the courage to look at him again. "You know how my business is booming now. I've even hired a damn secretary to help me keep up. I've had to add to my stable of topless maids too."

"Congratulations. But how does that help me?"

Ignoring Bob's sarcasm, George grinned wide, showing all his teeth.

"I'm coming to that! There's one girl I just hired; little Kayla Leigh. She's so new I haven't had time to add her picture to the others yet.

She's young; twenty-five to be exact, with long blonde hair and huge brown eyes. A real innocent type. She's kinda' a late bloomer too. Her thirty-six inch tits are the firmest I've ever seen, and those nipples of hers; so help me God! If my bride wasn't so mean, I would've tried something with her the moment she walked in. I mean, she was dressed real nice, wearing a damn three-piece white silk suit, for Christsake. I thought she was lost at first and had wandered in here by mistake. But when she took off her jacket and I got a look at those breasts of hers poking through that white silk blouse, I thought I'd died and gone to heaven. I swear those nipples take up a full quarter of her breasts. And they're very responsive too. When I took her picture, I accidentally bumped against her, you know, then started to steady her. Only, clumsy oaf that I am, my hand missed her arm, and cupped her breast instead. Well, you know me. Of its own accord, my thumb brushed her nipple and it hardened right away." He sighed heavily. "I mean it, Bob. She's the sexiest damn thing I've ever seen."

Bob laughed. George was an expert photographer and had never been clumsy in his life. "She sounds good, but she's only twenty-five?

Hell, I'm ten years her senior. Don't you have someone suitable who's a little older? Someone more sophisticated with some sexual savvy? I was thinking more late twenties, early thirties."

"Pardon me for saying, but it doesn't sound like you can afford to be too picky. And there are advantages with a younger woman. For one thing, you can train her exactly the way you want."

In spite of his reservations, Bob felt his heart speed up, his interest increasing. "So this girl, Kayla, will do *everything* I say?"

Without warning, he remembered his fat mother with her bleached blonde hair in huge curlers, her old terry cloth bathrobe tied around her, arms crossed, tapping her bare foot with a cigarette dangling from her lips as she stood in the hall. Like a traffic cop, she stood there, the pudgy fingers of her right hand invariably pointed to him first, waving him into the bathroom, ignoring his father who sprinted awkwardly down the stairs with his legs held as tightly together as he could hold them and still move. No wonder his father had prostrate trouble. Bob's mother never let him go to the bathroom before he left for work, not caring he had an hour's drive ahead of him, and, dammit all, he took it!

"Well, not everything," continued George. "You don't want a doormat, you know. Doormats have no spunk in bed."

Bob took another sip of stale coffee. *She will if I train her right.* But he kept his thought to himself.

"And another thing," continued George, "you said yourself you need someone with money problems too, right? Big money problems, if I'm reading you right. Kayla Leigh has more than all of my other girls combined. I mean, she checked out okay. Her background's solid. It's just that… well, she has a 'thing' for the finest money can buy. Her credit rating's the lowest I've ever seen. All her credit cards are maxed out and over-due. The P.I. that works with me found out her apartment manager is threatening to throw her out. Seems the poor girl's three months behind on her rent, and the repo man for the car dealer's about to get his orders to take her brand new Volvo. She's desperate."

Desperate? Bob started perspiring heavily, and his heart pounded. *Like Dad had been that time when he'd tried to win back the food money he'd lost in a 'friendly' game of cards before he got to the store?* To this day, he still remembered standing beside his mother in the police station, and how his father looked in his torn jeans and white tee-shirt with blood stains on it. His eyes had been nearly swollen shut, and his nose broken. The discoloring flesh had created a strange jigsaw patterned mask of purple, blue and magenta across his face. But his father had held his head high and his shoulders straight, despite Bob's mother glaring at him out of eyes narrowed to slits, as he tried to explain to his wife what had happened.

What had made it worse was Tommy, who was in Bob's third grade class, spotted them walking out of the jailhouse together, and had called him a jail bird the next day, in front of everyone. Bob had slugged him, of course. Then he'd had to endure his mother's wrathful nagging. She'd berated him for starting to be like his dad, and had threatened to refuse to love him if he continued. For an eight-year-old, it was a mortifying experience. The best thing to do was be a law-abiding citizen, at least enough so you didn't draw attention to yourself. It was a hell of a lot safer.

Shaking his head, Bob came back to the present. "She's not into booze or gambling, is she?" he asked.

"Hell, no!" said George. "You think I'd take her on if she was?"

"But what I don't want is someone drawing unfavorable—"

"Look, it's simple. Kayla just likes fancy clothes, luxury high-rises, expensive jewelry and great cars; that kinda' crap. But she doesn't have the patience to wait until she can afford them, so she got in over her head. That's why she came to me. I've got a reputation for paying my girls real quick, in hard, cold cash." He smiled wide. "All they have to do is go topless and clean a few lousy homes that don't really need it, if you get my drift. And for that little bit of work, they get to keep half of what I charge the clients, and keep any tips they make for themselves."

"How commendable," he muttered, deciding to slug him if he asked him to invest in his business. "But I'd like someone with a little sexual savvy. The last thing I want is to go to bed with a naïve, wild-eyed innocent who still believes in romance and love, for God's sake. What I'm offering is a business proposition, period. I don't want anyone with illusions about what they're getting into."

His eyes clouded as he remembered that overcast day in the spring of his junior year. *Remember, son,* his father had said, walking out of the garage, zipping up his pants after he'd screwed the girl Bob had thought he loved, *confusing love with romance is dangerous. It's how women trap men.*

George grinned as he opened a drawer and slid a couple of glossy eight-by-tens over the desk. "Look at this girl. Just look! I haven't even sent her out on a job yet. I've been looking for just the right client so as not to scare her off. My point is, she's not familiar with the rules. Usually, I don't allow any funny business. No hanky-panky. But Kayla doesn't know that. So let me send her over to your place and you feel her up a little. She won't know you can't. She'll think it's just part of the job." He leaned back. "If you tried any of that crap with any of those girls you've been leering at, you'd get your face slapped, and hard. However, I'll let you have Kayla on one condition. If you decide on her, I get a generous finder's fee of five hundred and fifty bucks."

"Are you out of your mind? Do you know what you're..." Bob stilled as he looked down at the picture of the blonde. Her peaches and cream complexion in her heart-shaped face was flawless. But, although her pink lips were smiling, the smile didn't extend to her large brown eyes, which seemed to be drilling holes in the camera lens. *Challengingly.* If there was one thing he loved, it was conquering challenges; meeting them head-on. Especially if the challenge came from an attractive, shapely young woman. Like this one.

He could easily imagine getting behind her, holding her close to him despite her resistance while one hand cupped a firm breast, teasing her nipple with his thumb while he ran his other hand into black silk panties. He'd rub her clitoris slowly while lightly nipping her silken neck and shoulders until he felt her pelvis tilt in anticipation of its climax. Then, he'd spin her around, kiss the hell out of those luscious breasts of hers, then ease her down over his knees, licking that firm ass of hers, then spanking her for being such a naughty girl; for making him want her like he did.

As his eyes continued traveling down past her golden, fashionably cut shoulder-length hair, which looked wind-blown and sexy as hell, he zeroed in on her thrusting breasts, and his penis stretched in approval. God, he was hard as a rock, wanting to wedge his penis into her, fucking her senseless with his lips firmly fastened on those pert nipples.

Damn! She *was* built, just like good old George'd promised! Her firm breasts were a good six inches larger than her tiny waist, and those long skinny legs of hers were a turn-on. He could easily imagine them around him, squeezing hard as he pumped her, feeling her clamp that tight little vagina around his throbbing penis.

"How much for the night?" he croaked hoarsely, then quickly cleared his throat. "A hundred? Two? Keep in mind this'll just be a test. If there's not the right chemistry; if she's too stand-offish, too shy, too slow, I'll have to try someone else. I can't afford to waste time on someone not right for the job."

George raised his brows, with a rueful expression on his craggy face. "After all this time you don't know how much I charge? I'm crushed, Bob. Just crushed. But don't worry about the damned fee. Not tonight. If you like her, and decide she's the one for what you've got in mind, just give me the seven hundred we agreed on. That's it. No added charges."

Bob choked on his coffee. "We agreed on five hundred and fifty."

"Price just went up. Take it or leave it."

Draining his coffee while George answered the phone, Bob remembered his late aunt. If it wasn't for her and her stupid will, he wouldn't be in this mess. But despite her being a spinster, she was one hip broad who didn't miss a trick. For one so old (she had been at least fifty) she'd had great eye-sight. He remembered spending the day with her when he was six. Because he liked her so much, and wanted her to like him, he also wanted to get along with her kitty, Tabitha, a huge Siamese. A sweet-natured kid, he'd softly petted her silky fur, cooing to her in what he thought was a sweet voice, telling her how pretty she was, and how smart. While it surprised him she growled instead of meowing like a normal cat, he'd taken it in stride. They were, after all, in New England. Maybe, he reasoned, cats just spoke differently clear up here.

At first, Aunt Hortense had watched him skeptically, then she'd relaxed as the cat stopped swishing her tail with her ears pinned back. It was all right with him that she watched them so carefully. He was a stranger here and not familiar with their customs and things. But when his aunt went to turn off the kettle in the kitchen, he decided maybe Tabitha wanted to play; and that's when the trouble began.

He had no idea how territorial cats are about their possessions, so when he reached into the big bag of colorful yarn and threw a ball of bright red under the kitty's nose, he was surprised when Tabitha reared back, pinned her ears back again, bared her fangs, and spit at him with narrowed green eyes. The way she started growling too, startled him, since it was deeper than her growls earlier, and was continuous.

"How are you and Tabitha getting along?" called his aunt from the kitchen. "Everything still okay?"

"Sure," he shouted, jumping back as Tabitha lunged straight for him, jumping up on him, then chasing him to the fireplace, where he had no choice but to climb the unevenly-spaced bricks, hanging onto the mantle for dear life as the cat paced back and forth on the hearth, her eyes glued on him.

"What the heck?" screeched his aunt, nearly dropping her silver tray laden down with steaming tea and sweet-smelling treats, as she rushed to pick up her kitty and comfort her. "Why are you scaring Tabitha?" she demanded. "Get down from there, this minute!" Although he was bewildered by her thinking he was scaring her cat instead of the other way around, he obediently jumped down. His aunt calmed down and he drank his tea beside her and studied the cat. She was one cunning creature, acting loveable and purring when Aunt Hortense was around, then turning into a spoiled little monster when her back was turned. *Well, two could play at that game*, he decided, waiting for his chance to get even.

It didn't take long for him to get it.

When his aunt answered the phone, talking to whoever it was, with her back turned to him, he had seen his chance to get back at Tabitha, who was now asleep. Grabbing the cat before she could react, he stuck her deep in his aunt's knitting bag, burying her under the numerous balls of colorful yarn.

Unfortunately, the cat was quick too, and, before he knew it, balls of yarn exploded from the bag, bouncing helter-skelter across the floor as the cat shot out of the bag, shaking itself out of the offending yarn, then looked around. But Bob didn't give her the chance to get even, and instead took off, running as fast as he could...careening head first against Aunt Hortense's legs. Continuing on with her conversation and without looking, Aunt Hortense literally seemed to jump across the room, swinging a strong arm, to slap some manners into him. After that, Aunt Hortense never asked him to spend time with her again.

"Deal?" asked George, hanging up the phone. "Or not?"

Bob nodded. "Hell, yes. If I don't produce a child, the money goes to build a damn orphanage for stray cats. The site's already been picked right beside the park of my own subdivision. That's to punish me, I'm sure, if I don't do what she wanted. I'll have to either look at it every time I go in go in or out, or move away. Something I'm not about to do."

George's eyes widened. Then he laughed. "Oh, boy! Does she have it in for you, or what?"

"I don't see what's so damn funny. It's not like I knew her well. I only saw her a few times when I was a kid...and stayed with her for a few hours once when I was six and again for a couple of days when I had leave while I was in the Army. But, apparently, she remembered me. I think she was impressed in spite of herself. She kept telling me what a handsome young man I'd turned out to be, but how surprised she was that I hadn't married yet. To insure I would, I think, she made it clear in her will that her lawyers have to interview my 'wife' and satisfy themselves everything's legit. At that point, they'll advance a quarter of the money. I'll get the remainder only when my bride gives birth. And if she doesn't give birth within the year, I have to pay back the damned money they extended. I don't think she died at this time of year just for spite. But that's how it's turned out. It's already April. If I can't knock up my new wife by next month, I lose it all. And if she's as much as a month late, I've lost it all too."

George nodded, studying the calendar with the girly picture on the wall. "Your chosen victim should give birth by Christmas. But since this'll be her first child, who knows? Some women carry ten months."

"Exactly, and it's that kind of risk that scares the hell out of me. I've got to get started right away. I can't afford a woman who might have any reservations about this. She's got to be willing to do nothing but screw for a while, have my kid and then give me a divorce a few months after the kid's born. But I'll make it worth her while. She can even keep the kid."

Looking absently at his nails, George frowned as if he disapproved of them. "A hell of a lot more money's involved here than just a few paltry hundred, right?" Bob nodded curtly. What the hell? Why shouldn't he spill it? He knew

George would find out sooner or later anyway. "Twenty million dollars. That's what I stand to gain if my plan works. Twenty million beautiful greenbacks!"

George's face turned so red, Bob was afraid he'd have a heart attack right then and there.

"You can see why this is so important, right?"

"Sure as hell can," George breathed heavily. "I never knew anyone in your family had that kind of dough. Comes as kind of a shock."

"Well, hell, it did to me too."

As George's secretary came in with papers for him to sign, Bob remembered the first time he and his parents had driven up there for a 'fun' family vacation.

It had been his first time to meet his old great aunt on his father's side. His parents, as usual, were arguing; this time about how much gas they'd need to get back to a town that resembled civilization. He remembered they'd turned onto the long, badly pock-holed graveled drive-way, and had made their way to the huge old house that hid behind some trees, with only its red brick chimney visible. Bob had been fascinated by all the trees that looked like they extended for miles in all directions. He'd wanted to explore them while his parents were talking with his aunt. But they had other plans, and promptly put him between them, keeping him there with his mother's hand on one shoulder and his father's hand on his other shoulder. He'd only been four at the time, but he remembered it vividly.

When an ancient-looking, bald-headed man dressed in a tuxedo opened the biggest door Bob had ever seen, he tried hard to escape from his parents and hide in the safety of their car. But when they were led through the longest hallway he'd ever seen and he'd seen the huge old woman with the bright red lips and the greenest eyes he'd ever seen amble toward them, and she had reached down for him with a grin, he had been paralyzed with fear. He'd been so terrified he'd had nightmares for over a week. As George's secretary left, Bob continued. "When we moved down here from Ohio, when I was ten, I never saw her again, 'till I was in the Army." George let out a low whistle. "Yeah? Well, you must've made some kinda' impression on the old broad. So do what you gotta, and don't worry about anything. You've got old George to help you now. Don't even think about the money for tonight or for however long it takes to convince your chosen victim to go along with your plans. I trust you. And if Kayla proves not to be the right one, try another of my girls. Hell, try 'em all."

Reaching into the tall metal cabinet behind him, he grabbed another stack of glossy nudes. "These are duplicates of what you've got over there. Take 'em. Study 'em. If another girl catches your eye, just call. But," he grinned, "I trust you'll be just as generous with me as I am with you. So you'll understand why my finder's fee just rose to ten thousand, payable after you get your dough. Hell, I'll even deduct the seven hundred we agreed on, and which you'll pay me once you decide who you'll pick. Hell, who knows, maybe you'll throw in a little bonus for yours truly too. Not that I'm pressuring you or anything. It's just a thought. One that'll keep me patient for as long as it takes you to make up your mind." He grinned archly. "Just as long as you do it damn quick."

Standing, getting his keys out of the back pocket of his jeans, Bob ground his teeth.

If there was one thing he hated, it was being out of control. Not only had he received the call from the lawyers at the ungodly hour of seven a.m., he was told, in a voice that sounded like a machine gun firing, about his aunt's death and the need for him to come to their office the following Thursday. They had refused to reschedule for a more convenient time for him, forcing him to cancel an important meeting with a prospective home buyer who was thinking of using him as their architect. But it seemed in the past two weeks, since great-aunt Hortense's lawyers had first contacted him, he'd had no control over anything.

"Let's go with victim number one for starters," said Bob. "Have Kayla or whatever the hell her name is at my place around seven." *That was one hurdle over with,* he thought. *Only a few more to go.* "But don't spill my plan. I'm not making an offer until I've sampled the merchandise. Let her think this is just a job."

"Of course, old buddy. Of course! She'll be wearing a black satin skirt, black lace panties, black hose, spike heels and a smile. Nothing else. So she'll be real easy to recognize."

As satisfied as he could be under the circumstances, Bob went out, listening to his friend muttering something unintelligible. Alone, George studied Kayla's picture. Although she was luscious, she was also, unfortunately, stand-offish. But then she was inexperienced in the ways of the world. Chances were, though, she could be easily bluffed, especially if the lure was money. Not that he'd tell her Bob's plan, of course. But a few white lies would work wonders, if told in the right way.

Chapter Two

Driving up in the wide driveway beside the large two-story beige brick house, Kayla glanced around. No one, thank God, was standing at any of the windows in any of the huge, two-story houses nearby. No one was on the sidewalk either, or in any of the yards, as far as she could see. No one was coming out of their doors. No cars were coming down the wide, two-lane street. *So far so good.*

Pulling down the spotless white visor with the mirror on the back, she quickly smoothed her long, unruly, softly permed blonde hair, then pushed it demurely behind her ears. The last thing she wanted was to have her hair get in her face while she cleaned for her very first client. She had to do a good job. She just had to! Studying her tense face, she smoothed the wrinkle line between her brows, then quickly, before she lost her nerve, opened the door with one hand and stepped out of the car.

Glancing around suspiciously, she unbuttoned the top two buttons of her brand new black leather, ankle-length trench coat. It was hot as blazes. But it offered protection from any prying eyes that might spot her skimpy outfit underneath. This is just a job, she assured herself, very aware of her bare breasts and sensitive nipples, which were being teased by the soft satin lining of the coat while she got her new Easy-rack, filled with cleaning supplies out of the back. It was an important job, to be sure. There would be a brand new hundred dollar bill, at the very least, waiting at the end of two hours. But still it was just a job. All she had to do, Mr. Griffin had assured her, was to smile, act friendly, and do her very best to please his new client. If she relaxed enough, she could, at her discretion, stay longer than two hours, increasing Mr. Griffin's fee and hers at the same time.

An additional hundred bucks an hour was a hell of a good incentive to at least try to make the best of it.

Pushing the automatic car lock button on her key ring, she dropped her keys into her rack and glanced at her shiny gold-link watch with twelve sparkling diamonds around the perimeter of its midnight blue dial. Seven on the dot. Good! She'd been told Mr. McKnight didn't like to be kept waiting.

Her brand new black patent leather high-heels clicked sharply on the cobbled stone walkway, as she quickly unbuttoned the third button on her coat. No one was watching her, she assured herself, glancing covertly around again. No one but Mr. McKnight knew what she was wearing underneath her coat, so there was no reason to feel self-conscious. Lord knew she wanted … she *had* to make a good impression on her first client ever, so Mr. Griffin would be pleased. He'd told her all his customers had favorites. If they liked a girl, they'd always ask for her, and only her; and she'd be assured of making at least a tidy sum paid in cold, hard cash each and every week. If she cleaned enough houses, she'd be able to take her time looking for a new secretarial job during the day, while paying enough on her apartment and her bills to keep creditors and her manager, the mean old bitch, satisfied.

***

At the sound of a car in the driveway, Bob looked up from the architectural plans for the new subdivision twenty miles to the north. Peeking out the corner of the long, narrow window by the door, he stiffened. The pristine white Volvo was a dead giveaway. Kayla Leigh. And right on time. Damn! So soon? How'd time passed so quickly?

He glanced around as he absently straightened the papers. The slow romantic CDs were ready. And the champagne was chilling in the golden ice bucket on the black leather bar, with two cut crystal champagne flutes next to it. If the girl was as attractive as George claimed, and she proved amenable to his plan, they'd both have good reason to celebrate.

Unfortunately though, the place was just too neat. Against his better judgment, and hating to do it, but determined to create a good ruse in case he didn't choose her, he turned the high black leather tufted stool, on which he'd been sitting, upside down and tore the three large white leather cushions from the couch and the two cushions from the matching arm chairs, throwing them all haphazardly on the floor. Opening his teak wood supply cabinet, he swiped his hand over both shelves, spilling their contents haphazardly on the white carpet.

Racing to the bar, he grabbed as many liquor bottles as he could, and set them on his glass-topped coffee table. He went to the two smoked glass-topped matching end tables and took the two thin-based chrome lamps off, carefully setting them on their sides on the floor.

Rushing into the immaculate kitchen, he grabbed a couple of cans of beer from the fridge and emptied them in the sink to get rid of the antiseptic cleaner's smell. He smashed the cans on the white tiled counter, then emptied the trash can in the middle of the red tiled floor. As he was debating whether or not he should wreak havoc on the master bedroom, the doorbell chimed. Dammit, there wasn't enough time to go upstairs and tear up the guest bedrooms, much less the den.

Taking a moment to compose himself as the doorbell sounded again, he studied his reflection in the mirrored foyer. For a guy thirty-five, he didn't look too bad, he decided, pushing back his light brown curly hair and tucking his tight white knit shirt into his tailored jeans. She was awfully young, but he was in pretty decent shape, thanks to the new home exercise gym he'd recently added. The stuff'd cost a fortune, and had nearly maxed out over half his credit cards, but was well worth it. Hell, if Kayla was the one he picked, he might even put some exercise equipment in for her too. Even pregnant women needed to exercise.

"Mr. McKnight?" asked the little blonde as he opened the door. "I'm Kayla Leigh," she whispered, glancing around furtively. "From the … um …cleaning agency. I believe you're expecting me?"

Bob hid his smile, his heart going out to her as he extended his hand and led her inside. With her eyes wide with fear, she blinked several times before meeting his gaze. She was scared half to death and shaking slightly. She was a lot smaller than he'd expected, only coming up to the middle of his chest, and had a small-boned, dainty build.

He'd always been partial to little things…with the exception of cats. It was gratifying to see how strong they could become with the right amount of nurturing. His mind drifted unexpectedly to the baby bird who'd spiraled down on his patio last year. He remembered how bravely it had tried to defend itself, mistaking his interest for intending harm. Its frantic squawking was heart-breaking. Like Kayla, the baby bird was shaking with fear. But by talking to it soothingly, letting it get used to him enough to trust him, then feeding it watered down canned cat food with an eye dropper, it soon came to have faith in him. It was then he'd mixed a sleeping potion into its food so he could examine its broken wing, and gently reset it. Maybe he should've taken it to a vet, but he had wanted the chance to try to fix it himself. He had named it Allie, figuring that could be a boy or girl's name. It had become a pet, chirping happily from its high perch the moment he walked out onto the patio. He was proud of his handiwork. The perch area had enough room for it to eat from the feeder he'd bought at a pet store, and to exercise a little. It even got so tame, it'd sit on his finger. He was content to let it stay as long as it wanted, but one morning, after greeting him, it surprised the heck out of him by flying high, doing a couple of loops in the air, then flying away. He'd become real fond of that little bird. He could've replaced it, he supposed, by buying a bird at the pet store, but somehow it wouldn't have been the same. And he liked to think one of the birds he heard every morning was Allie.

Coming back to the present, he noticed Kayla had set down her cleaning supplies and was starting to unbutton her coat, darting furtive glances at him. Although she was obviously shy, there was something in her gaze which intrigued him, and he sensed a high degree of intelligence.

"Would it make it easier for you if I closed my eyes?" he teased. "Or you could pretend I'm a doctor checking you over."

Looking puzzled, she finally smiled, catching on.

"You're right on time," he murmured, trying hard not to stare at her slowly opening coat as a tantalizing view of a perfect female body was revealed.

"This is my first job doing this," she whispered, hoping it explained her awkwardness.

"I know. Just take your time. There's no need to rush." Truth be known, her slow, unskilled movements were more erotic than anything he'd ever experienced. He felt seventeen again, wanting her so badly it hurt. But he didn't dare voice his thoughts. She was nervous enough as it was. If she'd had any idea of how hard his penis was, she would've run out of there. Fortunately, she was too shy to even look where she would've seen evidence of his desire against the rough denim fabric of his jeans.

Although Kayla was grateful he was being so kind, his green eyes had enlarged slightly, clearly showing his sexual interest. And he hadn't once looked at anything but her since she'd started unbuttoning her coat. That made her even more awkward, her fingers fumbling badly with the buttons.

Watching her success with the last of those infernal buttons, Bob quickly eased behind her to help her shed the thing.

Kayla involuntarily stiffened as she felt his gentle fingers close around the collar of her coat, gently brushing her neck and shoulders as he pulled it down, then slowly over her arms and completely off her.

"Relax, dear," he urged. "I won't bite. Unless of course, you want me to." Feeling tingles travel up and down her spine as her heartbeat increased, she felt drawn to him like a magnet, and leaned slightly back, as need became more important than logic. She could just imagine this good-looking stranger sucking and lightly nibbling her breasts, screwing her right then and there.

Hiding his satisfaction at her receptiveness, as he hung up her coat in the large cedar lined closet, he watched over his shoulder as her nipples beaded tightly. She was ready for him now. Just as ready as he was for her. Soon, very soon, he'd make her an offer. Mentally, he relaxed a little. He'd made his choice. Next on the agenda was getting her to accept it.

Turning to face him, Kayla was more aware of her body than she'd ever been in her life. He was close enough to her she could feel his body heat which intensified his fragrant after shave.

For a long moment, they stared into each other's eyes, not more than six inches apart, with their expressions bland, but their eyes enlarged. It was, she knew, the beginning of the mating game, as irrational as it was, considering she was there to do a job and they'd just met.

Feeling more alive than she'd been in a long time, she stopped questioning it and instead followed his lead, running her eyes over him as he'd started doing to her.

He wasn't only good-looking with lots of light brown curly hair framing his handsome, square-jawed face, he was downright virile looking, with his huge green eyes reminding her of a lion. He had a great physique. His broad shoulders and well-muscled biceps, partially visible beneath his short sleeves, were deeply tanned. His tight knit shirt outlined the planes of his muscled chest, then tapered down to a trim waist. He was tall too, well over six feet. She'd always been attracted to tall men.

For some reason, she'd assumed Mr. Griffin's clients were all dirty old men who'd be leering salaciously at her; maybe even drooling, wheezing old geezers who'd quickly back off at the slightest challenge. This tall, well-built man, she realized, wouldn't.

His erect posture with his broad shoulders firmly back, his calm demeanor as he met her eyes when she looked up at him, his very closeness, standing within inches of her, were all unnerving. Self-confidence literally radiated off him.

Were all Mr. Griffin's customers this good-looking? Dear God! She hoped not. There was only so much excitement a girl could take.

Afraid he'd give into the temptation to screw her right there, Bob turned away abruptly, trying to will his stretching penis into submission. He wanted to push her against the nearest wall, pull down her black lace panties, and plunge his penis deeply into her. But while it'd sure satisfy the hell out of him for the moment, it'd probably scare her so much she'd bolt half-nude outside, where all his neighbors could see what was going on. Later, they'd have fun and games. But not yet. Not this soon.

"You have a lot to clean up," he barked, sounding harsher than he'd intended, as he headed into the living room. Realizing how dictatorial he sounded, he paused, getting himself under control. "But I'll help," he assured her, keeping his eyes off her breasts with an effort.

Puzzled by his quick change of mood, going from seduction to strictly business in what had to be record time, Kayla picked up her case of cleaning supplies and followed him. What she wanted was to get out of there as fast as she could. But she couldn't. She needed the money too much. She wished she knew the rules of her new job, though. When Mr. Griffin hired her, he'd said he'd give her some guidelines to go by. Unfortunately, this assignment had come up so fast, he hadn't had time to tell her what they were.

Aware of the moisture between her thighs which had been brought about from his nearness and her wayward thoughts, she quickly strode into the living room as fast as she could in her precariously high heels. "I doubt if you're supposed to help. I think you're just supposed to watch." "That wasn't my understanding," he countered.

"Well...I guess you can then...if you really want to," she said, stepping over one of the large couch cushions to get to the scattered supplies beyond.

"I want to...do a lot of things with you," he muttered, joining her, getting down beside her, leaning close, swiping a large package of tracing papers out of her reach to get her attention. "But right now, I'll settle for you slowing down and relaxing a little. I'll even double the pay for tonight, if you do."

What the hell, he wasn't paying a dime for her tonight. "Personally, I prefer to go slow and thorough, taking my time … with everything. And I like my women to be the same way."

He'd double the pay? Was he serious? "Are you sure that's all you want? I mean, I'll be glad to do it like that, but—" Then she stiffened, wanting, but unable to move away, as he gently trailed his fingertips down her arm. She was intensely aware of his broad shoulders close to her breasts as he held her eyes.

"That's all I'm asking you to do," he whispered seductively, his warm breath fanning her face. "Just relax, sweetheart. For now." Kayla swallowed visibly and looked away, slowly gathering some scattered design books. Playing the mating game was one thing. That, in her opinion, was harmless flirting. But seduction was quite another.

He was up to something. She knew he was. But what? She should've questioned her friend, Darlene, more about Mr. Griffin's operation. From the way Darlene had talked, she'd assumed it was a high-class place, with no touching or affairs allowed. Obviously, she'd been misled.

"Drink?" he asked. "You look like you could use one as much as I can."

She really needed to get hold of a copy of Mr. Griffin's rules! There were all sorts of things coming up here that she wasn't prepared to handle. "Maybe I'll take a gin and tonic. A very small one." *And nurse it.*

The truth was, she didn't care much for drinking. She never had. To her, all liquor tasted the same, like castor oil. The only times she drank was when she was with someone else who did, and then she did it so she'd fit in. But she never had more than one and instead kept adding ice and water to her first drink so it'd look like she was drinking more.

Bob took a good stiff belt of Jack Daniels straight, then mixed her drink. He should send her packing. If it hadn't been for the unmistakable signal that she was attracted to him, he would have. But the way her eyes kept straying to his lips as she repeatedly leaned towards him, the way her nipples beaded instantly whenever he touched her, and the way her eyes enlarged slightly as she looked at him were clear signs she wanted him to take her to bed.

But there was something holding her back. She didn't approach him unless he approached her first. She didn't touch him playfully to see how he'd respond. She didn't even talk to him while she cleaned.

But she was a quiet young thing, so maybe that was just her nature. That was fine with him. He was kind of quiet too. He was rarely the life of any party. He'd bet she'd never been either.

She was bound to be a little shy, considering they'd just met. He was nervous as hell too. If it hadn't been for him having to get married quickly, he'd have been content to take it slow.

Surely she was used to having men look at her, with her attractive sweet face and that terrific body. She did seem a little self-conscious, but, considering this was the first time she'd had to be half-nude for a damn job, that was natural.

Was she afraid she'd get fired if she didn't clean his house properly? She seemed so damn conscientious about it. He had to give her credit though. In no time at all, she'd scooped up all the books and other papers on the floor and was now stacking them in neat piles all the same height in his supply cabinet as he fixed their drinks.

His eyes zeroed in on her breasts again, which were bobbing and swaying seductively as she bent over his slanted work table, organizing everything. He could see why George was doing a brisk business. Just watching a half-nude woman work was as enjoyable as hell. But this woman seemed hell-bent on cleaning everything until it shone, reeking of polish and cleaner.

He sighed contentedly, watching her rotate her shoulders, moving those luscious breasts in a slow circle. Unfortunately, she didn't seem to be doing it to entertain him. The way she frowned as she moved them, it was clear as hell she was tense. But that was good, in a way. It should make her more responsive to getting laid tonight, which was a great stress-reducer. Besides, he had to test her to make sure they were sexually compatible. He wasn't about to be tied to a woman for nearly a year if she wasn't physically well-matched. He did have a strong sex urge which was damn inconvenient, living alone like he did. That was the worst part of being a bachelor. No sweet young playmate, ready for sex.

This woman should be able to satisfy him in every way. The way her little hips were wiggling, as she walked to capture a stray paper that floated out of her reach, stirred his imagination, keeping him hard as hell. He dearly loved those long skinny legs of hers too, especially clad in those black silk stockings.

But he had to do something to motivate her in the right direction quickly. There was no way he'd take the chance of being saddled with a frozen ice princess.

Her aloofness was challenging, but surely that barrier could be broached if he used the right bait. She'd be well worth whatever effort it took.

"Your drink's ready," he called, raising his glass in a mock salute, downing his own quickly. "But tell me something," he said, as she seated herself on a black leather stool. "Why are you doing this? Cleaning people's houses dressed like that? With your looks and um, other assets, I'd think you'd try for something better."

Taking a sip of her drink, which was so strong it made her eyes water, Kayla promptly put it down. Did he honestly think she *liked* doing this, letting strange men ogle her breasts, knowing there wasn't a damn thing she could do about it? She was looking forward to it as much as getting the plague. But she'd be damned if she'd admit it to a stranger who was paying her to do that very thing.

"There's nothing wrong with good, honest work. As long as someone's willing to pay me for it." That, at least, was true, as far as it went. The only problem was, she didn't know if what she was doing could technically be classified as work. She felt more like an entertainer than a worker.

"You call running around half-nude good, honest work? Besides, from what I understand," he continued, as she parted her pretty lips, "the pay's not all that good. You could make a hell of a lot more doing other things."

"It's all relative," she shrugged. "Even if you decide not to double it like you said, two hundred dollars means a hundred bucks an hour. To me, that's good pay."

"It's chicken feed compared to what I'd pay you if you worked for me personally."

She hated to ask, but was too curious not to. Taking another sip of her drink for courage, then putting it down in front of her, she studied him. "Doing what?" she asked, archly.

Bob handed her drink to her, silently urging her to drink more. "I'd be willing to pay you two million dollars, with a retainer of ten thousand now," he said, evading her question, planting his bait. "and I'll pay all of your expenses; everything, including medical and dental bills for the next, say, twenty or so years, rounded off." That, he'd figured, was competitive in today's market. "That includes of course, any, uh, incidental expenses." *Like our child's.* "I'll be responsible for those."

For a moment, Kayla stared open-mouthed at him. Then she took a big gulp of her drink. "I'm sure I didn't hear you right. For a moment there, I ... would you repeat that?"

Bob hid his smile. The fish had not only taken the bait, but his hook had sunk deep. "You heard me," he said, gallantly taking her elbow, steering her to the couch and lugging a big pillow back in its place. "And it's easy work, Kayla. I think you'd like it."

Kayla sat down beside him, and quickly took another swallow of her drink. "Doing what?" she repeated.

Bob grabbed his checkbook and a pen off his desk, then sat down next to her with their thighs touching. "Here's the retainer," he said, writing out a check. "With the two million, I'll deposit it to whatever account you choose by the end of the year." *So I can take it off my taxes, right away, which are going to be huge.*

All that money was making her head spin. It was hard to keep it straight. But she had to give him credit. He had it all figured out.

Unfortunately, he was still evading her question. And that made her edgy. But she couldn't just turn it down ... at least not without knowing what kind of a job he had in mind. That kind of money would make her not only solvent, but wealthy; especially with him paying all her living expenses. "What makes you think I have the skills for what you have in mind? I'm sure sex is a part of it. It has to be. But there's something else to it too, isn't there?" She met his eyes. "What is it?"

Deciding she needed further enticement, Bob ignored her for the moment, and calmly wrote out the check for ten grand, leaving her name blank, and dropped it in her lap. "I'm in my late great-aunt's will, and I stand to inherit a lot of money." That's all he'd ever tell her about the amount, he decided. She didn't need to know how much.

Kayla picked up the check with shaking hands. *Dear God!* All those zeroes at the end seemed to grow, looking larger than life. It wasn't that it was such a huge amount itself that astounded her, it was the timing. She was at rock bottom with only twelve dollars in her checking account, and the service charge of ten dollars a month was due to be deducted next week. She had very little to eat in her kitchen. Even her apartment might not be there next week, as the apartment manager had threatened to throw her out unless she came up with the rent money. Even the car dealer had warned her he'd have to take back her car if she didn't catch up with her payments.

"I've got to meet certain requirements to get that money, Kayla. I've got to get married, get my new wife pregnant and have her give birth to my child by the end of December." He searched her eyes. "Are you woman enough to do the job?"

Chapter Three

Kayla felt numb and disoriented, looking from Bob to the check, then back again. Was he insane? There was no way a rationally thinking stranger would want her; *her*, of all people, to have his baby…by the end of December. It didn't take a rocket scientist to figure out that was only nine months away, and sometimes it took years, not just months for a woman to conceive. Add to that another nine months for her to deliver and God alone knew how long it all would take. "Do you want me to promise something like that? Because if you do, I'm sorry. I won't do it. I can't. I'm not going to make a promise I can't keep."

"I think you can do it if we get started right away. I know it's awfully soon. But we've got to at least try."

Sensing she needed a little more enticement, Bob put his hand on her thigh and squeezed it gently, as he looked deep into her eyes as if she was the only woman on earth. "When our baby's born, you'll get all that money deposited to whatever bank you choose. That's a lot of money for such easy work. And I'll cover all doctor and hospital bills connected with the baby's birth too, since you'll be my legal and faithful wife, living here with me. Then, after the baby's born, you'll give me a divorce, keep custody of the kid, and we'll go our separate ways, with me continuing to pay all your living expenses, and that of our child until he's out of college, which of course, he'll attend."

Kayla's mind was spinning so fast she was dizzy. Was this really happening? *To her?* She'd never been lucky before. She had never won anything in her life. And now, here she was getting a check for ten thousand dollars from a man she hadn't known existed a couple of hours ago. She should've been asking questions. She should've been suspicious, or at least cautious. But…accepting this check would keep away the very real fear of being homeless and out on the street, being at the mercy of God only knew what nut, and having to walk the streets constantly to keep from being arrested for vagrancy. With her parents dead, no sisters or brothers to rely on, no family whatsoever, and friends who'd moved so long ago she'd forgotten their addresses, she was terrified.

Bob could almost see the wheels whirling in her mind. Was she really that desperate for money? Her eyes were huge as she stared at the damn check. Her face was pale. And she was shaking like a leaf. Reminding him… of that little baby bird he'd taken care of a few months ago.

In her own way, Kayla was just as helpless. Just as frightened. Could he nurture her to help her reach her full potential? Would she let him? Or would she resist? It would take a lot of patience, which he wasn't sure he had. And people were a lot more complex than birds. But still… he wanted to try.

He put his arm around her shoulders, gently rubbing flesh as soft as silk. He sniffed her neck. Her perfume was alluring, too. It was a subtle floral scent, but just as potent in its own way as some of the stronger perfumes some women wore.

He hated like hell to rush her at such a time. *Damn Hortense to hell!* But then, if it hadn't been for her will, he'd never have met Kayla, and never would have had the chance to help her. There was no such thing as coincidence. He firmly believed that everything that occurred happened for a specific reason.

"Considering the fact there's so little time," he murmured, running his hand a few inches up her thigh, "that means we'll have sex at all hours, so I need to know if there's anyone who'd object to our relationship. Even though it'll be strictly business between us, another man in your life would complicate matters. Few men would understand the nature of such an arrangement."

"Is this really on the level? You're willing to pay me this much money?"

"Absolutely. If you agree."

"There's no one," she admitted, still reeling from shock, sitting back, trying to make sense of out what seemed like a miracle. "I don't have a boyfriend or even anyone I date on a regular basis." Never in her wildest dreams had she expected this. She wouldn't get kicked out of her apartment now. She could pay several months in advance, pay off her car and credit and charge cards, and still have plenty left over.

Before she could think of any objections, Bob pinned her to the couch, with his weight pressed against her and kissed her softly, slowly tasting her lipstick, deeply inhaling her clean, gin-scented breath. "What do you say?" he whispered, kissing her again, running his hand softly over her bare breast, cupping it and teasing her responsive, peaking nipple with a feathery light touch. "Do we have a deal?"

Feeling a piercing thrill shoot right through her, Kayla nodded, not trusting her voice enough to speak. Not only had all her financial problems been solved, the man of her dreams was kissing her again, making her feel loved, caressing first one breast, then the other, arousing feelings in her she'd thought had died. It had been so long since she'd allowed a man to get close to her. She'd been so intent trying to make it on her own, she'd rarely dated, much less let a man get this close. Forgetting about the checks, she dropped them and wound her arms around his neck.

"I'll take that as a 'yes,'" he murmured, kissing her soft lips again. "I know it's a lot to absorb, but everything will be fine." Hugging her tightly, he felt the crush of her firm breasts against his chest as she kissed him with surprising fervor, exploring his taste with her flicking tongue.

Letting him spread her legs, she watched him slide down between them, running his hands over her back. He pulled her toward him and sucked her nipples gently, laving each in turn with his tongue. Spiraling out of control, she was lost in the wonderful haze of being made love to by an expert. Whatever else he was or wasn't, this man knew his way around a woman's body. And all he asked what that she submit to him in this wonderful way? How could she possibly refuse?

Bob glanced up at her heavily lidded eyes. They were huge. He kissed her nipples again. Both were peaked into hard little buds. He hid his smile and quickly crossed his hands over his chest, jerking off his shirt with record speed. As innocent as she looked, she had fire in her. Soon, very soon, she'd be ready for him to brand her as his by fucking the hell out of her. Once she did that, she'd be reluctant, he knew, to pull out of the deal, even if later on she was so inclined.

Stroking her thigh just above her garter, he edged his fingers into her black panties and stroked the growing, pulsating nub between her legs.

Predictably, it was slick, her cum spreading over his fingers, engulfing them. Even if she did have some loser somewhere that she thought she loved, he hadn't been taking care of her. As wet as she was, as needy, it was clear she hadn't had sex in a good, long while.

Taking gentle hold of her waist, he squeezed it, kissing her breasts again, sucking and blowing, then kissing her collarbone and her creamy shoulders, as he pulled her down on the floor beside him. "It's okay, baby," he murmured huskily, bracing himself on one hand, looming over her as he took firm hold of her ridiculous skirt and, with one knee holding it in place, ripped it off her little hips. "Relax. I'm going to take very good care of you."

"Entwining her arms around his neck, Kayla arched her back, wanting to feel that thick mat of dark hair against her. She wanted him more than she'd wanted anything before in her life.

Leaning more heavily down on her, kissing her thoroughly again, he jerked off her panties, then his jeans as she squirmed against him.

Instinctively, she positioned her body to his, her breasts teasing his nipples, her enlarged nub nuzzling the sensitive tip of his penis, which was stiff and pulsating against her as it popped out of his shorts, causing him to nearly lose control right then and there.

Gently taking hold of her hands, disengaging them from his neck, he gently but firmly pushed them over her head, causing her breasts to surge out to his warm, welcoming lips, as his penis surged deeply into her, to hell with his shorts. Why not? He'd done it all ways; in all states of dress and undress. Her little ass was so tight and so wet, it quickly clamped down around him, squeezing so hard, he was powerless to do anything but give her what they both wanted.

Bracing himself on his hands, he pumped slowly, his penis sliding in deeply, holding it as she squeezed, then edging back out, going in quickly again. Although his intention had been to bring her to the brink, then pause several times before going for the climax, his penis had other plans, and kept pumping her for all he was worth. He'd had experienced women before, but Kayla was different. Arching her back repeatedly, spreading her legs wider to give him access to deep inside her, she apparently needed all of him inside her, pillaging her, touching her in places which had been, judging from her response, too long ignored. Who was he to refuse? He'd always been a sucker for an attractive woman with firm breasts. At the moment, he'd have given her anything in the world she asked for.

He sweated heavily as he pumped. The sweet aroma of his sperm and her cum mingling wafted around them, as he continued fucking her faster and faster, losing control, reveling in it.

Despite her youth and relative inexperience, she was the best lay he'd had in years.

Then he lost it completely, pumping her hard. Pumping her fast. Banging those hips of hers hard; grinding them into the floor and surging down against her so forcefully, she slid up a couple of inches.

But Bob was equal to the task of following her. Pushing down on her with his chest, he pinned her body tightly under his, plunging into her again and again. To hell with being a gentleman about it. His penis was in charge now. As it surged in faster and faster, harder and harder, Bob gave in completely to the earth-shattering climax which was better than anything he'd had in a long time

***

Kayla bolted straight up, startled out of a deep sleep by a rip-roaring snort directly into her ear. Taking a few calming breaths to get her speeding heart under control, she turned her head, trying to focus her bleary eyes. *Dear God!* A strange man was sleeping beside her! And except for wearing a pair of shorts, with his penis sticking out, he was nude! And she was dressed strangely too, wearing nothing but black silk stockings!

Jumping up, she shook her head, trying to clear the mental cobwebs.

Now she remembered. She'd started a new job as a topless maid... and Bob McKnight owned this house, which she'd been starting to clean, until he'd diverted her attention by giving her two checks as an advance for... damn! She'd been tricked! All that talk about marriage and babies and money had been a ploy to get her to have sex with him. She'd been so dazzled by it and the man's kissing skills, she'd done exactly what he'd wanted...she'd slept with him. Hopefully, he wouldn't tell Mr. Griffin about it, but then the way her luck had been going lately, he just might, and she might get fired as a result. *Damn!* She had to get out of there, she had to think.

Remembering him putting her coat into a closet, she strode to it and jerked it off its hanger. Then she stilled. *Dear God!* She'd had sex? But she wasn't on birth control pills. She hadn't been for two years now, ever since she'd broken up with Harvey Anderson back home. What if she'd gotten pregnant just now? By a man she'd just met, who had one of the most original lines she'd ever heard?

With shaking fingers she buttoned her coat up to her neck. But where had she put her keys? Feeling her panic building, she frantically searched her pockets, turning them inside out. Dear God, had she locked them in her car? Again? That made the second time this week.

Nervously smoothing her hair, she crouched down and touched Mr. McKnight's warm shoulder. "Are you awake? There's some things we need to talk about."

She sat back, waiting expectantly. But he didn't move a muscle.

Leaning closer to him, she tried again. "Mr. McKnight, please wake up. We have to talk!" Taking hold of his arm, she shook him as hard as she could. "Mr. McKnight!" Jolted awake by a woman's anxious voice and relentless shoving, Bob slowly opened his eyes. Then he smiled, remembering her and their lucrative deal. This was the woman he'd chosen to marry and to be the mother of his child. Unfortunately, his new bride-to-be didn't seem all that pleased.

Running his eyes over her, he wasn't too pleased himself. "Call me Bob," he chided, sitting up, raising his arms high over his head; stretching. "Might as well be on a first name basis. And take off that ridiculous coat."

"What I'm wearing is the least of our worries! We've got some big problems here." She swallowed visibly. "I know I'm to blame! I shouldn't have gone to bed with you. I don't make a habit of sleeping with men I don't know. I just got carried away by the moment."

"Fine. So what's your point?"

"My point? My point is I hope you don't tell Mr. Griffin what we did. This is my first assignment for him and I really need this job."

Had she forgotten she was working for him now? There was no way he'd let her work for George too.

"Another thing," she blurted, his silence worrying her. "I really should've told you before we did anything. I ... we ... I'm not on birth control pills. But don't worry. If something happens, it's not your problem. I just thought you should know...just in case." Bob suppressed his grin. She wasn't on birth control pills? That was great news. But unfortunately Kayla looked close to tears. Didn't she remember part of their arrangement was for her to get pregnant as soon as possible?

"Don't you understand? You—"

"Not really, no. I don't," he interrupted her. "I don't see any problems other than you wearing that god-awful coat. You have no idea how strange you look in it. It's not cold in here." He winced, his stiff muscles protesting the movement as he reached for his jeans. Next time, they'd screw in his bed or on the couch, not the damn floor.

"But—"

"You do remember me giving you that check for ten grand, don't you? And about my needing a wife and her getting pregnant? Does any of that ring a bell?"

"Of course it does," she said watching him get dressed. He had a great body. Not an ounce of fat anywhere. "How could I forget? But I also know a line when I hear it." She smiled wistfully. "It's a great one though. Very original."

"Original, hell. What I told you is the truth." He rotated his shoulders, trying to get the unaccustomed kinks out. "From here on though, we'll fuck on something soft."

"Surely you don't mean this thing's on the level? It's not just a line?" "That all depends on whether you take off that damn coat or not. If you insist on wearing it all the time, the deal's off."

She hesitated, then started unbuttoning the dang thing. "How much time do I get to decide?" she asked, following him out to the kitchen. "I realize you want my decision quickly, but you'll give me a few days to think about it, won't you?"

He laughed. "By going to bed with me, you already gave me your decision. You've got to give birth by the end of this year. We don't have time to waste and play games."

"But you haven't proposed. And I need time to plan a wedding."

"I'm not going to propose, Kayla. We have a business arrangement, nothing more. As for the wedding ceremony, that's no big deal," he shrugged, measuring out coffee grinds and pouring water in the pot, "We'll work it in soon, after one of my daily meetings with my new clients. We'll go to a justice of the peace downtown and say our vows. The important thing's getting you knocked up, and the most efficient way to insure that is getting you moved in right away. How much stuff do you have? Do you think we can get it in one trip using both cars?"

Kayla's heart sank. All her life she'd been dreaming about a big church wedding. "Dammit! What about love? What about—?"

Taking hold of her shoulders, Bob jerked her damn coat off. "First things first. I'm burning this," he said, holding it high, keeping it out of her reach. "Second, your job description is fucking me, getting pregnant, marrying me, then giving me an uncontested divorce after the kid's born. Mine's giving you and our future kid my last name and fucking you. Love doesn't enter into it."

"But marriage is a big step," she hissed, jumping up; trying to swipe her expensive coat out of his hands.

Raising her coat high overhead, Bob watched her breasts jiggle as she jumped again, trying in vain to get her stupid coat. They needed to get her moved in tonight. A single girl who lived in an apartment shouldn't have much, he reasoned. Unfortunately, his penis was fully erect, watching those bare breasts shake again as she jumped. But, what the hell? They had plenty of time. The night was still young. Chances were it wouldn't take more than a couple of trips at the most to get her stuff. "I'll give this to you after you give me something I want," he murmured.

Kayla stilled. She didn't like the look in his eyes. The way he was staring at her breasts instead of her face unnerved her. His green eyes had darkened and glittered like emeralds. And the planes of his handsome face had hardened.

"What do you have in mind?" she asked, backing away.

Tossing her coat over his head in back of him, he grabbed her waist as she ran for it. "These," he softly growled, pulling her close, rubbing his face on her breasts, kissing them, licking them, nibbling her nipples which were hardening quickly. "You give me these every time I want, and we'll get along fine."

Before she could protest, Bob seared her lips with his own, his tongue darting and exploring every inch of her mouth. It differed from his earlier kisses, she realized, as he picked her up bodily with one hand, letting her feet dangle several inches above the floor, cradling her skull with the other, keeping his lips on hers. This kiss was forceful to the point of being harsh, and much more possessive than his earlier ones. She wasn't afraid of him. Exactly. But his change took her by surprise as he pinned her against the wall, keeping her body in place with his weight.

"Put your arms tighter around my neck and your legs around my waist, sweetheart," he whispered, coming up for air and unzipping his pants. "I can't wait any longer."

Dear God! He wanted sex standing up? She'd never done it like this before.

"Do what I said, Kayla. Now!"

Hesitating for another few seconds, she finally put one leg around him. "Don't let me fall," she pleaded, as she felt his hand on her bottom, steadying her as she wrapped her other leg around him, holding on for dear life. Sex was supposed to be fun. This way, it wasn't. Not only did it feel strange, it was awkward as hell.

Feeling his other hand slide between them, guiding his penis inside her, she wobbled precariously, until he put his other hand on the other side of her bare ass, pushing her closer against him.

His penis slid in deep. "Comfortable?" he asked, glancing down into her eyes.

What did he expect her to say? No? She nodded, hoping her fear of falling wasn't apparent.

"Relax," he murmured, his penis starting to move more inside of her, setting up a rhythm. "Sex is great, no matter where or how you have it."

Did he really believe that? She wondered, still holding on tight.

But as he continued moving, teasing her clitoris by pushing his penis deep inside her, stopping, then continuing, her fears started to vanish as her body began to respond. This way of having sex would take time to get used to, she decided. As he started pumping her faster though, rubbing her slick clitoris harder, she found herself concentrating on his movement and forgetting her fears. This way of being fucked wasn't half bad. In fact, it felt pretty damn fantastic.

Feeling his hips slam repeatedly into hers, her body took over and her ability to think vanished. All that mattered now was getting that intense release they both craved.

Chapter Four

Breathing heavily, Kayla's legs fell from Bob's waist of their own accord, and wearily, she sagged against the wall with Bob leaning against her. If someone had told her this morning that the scent of a man's sweat could be sexy, she would've laughed. But oddly enough, it smelled better right now than any expensive after-shave or cologne she could think of.

"Something tells me we're going to get our exercise," he said smiling, softly kissing her lips. "Not that I mind. But I'm exhausted. I thought I was in better shape."

"You're in good shape," she smiled, kissing his broad shoulder.

He pushed himself away from her, heading toward the cabinets. "Yeah, well, thanks, but we've got to get this mess cleaned up in here. I'm not looking forward to doing any more work, but we need to get you moved in tonight. Can we get all your stuff with both our cars in one trip? I've got a jeep with a lot of space in it."

Kayla looked longingly at her coat, which was clear across the room by the door leading to the garage. "Tonight? I'm not exactly dressed right for it." Truth be told, she was freezing now that he'd moved away.

Following the path of her eyes, Bob quickly took off his shirt and tossed it to her. "You will be with this on."

She caught it easily, holding it in front her, studying it. "You're kidding, right? It hangs down to my knees."

Pouring two mugs of freshly made, steaming coffee, he automatically gave her one. "Why do you think I made coffee this late? It's going to be a long night. I'll get you something to wear underneath it in a minute. I've got some women's stuff in my closet from a few dates who'll never reclaim them. Something's bound to fit you enough for you to wear it to work in. I want you to know though; I'm a better housekeeper than what you've seen so far. Believe it or not, I don't usually have trash stacked up like this in my kitchen, and it generally smells like disinfectant, not beer."

But Kayla wasn't paying any attention. He had *women's* clothes in his closet? *Why?* Setting the coffee on the counter, she quickly put on his blasted shirt that came down to her knees with the sleeves coming down to nearly her elbows, fitting her like a shroud. "There's not something you're not telling me about our arrangement, is there? Like another woman being involved?" If there was kinky stuff going on, she'd kiss him good-bye…quickly.

"I'm not a saint, Kayla. I've never pretended to be. Sometimes women have stayed with me overnight and forgotten things. I hang onto them for a while in case they remember, and want them back."

"Any of them stay recently?" she asked sweetly. Surely he wouldn't be entertaining any more of them while she was here, but it was best to get such things out in the open now.

"That's none of your business," he laughed. Getting the broom and dustpan out of the tall closet at the end of the room, he tossed the dustpan to her.

Resigned to her mundane chore, she bent down, holding it in place as he swept. Should she press him about the women? Surely he'd stop having them over after she'd moved in. But there was another problem. She wasn't all that certain she wanted to move in any time soon. Not now. She liked her life just the way it was, with the exception of her money problems. "Why's it so important I get moved in tonight? What's the rush?"

"Don't give me a hard time, okay? I have to see a client Monday morning, and I want you to have one day to settle in while I'm around, in case you need anything. You can have either one of the two guest rooms upstairs. They're already furnished, of course, but they're small and you might want something changed, added or whatever. If we move you in tonight, we'll be able to go to the mall right away and get what you need."

"Hold it! About the room upstairs. It's just for my things, right? But I'll be sleeping with you in the master bedroom."

"Nope." Hauling the filled dustpan over to the trash basket, he slipped a new plastic liner into it and emptied his trash. "I sleep alone. Always. Except when I'm entertaining. Even then, though, I don't sleep with anyone all night. I take my dates home, or send them there in a cab if they don't live too far."

"Fine, I can understand that. Sort of. But those women aren't your wife, like I'll be. So why shouldn't I sleep in the master bedroom with you? I mean, I've never been married before, so I might have my facts wrong, but I've heard married couples share the same bedroom."

"Ah, but most couples have a real marriage. The husband doesn't generally pay his wife to marry him, sleep with him, and have his baby. Technically, that makes you my employee and me your employer, and as your employer, what I say goes."

Kayla was strongly tempted to grab the broom from him and hit him over the head with it. "I thought you said lawyers were going to be involved. Won't it look a little odd if they find out we're sleeping in separate rooms?"

"They're not coming here, Kayla. We have to meet with them at their office. They just want to assure themselves things are moving along like they should. So, unless you specifically tell them, which you'd better not, they won't know."

"But I'll know! Call me strange, but I feel very strongly about this. Can't we pretend we're a real man and wife? At least for a while? Until we get used to each other?"

Bob glared at her, as her sweet face was replaced by the face of his mother, who used to try to come into his room nearly every night after his fifteenth birthday, claiming she wanted to sleep with him instead of with her husband. He could still hear her whiney voice on the other side of the door, claiming she loved him and begging, night after night, for him to unlock his door and let her in. Why his father never heard her and made her stop, he didn't know. Or maybe he did, and by ignoring it, had dealt with it. Whatever the reason, his father agreed to let him go into the Army at seventeen, after which he entered the university and stayed there, never looking back. Though he eventually returned to Houston, he hadn't seen either of them since.

"Bob?" asked Kayla, alarmed by his sudden silence and the odd look in his green eyes. "Look, I don't want to start an argument or anything, but—"

"Do you love me?" he whispered, interrupting her, his voice lethally soft. *Like my mother, the bitch, told me she did?*

Kayla stilled. What an odd question. There was something in the way he asked it too that made her skin crawl. "I…" Her voice trailed off. Bob was rigid. His face was pasty white. He hadn't blinked. And he looked like he was controlling himself by only a thin thread. He looked ready to pounce if she said the wrong thing. She'd always believed in trusting her gut instincts. And right now, her gut was telling her to tread softy...*but why?* "I...don't..." Damn, she felt so sorry for him. Pain was so visible in his huge green eyes; it hurt to look at them. What had scarred him so emotionally and psychologically? Physically, he was here. But mentally, he seemed far away. Even his voice had a strange, unreal quality to it. Yet he was talking to her, somehow keeping track of whatever he was seeing in his mind, and playing it off against her.

"Do you or don't you?" he persisted in that strange voice, looking like he wanted to kill her.

"No," she answered honestly, wondering where she'd put her car keys, wanting to get the hell out, but at the same time, wanting to stay and comfort him...if it was possible to do so.

Bob blinked, his eyes slowly refocusing, looking confused.

Kayla didn't have a genius level I.Q., but she realized he'd suffered some kind of trauma in his past that he'd never come to terms with. He'd just been reliving it. Yet he had enough presence of mind to somehow keep track of things going on around him. But what did love have to do with it? There was no disguising the relief that showed clearly in his eyes now. Was he that afraid of it?

"How much stuff do you have?" he asked as if nothing unusual had happened. "Can we get it all with one trip if we take your car and my jeep?"

She took a sip of her coffee, stalling for time. She had her own crisis to deal with. Her apartment manager had told her she had to pay her back rent by midnight, or get kicked out. So...where did she want to go? Here or on the streets?

She didn't know any one well enough to beg for a place to stay, except maybe at Darlene's house. But she didn't think Darlene and her new husband would like her barging in there for a few days. This job was supposed to have been her last chance to keep her apartment; and she'd just blown it big-time.

"Kayla?"

She glanced at him. He didn't look homicidal now. But then, how exactly did killers look? Was there a way to recognize them? As long as she kept telling Bob the truth; that she didn't love him, things would probably be fine. Besides, she'd have the whole upstairs to herself, from the way he talked. It'd beat the hell out of trying to cram all her stuff in her car, and sleeping there until she figured out what to do.

"Kayla?"

Absently, she drained her coffee and automatically started rinsing out the cup. She never thought she'd see the day when she was grateful her parents were dead, but today she was. This way, they didn't know their little girl had fallen flat on her face in the big city, especially when she'd been doing so well the one time they had visited her. Of course, her prosperity had been short-lived, but she'd never told them that.

Too bad there weren't any jobs in Odessa, or she could go back there. Unfortunately, her best friend from there, Suzanne, had gotten married and had settled on the West Coast. If Suzanne had still been there, she would've put her up for a while, no questions asked.

"Kayla!" shouted Bob, gently touching her shoulder.

"Dammit!" she hissed, jumping so violently she nearly dropped the cup. "Don't you know better than to sneak up on people? You scared me half to death."

He had scared *her?*

"Is there something in particular you wanted?" she asked, taking a patterned paper towel off the roller and drying her cup.

"I've been trying to get your attention for the past few minutes." He stifled his sigh. "Can we get all your things in one trip from your apartment if we use both our cars?"

She nodded. "I think so. But let's not advertise I'm moving when we go there," she suggested. *In case my manager finds out and tries to keep us from taking my things.* "Now, I need to finish getting dressed. We need to get in and out of there quickly," she said, as she turned and headed out of the kitchen. "The things you were talking about are in your closet? I can find it."

Catching up with her, Bob spun her around. For such a sweet-looking little thing, she was awfully pushy. "My room's off-limits to you. Call me selfish, but you're not to go in there unless I invite you there to have sex. Understand? But what in the hell are you talking about, we don't have much time? It is your apartment we're going to, right?"

"Of course it is! But what do you mean you're going to *invite* me to have sex with you? I'm going to be clear upstairs, remember? What are you going to do, send an engraved invitation by carrier pigeon?"

He shrugged. He knew she wasn't going to like his reasoning. But she would have to deal with it as his paid employee. "You have a cell phone, don't you?"

She glowered at him as what he'd said sank in. "Don't tell me you actually expect to call me on the damn phone! That's absurd! Legally, I'll be your wife. I'm not going to be treated like a whore you call on the *phone* whenever you get the urge."

"There's nothing wrong with whores," he threw over his shoulder, striding to his closet. "A lot of them are real class acts. But don't worry. I'm paying you a lot more than I've ever paid for any of them."

Damn! That hurt! Batting back her tears, she rushed after to him. "Of all the nerve!" she hissed. "I've never sold my body for sex in my life!"

"I'm not saying you did," he said, rummaging through the hangers at the very back of his closet, which contained numerous women's sweaters and blouses in various styles and assorted colors, and pairs of slacks and jeans, all neatly pressed. "But I'm paying you a heck of a lot of money to do as I say. In this case, that means fucking when I want, however I want." He sighed, feeling drained. "I mean look, Kayla, I like you. I really do. I've chosen you to be my wife. But there are certain limits you have to abide by living with me."

Kayla had never wanted to murder anyone in her life. Until now. "Damn you, *Mister* McKnight! I may be destitute. Now. But I won't always be."

She was destitute? Not just desperate as George had claimed? "You can relax about your financial situation, thanks to me, if you behave yourself," he muttered, throwing her a pair of jeans and some chartreuse knitted bedroom slippers and taking a clean, freshly-pressed shirt for himself. "So let's get this over with. Anything we can't bring back here in one trip, we leave."

"We're going to have to limit it to one. Two would be too risky. But I'm wearing my coat over this outfit. I've got an appearance to maintain to get by the doorman and night watchman."

"What? You'd rather they think you're crazy than badly dressed?"

"So they won't call Mrs. Blithers, my manager. Kurt, the doorman at night would call her if he got suspicious. They are buddies."

"Your manager doesn't want you to move out? But I thought you owed her rent. I'd think she'd want you out."

"She might. But she might also be planning to keep my stuff for the back rent I owe. I'd just as soon not take the chance."

"How much do you owe?" he asked, watching her struggle into the oversized jeans, handing her the belt from his robe which she tied around her waist keep them up.

She hesitated. She didn't want to tell him. Even *she* thought she was being extravagant living there. But after she'd gotten what she considered her dream job, as personal secretary and assistant to the chairman of the board of a prosperous oil company that had transferred their headquarters to town, she'd worked only three months before she moved in to her dream apartment…lying…well not exactly lying, but more like stretching the truth, on her rental application. Because she'd looked so prosperous, Mrs. Blithers hadn't even bothered to check her information. She'd rented the apartment in good faith, never dreaming two months later her boss would be canned, throwing her out of a job too.

"You have to keep in mind it's a bargain for all you get. Crystal chandeliers. Silk covered walls to match the floor to ceiling drapes. The entire walls of my bedroom and living room are glass, and have a spectacular view of the Galleria. I have patios for both, of course, which can be turned into one by—"

"Never mind the sales pitch. How much?"

"Two thousand," she whispered so low he could barely hear. "But that includes part of this month's rent too. You don't have to pay it for me, though. I think if we're quiet and don't arouse suspicion, we can get most of my stuff out by using the back stairs with no one the wiser."

Bob raised his brows. *Good Lord, she was larcenous.* What kind of a woman had he picked? "I'm not going to worry about that now," he said, getting his keys, his check book and his wallet. "We'll deal with it as it comes."

Taking one last look in the mirror, she winced. Not arousing suspicion would be hard, even with her coat on. But quickly she discarded the darn slippers for her spike heels. They were uncomfortable and looked strange with her odd outfit, but not as strange as the slippers. And if they could get into her place, she'd change anyway, so she wouldn't have to endure the pain long. Unfortunately, her hair was badly mussed and her mascara was smudged and her lipstick had long since vanished, making her look as pale as a corpse. She had things necessary to repair her face, but they were locked in the car and she had no idea where her stupid keys were. And they were in a hurry. He was going to be furious when she told him she'd lost her keys.

***

"You what?" Bob exploded several minutes later. "How could you be so careless?"

"Wait just a damn minute! I didn't do this deliberately to thwart you. I was nervous when I first arrived. I was coming to work half-dressed in a house I've never been in before, to work for a man I'd never seen in my life. I felt more than just a little vulnerable. The least of my worries was my stupid keys."

Bob ground his teeth. "Have you searched everywhere? Have you retraced your steps? Looked in the pockets of your coat? Your cleaning supply rack? Everyplace you were from the moment you got out of your car?"

"I've searched my coat pockets. That's where I'd have put them. It's the most logical place."

"Take this," he barked, giving her a huge flashlight. "Make sure you didn't lock your keys in the car. If you did, we'll break the damn window to get them. If they aren't there, search every step you took coming in. They might have fallen out of wherever you put them. While you're out there, I'll go through your coat again and your rack."

Bob's temper came as no surprise. She'd known he'd be upset. The thing was, she was upset too. She just showed it in a different way. She always got quiet when she was worried, trying to think, to figure things out. But maybe it wasn't a good thing to be like that, because people seemed to pick her for an easy target because she was so quiet; and she was getting damn tired of it.

Did it go back to her mother? She'd always cautioned her that "Ladies don't shout. Ladies keep their tempers. Ladies don't cross their legs at the knees, only at the ankles. Ladies always eat with a napkin. Ladies don't get dirty." Then the damn nuns at the school she went to expanded the Ladies Rule to include sex. "Ladies don't have sex with men they aren't married to. Ladies don't do 'it' in motel rooms. Ladies don't do 'it' in cars." And the thing was, she'd bought into the concept. No wonder her first affair had been so disastrous. Not only hadn't she been married to the jerk, they'd had sex in motel rooms.

She took a deep breath, inhaling the fresh air as she went outside. It was a beautiful night, ironically, made for romance; with a full moon so large she felt she could touch it, and millions of bright, twinkling stars in the sky. She loved this time of year here in Houston. Usually. But not tonight. With winter's grasp long-gone, it was still early enough in the year to have cool nights and warm, but not overly oppressive hot, humid days. Maybe that was part of her trouble too. She was too easily appeased.

Hoping none of Bob's neighbors could see her, she held the flashlight well away from her and ran its bright beam over the huge lawn, which was neatly cut, with not a blade of crabgrass in sight. The row of flower bushes along the perimeter of the house was perfectly trimmed, and the camellias were about to bloom. She could see the little white buds nestled deep in their cocoons of round leaves. Did he have a gardener? Or did he like to do gardening like she did when she'd lived at home?

Maybe he'd let her do that here. It'd give her something to do when she wasn't bowing and scraping, carrying out his every wish.

Shining the light ahead of her inside the windows of the car, her heart sank. Her keys weren't there! She tried to open the door to check the floorboard but, predictably, it was locked. That meant she had to have taken her keys into the house. Her car didn't lock without her pressing several buttons on her key ring as part of the car's alarm. But where were they?

Squatting down on the driveway, she looked underneath her car. Maybe she'd dropped them and they'd somehow bounced under it. She should have heard them clink if they had, but then again, she'd been so nervous, she might not have noticed. But nothing unusual was there, just a slight rust stain.

Walking back, she again aimed the beam of her bright light all around and her heart sank. Her keys weren't anyplace out here. If they didn't find them inside, Bob would have to pay a locksmith to come out and make new keys. He'd have no choice. But he'd be enraged! Well, so be it.

Letting herself back in, she nearly ran into Bob who was lounging against the wall in the entryway, holding her keys twirling her key ring around on his finger. "They were in your cleaning rack, Kayla. You didn't look hard enough before, or you'd have seen them."

Deciding not to tell him she hadn't looked in there at all, since it wasn't the logical place, she tried to hide her relief at locating them, striving to look as blasé as he was. But she knew she was failing miserably. It was going to take a lot of work to change herself, but, dammit all, she had to try. She was tired of being everyone's door mat.

"Ready?" he asked, throwing a few empty boxes at her. "I'll follow you, but go slow. The cops out here love to give tickets."

Chapter Five

Pulling up in the well-lit, wide, curving driveway of her luxury apartment building nearly an hour later, Kayla felt her heart break. She loved this place so much, and now, less than a year after moving in, she had to leave. Nestled in the middle of the exclusive area of River Oaks, the white brick building stood twenty stories tall, with every apartment having its own covered patio stretching from the living room, with its huge marble fireplace, past the master bedroom, and on to the smaller guest bedroom.

Stopping the car as the door man ran out to get her car key, she took it off the key ring along with the alarm, so that the parking attendant could take care of her car. Although his eyes widened when he saw what she was wearing, he quickly got himself under control. His expression composed itself into a bland mask. Thank goodness he recognized her. If he hadn't, she might have had to explain to one of the twenty-four hour security guards what she was doing dressed like this, trying to get in here.

She grinned at Bob when he joined her a few minutes later in the marble floored foyer. His eyes were huge as he looked all around, gawking like a tourist. "Like it? It has tennis courts, a fully equipped gym, parking attendants, and even a private club downstairs."

Bob stared at her, incredulous. No wonder she was in debt. Driving a new Volvo, living in an exclusive, very expensive high-rise, and no telling what all. And worse, she still acted like money was no object. But she wasn't stupid. She didn't seem to be the frivolous type, either. Maybe she had simply been dirt poor as a kid, and living in a place like this helped alleviate the feelings of inferiority brought on by poverty, he thought.

"I used to have a roommate I found through roommate-dot-com." she said. "For the first three months I lived here. I was really relieved when she moved back home to save up money for her wedding, though. She was very noisy, coming in at all hours of the day and night. I've been looking for another roommate, but no one wants to pay five hundred dollars a month to share an apartment."

"So you have a two bedroom place?" He asked, as they got in the thickly carpeted elevator. No wonder she wasn't happy to have a small guest room, when she was used to all this. It had to be a painful wake-up call to reality.

She nodded. "I really love it. Whenever I got depressed, I never stayed that way for long. The view from the tenth floor where I live is great. Wait 'till you see it. It's spectacular. And my garden tub with the eight spray jets is a great relaxer too. I used to stay in it for hours at a time. It's hard to stay tense here."

Bob didn't let his surprise show. She had no idea how much she'd just revealed about herself. She didn't appear to be nervous and depressed. But she obviously was. A lot, apparently. Was it because she knew she couldn't afford this place? Or was there something else? She was attractive, with an excellent figure…but she seemed to lack the self-confidence he'd expected from someone who'd been a secretary, and who'd chosen life as a single girl making it on her own. She had a temper, but didn't lash out except to defend herself, and even then, she wasn't all that skilled at it. And adding to it was the fact that she seemed to know she lacked what it took to be successful. *Poor thing.* She was as helpless as the little bird he'd helped. He wondered if he could he help her, and wondered if he had what it would take? In the end he decided he didn't know. Not yet.

The narrow hall was deserted when they stepped out of the elevator at the tenth floor, onto thick royal blue carpeting. Small, expensively framed oils done in soothing shades of blue adorned the long ivory walls. Although he couldn't see them, he was willing to bet there were security cameras hidden up here.

"I fell in love with this place the minute the manager first showed it to me. I rent most of the furniture, though, so we don't have to worry about taking any of that. I can call Logan's on Monday, and they'll come up here and remove it. I don't have a lot of linens, just a few sets…I don't suppose the beds upstairs at your house are doubles, are they?"

"No," he smiled, "but don't worry about linens for them. I'll be glad to furnish them."

She figured as much. He was well-prepared for almost any eventuality, apparently; totally unlike her. She envied him. But his ability contrasted sharply with hers, making her feel inadequate. She'd always envied older people, ever since she could remember. They always seemed to have their act together.

"Other than that, there are my books, bookshelves, my home entertainment center, a few place settings of china, and all my clothes and shoes. In addition to my walk-in closet, I use the two hall closets here as well. I don't think one closet in a small guest bedroom will hold them all. That might present a problem, huh?"

Dear God! It sounded like she had clothes to start her own second-hand store. But he knew where she was headed. "Your books and shelves can go in both guest bedrooms or in the hallway up there, if they need to, I guess. The china you won't need. We'll store it in my attic. If I like your entertainment center, it can go in my den. But we'll have to wait and see about your clothes. If you have too many to fit into both closets upstairs, you'll have to give some away or sell them at a second-hand store on consignment. I'm sorry, but there's no way I'm sharing my closet with you. I built and designed my house for one person. Me. In the two years I've lived there, I've never had a guest, but figured if I ever did, having two small rooms instead of one large room would discourage long stays."

She stiffened, proudly squaring her shoulders, looking oddly endearing in his oversized shirt, stuffed so tightly into that coat of hers it made her look lumpy. He wanted to hug her and assure her everything would be fine. But, dammit, he was paying her a hell of a lot, and would be taking care of her financially for the rest of her life. Surely it would be worth it to her to make a few compromises.

"Sounds like your plan worked," she sighed. "Until now." But she understood all too well. Her living with him was going to be an unexpected inconvenience. He'd put up with it only as long as it served his purpose, and as long as it was going to be temporary. They were alike in that they both liked living alone. She'd detested having a roommate. Unfortunately, she was going to have another one. Him. Stopping in front of a door with the gold embossed numbers of ten-oh-five, she ripped off an envelope and silently read the contents. "Looks like you're saving me just in time," she said, unlocking the door. "This confirms what I told you. Mrs. Blithers, my manager, will evict me at midnight if I don't pay two thousand in full tonight. So take a good look," she said, opening the door. "It's the last time either one of us will ever see this apartment again."

Bob studied her. Poor thing. She looked ready to cry. Quickly he put his arm around her shoulders, pulling her close as they entered. Expensive or not, this had been her home. Her place of safety. Her refuge from the world. And now it was gone. But, in spite of himself, Bob let out a low whistle as they entered.

Opposite the door, the entire wall was glass with floor to ceiling drapes of heavy white silk, completely open. In the huge, darkened room, it looked like they could walk outside into the night sky, with the large rambling houses and buildings far below. Facing south, the lights of the Galleria, with its multi-level hotels and shopping area, and the tall slender Niels Esperson building, lit the night sky. While closer underneath her window, numerous trees and budding gardens, lit by torch lights, gave the private parks an aura of mystery.

Watching her reflection in the dark glass as she turned on a Tiffany lamp in the far corner and looked around, his heart again went out to her.

Her eyes were hungrily taking in every inch, memorizing it forever. This was hers, dammit. It was where she'd belonged. Sure, she had expensive taste. But with many glass figurines of butterflies and unicorns scattered throughout, she'd turned it not just into a showplace, but had made it her own personal home.

The two twin Queen Anne chairs, a large Chippendale desk, and the four-piece sectional in white brocade were of superb quality, and…"You have a flat screen plasma TV?" He'd lusted for one since they'd first come out…and she had one!

Kayla nodded, clearly not all that impressed by it. "I hardly ever watch it. But it's part of my entertainment center. I'd like to take it though, along with my CD and DVD players and my computer."

"You bet we'll take it," he murmured, rubbing his hand softly around the sides of the thin screen, caressing it like a lover. "I've got just the spot for it in my den."

"Glad you like it," she said, heading into the bedroom to change her clothes. "If something else catches your eye, grab it."

Surprised by her generosity, but taking her at her word, Bob eagerly started sorting through her vast collection of CDs and DVDs.

***

Nearly three hours later, after so many trips up and down the back staircase she'd lost count, and a tense drive back to his house with her car packed so high with her things she couldn't see the rear view mirror, Kayla dragged herself into his huge house, carrying yet another cumbersome stack of dresses still on their hangers, going up more infernal stairs.

Unfortunately, life with her new fiancée wasn't getting off to the best start. Not only was Bob grouchy from all the packing and hauling they'd done, his bossiness was beginning to grate on her nerves. Worse, he looked so masculine with his five o'clock shadow, she was more attracted to him now than she had been when they'd first met. In spite of her exhaustion, she longed for him to hold her in his strong arms, and to feel those short whiskers on her skin. She wanted to taste them, to feel them with her tongue.

But Bob had other plans, the least of which was romance and cuddling.

"I don't see how a woman can have so many damned clothes," he roared, storming in with the last of her dresses. "Most of them are brand new. You'll never wear all these; there's not enough years left in your life." Angrily, he threw her clothes on the bed in the nearest room.

Leaning wearily against the door jamb, she felt ready to drop. "I already told you, I'll go through them to see if there's some I can give away or sell, or whatever. But I'll do it tomorrow. After we unload this stuff, I'm taking a hot shower and crashing."

"Oh, no you don't! You don't go to bed until everything is sorted, hung up, and neatly packed."

"Are you crazy? I'm ready to drop as it is! I'll be lucky if I can even stay upright long enough to take a shower. What's wrong with waiting until tomorrow? I'll have the entire day to do it then."

"This is my house, Kayla. I like a neat, orderly house at all times. You are just hired help. You'll do what I say, when I say it."

She glared at him. She'd never worked so damn hard in her life; her energy fueled by the fear her manager would catch them. She hurt all over, in places she didn't know she had. She reeked of the sweat pouring down in rivulets, soaking her hair, her light-weight cotton t-shirt, her white cotton shorts and even her tennis shoes. Her right arm was bruised from banging it against the metal stair rail of the back stairs in her apartment building as she careened around the corner too fast, nearly dropping the huge box she'd been carrying. For every one of his trips up and down the stairs, she'd made two. And they'd been successful. They'd gotten everything. But there were limits to her strength. "Damn you! I'm not your slave."

"You're not? I've bought and paid for you, lady, and you need to learn your place and stay there. I won't have clothes scattered all over the damn house, and I'm not going to tolerate any back-talk. You'll do as I tell you from here on in, and you'll do it without question."

Why was he doing this? He had to know she was worn out. He looked every bit as tired as she did. But he refused to give her any slack. "Of all the nerve! Contrary to your illusions of grandeur, you don't own me, and you never will. I may have agreed to your hare-brained scheme in a moment of insanity, but I never agreed to let you rule my life."

"You didn't?" His face was bland. His tone was lethally soft. But his words were clipped and distinct. Too distinct.

His abrupt change worried her. But she was too angry to care. "A wife isn't your possession! A wife has the same rights as her husband. Maybe even more so, inside the house.

It's common knowledge that a woman takes control of the inside of a house, while the man's domain is the outside." She swallowed visibly, alarmed by his widening, unblinking eyes staring hard into hers. His jaw clenched and his facial muscles tightened. Pushing herself upright against the door jamb, she cautiously backed up, just in case. "This isn't your house, dammit. It's mine! You don't control a damned thing."

God! He was so difficult to deal with. Was he just being obtuse, or what? In spite of her growing apprehension, her own temper was starting to flare out of control. "I was talking figuratively, not literally, dammit. Why do you have to take everything I say and pick it apart? You seem like an intelligent man. Start using your intellect for a change."

For a change? Without a word, Bob lunged at her, going for her knees and rearing up, he tossed her over his shoulder. "You're not my possession?" he murmured, storming down the stairs and into his bedroom. "We'll see about that. You can bet your sweet ass we will." Soundly, he smacked her bottom, then threw her on his bed.

Stunned, Kayla watched him snap off his belt, fearing for her very life. As he wrenched off his shirt, she saw her chance to get away and bent her knees, trying to get enough leverage to scoot off the bed, out of his reach.

But she was too slow. And he was surprisingly fast. Grabbing her ankles, he pulled her back to the middle. "You're right staying here," he seductively whispered, clutching her wrists as he unzipped and dropped his pants. "I'm going to do things to you now that I'd been saving for later. Things which you may not like right now. But we'll stay right here, doing them over and over again, until you do."

Straddling her before she could fight him off, he ripped open the demure plain, white cotton shirt she'd put on at her old apartment. But it wasn't the loss of her shirt that upset her. It was his temper, combined with his rough manhandling, which unnerved her. He was, after all, a stranger. She didn't know what he was capable of.

With her heart beating frantically, Kayla watched him reach over her, retrieve his pants and take out his pocket knife, flicking it open. "This won't hurt if you stay still," he warned, as she steeled herself and scrunched her eyes shut.

Dear God, she'd really done it this time! This man wasn't only a maniac; he was a dangerous, mean brute. *Dammit, Kayla*, she scolded herself. *You had to push him! Now look what you've done!* Feeling the ice-cold blade of metal edge between her breasts, slipping under the fastening of her new French cut lace bra, she flinched, her whole body jumping.

"What the hell's the matter with you? I haven't cut a thing yet."

Kayla kept her eyes closed tight. "But you will. You're a mean, spiteful monster. And I hate you. I hope you rot in hell."

To her astonishment, he laughed as he slid the blade of the cold knife up and the see-sawing sound of cut lace exploded in her ears in the otherwise deathly silent room. Hearing the plopping of the knife as it landed on the floor and feeling no pain, she opened one eye.

Pulling her wrists over her head, he stretched her out underneath him and wedged his knee between her locked legs, spreading them. Her golden hair spread behind her, her deep breathing causing those luscious breasts to move up and down slowly.

He'd never wanted a woman this badly or needed her so desperately.

Her distinct scent, warmed by the energy of her fear, inflamed him. He had to have her. He had to possess her, all of her. At all costs. He had to make her submit to his will, so that she shared his desire to burn in the throes of his passion. He'd do whatever it took to tame her and brand her as his and only his.

Continuing to hold her wrists, he jerked his arm down to cover her shoulders just below her neck, so that he pinned her in place. If she moved, he'd break her neck. For a moment, he stared into her eyes as a silent warning. Then he rubbed his whiskered cheek over her smooth, cool breasts, laving every sweet inch with his tongue, hungrily swallowing her sweat, reveling in the taste. He stared at those sweet, responsive nipples reverently, then gently took first one then the other between his lips, sucking greedily. Shoving his arm roughly over her neck more forcefully, as a warning to continue to hold still, he jumped onto his knees over her and rained light kisses over her flat stomach. Then he quickly jerked down her shorts. Taking hold of the prim, white elastic of her lace panties with his teeth, he pulled them down, inhaling her fragrant heated pubic hair, the color and texture of spun gold. He could tell by her continued flinching and the instinctive tightening of her stomach she'd never been touched so intimately. Too bad! Her struggling only inflamed his determination to control her.

She was his now, by God, and he'd damn well do whatever he wanted with her! Never had he had anything or anyone he could truly call his. Until now. And he was going to relish the moment of total possession.

Watching him, Kayla's heart pounded. Bob was treating her like a thing, rather than a person. He'd never been this rough with her, before. In fact, he'd been an exquisitely gentle lover. Until now. Was he going to do what she thought? How perverse! How sick! "Please," she begged as he took her clitoris between his lips, teasing it with the tip of his tongue. "Don't! I've never done this, dammit! No one's ever done this to me before. I'm not into this…this kinky stuff!"

She'd never done it before? For some reason he couldn't define, her confirmation of what he already knew delighted him. Never had a woman tasted so sweet. Or been so responsive. In spite of her heated denial that she didn't like it, her entire cunt was soaked. She liked it, all right. She just didn't realize it. But then he didn't care what she wanted either. She was his to do exactly whatever he wanted with.

"You're out of your mind," she continued, not caring at the moment if he killed her or not. "I'd rather be dead than to submit to this … this…" she sputtered, her words trailing off as he continued to lave her clitoris and a piercing thrill shot right through her.

He felt her nub grow hard, pulsating and throbbing as he openly licked her, his probing tongue seeking and finding her deepest crevices, and soaking them as he inhaled her spicy scent that was intensified by her growing heat. He exalted in the moment of possession, knowing he was the first ever to awaken her body to this carnal pleasure. He'd made an excellent choice by choosing her. There was a lot he'd teach her along these lines. And she'd submit, by God, or he'd know the reason why. "I warn you," she whispered, breathing hard, her excitement building at the decadent, flagrant way his tongue was licking her in places she didn't know she had. "You shouldn't…you … damn you!" Moaning, she arched her hips up higher to meet his flicking tongue and relentless lips. He laughed wickedly. She liked this, the little hypocrite. She liked it a hell of a lot.

"Want me to stop?" he mumbled against her, keeping the tip of his tongue firmly on her vibrating, slick clitoris with an effort, continuing to lick her, feeling her hips tense.

"No!" she moaned, arching up again to more firmly get more of her in between those magical lips of his. "Don't stop. Not ever!"

Letting go of her wrists and removing his arm, he cupped her ass, turning it up, sliding his tongue into her vagina as far as it would go, gently nibbling the sensitive, wet flesh which surrounded it. She was soaked, and tasted better than any of the paid whores he'd spent so much money on. Strange how an ordinary woman was more exciting than an expensive, experienced call girl.

Feeling her fingers entwine in his hair, pulling, smoothing, jerking, squeezing, then pushing his head deeper into her, he felt more alive than he had in a long time. Hell, his penis was as hard as marble, vibrating as wildly as her clitoris. Jumping over her, he quickly rammed his slick rod deep inside her. This was no time for a gentlemanly fuck. He had to have her now, as fast as he could. Pumping her like a steel piston rams a well-oiled engine, he was soon lost in the magic of the best climax he'd ever had.

And though Kayla thoroughly enjoyed it, something nagged at her from the edges of her mind. Something was not quite right here. But her body didn't cooperate to help her see what it was that worried her. Until the following morning.

Chapter Six

Although Kayla was normally a sound sleeper; never one to thrash around in her sleep or get up during the night, she kept dreaming she was running from someone. But while she kept looking over her shoulder, she couldn't see anyone until she rounded a bend in her dreams, crashing headlong into a huge solid object that woke her. It was then she realized from whom she'd been running, as she stared into Bob's open green eyes mere inches from hers. In the near darkness, they glowed so eerily that, to her sleep-fogged brain, they looked like something straight from hell. He looked as surprised as she was and quickly reared up.

"I'm leaving," she said, jumping up on the side of the bed opposite his, gathering her clothes as she went. "But next time, I'm bringing an alarm clock."

Bob opened his mouth about to object. They had to do something. But not that. He didn't get the words out, though. He couldn't as he stared in horror at the bruises on her shoulders and her tiny hips. She was walking oddly too, her thighs spread slightly apart. "Oh, God, baby!" he hoarsely whispered. "I'm so sorry. I didn't mean to hurt you like that. I didn't realize what I was doing."

Following the path of his eyes, Kayla gasped audibly. In her frantic desire to escape she hadn't felt any pain. But as she stared at the bluish, brownish spots on both of her shoulders and across her neck and collar bone, she suddenly felt sore. Her bottom hurt too. A lot. And she felt, dear God! Like she'd been raped! She looked at him, puzzled.

"Please believe me, baby, I—"

"Don't touch me!" she screeched, backing up as he neared. "Just leave me alone."

"I won't hurt you again, I promise."

"Stay away!"

The pain in his eyes was apparent as he stopped cold. "You don't have to be afraid of me, baby. Stay here, please, and let me make it up to you."

"When hell freezes over."

Bob sat down on the edge of the bed, holding his hands up. "I won't touch you if you don't want me to. But we have to talk about this. We can't live under the same roof with you being scared half to death of me."

She was tired, sore and dirty. And she had no place to go. Her apartment was gone. Her job was gone. And she knew it was only by luck that she'd evaded the repo man for her car. But by God, she still had a half tank of gas. That'd get her someplace far away from this miserable town and this maniac, if she drove fast enough. She turned from him. "It'll take me an hour to get my things together," she shot over her shoulder. "What I can't put in my car, you can keep."

She was reacting out of fear, Bob realized. And the accompanying adrenalin rush that often comes with it. In her condition she wouldn't get far. Hell, she might even crash in her attempt to escape. "I know about your financial situation, Kayla," he whispered, playing a hunch. "And so does George."

That stopped her cold. "Excuse me?" she asked, whirling back to face him. "George has everyone who works for him investigated. He and the P.I. who works with him know everything about you from the time you were born."

"And he told you? Why? And who cares, anyway? I can manage fine on my own. I have so far."

"Have you? Look at the facts. You have no place to go. You haven't eaten since God only knows when. You don't have any friends. No money. And the way we've been having sex, you could be pregnant right now with our child."

Feeling the blood drain from her face, Kayla staggered to the closest chair, collapsing on it, feeling dizzy. Good God! He was right! She could be pregnant right now! Ruining her life was one thing. But she'd be damned if she'd ruin a baby's.

"That doesn't give..." her voice trailed off, sounding hysterical. She coughed nervously and tried again "That doesn't give you the right to abuse me." "No, it doesn't. And I promise it won't happen again. But try to see things from my perspective. I've never had financial responsibility for anyone but myself. Never wanted it. And I don't like it. I'll deal with it, but it'll take some time.

Last night we were both exhausted. I know I pushed you, and I shouldn't have. But I wasn't thinking. I never dreamed someone so broke would have all that stuff, and using those damn stairs wore me out, and you too. I hadn't eaten all day either, unless you count the veggie burger I munched on while I was working on a developer's plans. So I plain wasn't thinking right, Kayla. Believe it or not, I've never hurt a woman in my life. I don't know what got into me, to be honest. I just…your… well, dammit, you have a good figure and I overreacted. I had to have you at all costs. But I usually don't get carried away like that.

It's the strain of getting used to all this, I think, that finally got to me. Yesterday morning, I was single. Then I was about to go to sleep with my new fiancée under my roof. It's going to take time for me to get used to sharing my house, Kayla. Not only with you, but with our new baby; when it comes. I don't know if you're familiar or not with the way divorce works in Texas, but it takes a year to get it finalized. You can move out before then, of course, but for the first six months of our baby's life, you'll still be here. Then you can decide if you want to move into one of my houses, or another one, but until then, we have to start thinking about where to place a nursery here; that kind of thing. Quite frankly, the thought of having a new baby scares me stiff."

In spite of herself, Kayla felt herself softening toward him a little. She hadn't realized he'd planned this so conscientiously, and was taking his responsibilities so seriously. "Do you plan to take an active part in raising him or her?"

"I'm going to assume all his or her expenses, of course. Feeding, clothing, doctor's bills, a private school; that kind of thing. And I think it's only right our kid knows who I am, and gets used to me enough so he or she won't be scared of me. Some kids are afraid of men, you know. I don't want my kid to be afraid of anything or anyone. But as far as care, you'll be the primary parent." She nodded. All that was so far in the future. Unless, of course, she was pregnant right now. Then it was only nine short months away. That time would fly by, she suspected. But for right now, she'd postpone leaving.

"If you raise your hand or hold me again and hurt me like you did last night, I won't be able to stay. You know that."

"That's a given. But I don't want you to be afraid of me in the meantime. The purpose of our arrangement is to make sure you conceive. Do you understand what I'm saying?"

"You want to have sex? Again? Now?"

He nodded. "So you'll be assured that I intend keeping to my promise of not hurting you again."

"I'm already a little sore."

"I know that. I'll be very gentle. I just don't want you fearing me. It's kind of like falling off a horse. If you get right back on, you won't be afraid."

"But I'm dirty, and hungry and still tired."

He got up, advancing toward her. "I know," he murmured, putting his arms around her, pulling her up. "But I've got a big shower with room enough for two, and lots of hot steamy water and plenty of soap." He kissed her lightly. "We'll eat right after."

She searched his eyes. He was looking at her honestly, with patience. He wouldn't push her, she realized. It'd be her choice as much as his. "All right," she said, hoping to God she could relax a little and stop feeling so tense. She knew he could be gentle. But before last night, she hadn't realized he had such a dark side. It was that knowledge that made her edgy.

"Ever had sex in a shower?" he asked conversationally, taking her hand; leading her into his bathroom.

"No. Have you?"

He laughed. "Everything I do with you has special meaning, baby. But everything we do, I've done before. And that's a good thing. It's important for me that you like it and I'm experienced enough to make sure you do."

Kayla laughed, sounding a little nervous even to her own ears.

"It's going to be okay, baby. Just relax and follow my lead. I'll take very good care of you."

Like he did last night? She wondered. But then again, maybe she was being too hard on him. He was so good looking he could easily arouse her with just a glance. He was tall and well built, and she had, until last night, felt safe with him. She had to at least give him the benefit of a doubt now. Not only for her own sake, but for their child which she could be carrying, heaven help her. She hadn't succeeded at anything in her life. How would she be as a mother?

"Ladies first," Bob smiled, bowing slightly.

She stepped into the huge frosted glass enclosure encased with gold-looking trim, large faucets and the biggest shower head she'd ever seen.

Watching him adjust the temperature and strength of the spray, she waited near the shower door; on the back of which was a huge terry cloth bath towel in dark green.

"I had this custom-made for me. I think you'll like it."

"It's lovely," she said, mildly surprised by the overhead light, high up in the enclosure, dimming as the spray increased. "Kind of romantic."

"Or peaceful. It depends on my mood."

She went into his arms easily, as he gently kneaded the base of her skull with his thumbs as he kissed her. "You're tense," he murmured, kissing her again. "Try to relax."

"Keep kissing me like this and I will."

But he didn't smile in response to her teasing tone. He knew she was still scared, and he didn't blame her. She was so young, tiny and vulnerable, and he knew he'd made a mistake last night. Trust was an essential part of making love and he'd blown it big time. Chances were, she wouldn't be able to relax completely for a while. It would take time to regain her trust, but get it he would. He could see in her eyes she wanted that too. Her longing to recapture the magic they'd felt earlier was clear in the way she kept searching his eyes.

Was she pregnant now? He wondered, slowly working his way down her luscious little body, his lips lingering on her surprisingly large breasts. He honestly didn't know. She might be. He'd read enough to know that within a week or two of conceiving, Chadwick's sign, a bluish tinge to the vagina and cervix would appear. But he wasn't going to share his knowledge with her. There was no reason to.

Glancing into her eyes, he noticed her eye lids were beginning to droop as he made lazy circles around her nipples, teasing the sensitive buds with his thumbs. But her little hands around his waist were ice-cold and held him loosely. She should have been making forays into his chest by now. But she was holding back. He was penetrating her defenses, but just barely.

Pouring some thick white liquid soap into her hands, he stood closer. "Make love to me, baby," he softly instructed. "Rub this into me, everywhere."

He'd changed the rules since last night a lot. This morning, he wanted her to be an active participant in sex. Although she'd never done it in this way before, she gamely let a little water mix into the soap and lathered her hands, beginning with his neck and throat, rubbing it in, rinsing it, then kissing it, inch by inch. The hot water cascading down felt soothing, washing some of her tenseness away, as she slowly scrubbed him. His shoulders were so broad, strong and well-muscled. But it was his chest which fascinated her. It was covered by thousands of hairs, making him look almost furry, with his pale, flat nipples nearly hidden. She made lazy circles around them with her forefinger as she reached up to kiss and suck them. She felt his stomach muscles tighten with his quick intake of air, and heard his moan of delight deep in his chest. His nipples tasted salty, but not unpleasant, their male scent mixed with the fragrant woodsy smell of the liquid soap.

Putting more into her hand from the dispenser, she stood back and slowly massaged soapy lather into the tapering curls of his hair leading down to his penis, which erected and elongated to meet her probing, gentle fingers.

"Don't go too slow, baby," he pleaded. "I can't hold off much longer." He'd never felt anything this erotic in his entire life. Her light touch, her awkwardness as she gently massaged him, trying to be thorough, for God's sake, aroused him as nothing before. The way she kissed and licked his nipples with the lightest tip of her tongue, probing into each crevice, had nearly caused him to come right then and there. But he wanted her to be comfortable with his body. He just hadn't counted on her being so damn conscientious about getting him clean.

Kayla didn't have to ask him if he liked it. She could tell by his nipples hardening, his stomach clenching, and his sharp intakes of breath, mixed with deep, rumbling groans, that he did. She looked at his penis. It was large, throbbing and dripping. He liked what she was doing. A lot.

Taking gentle hold of it at its base with her heavily lathered fingers, she started slowly massaging it upward, toward the sensitive tip. "God dammit, baby!" he growled, bending her over, curving her fingers around the soap dispenser holder on the shower wall. "Play time's over."

Kayla jumped upright. "Don't you dare enter me from the back!"

"I'm not going in your ass," he hissed, positioning her hands again; bending her over, keeping her down with his weight as he straddled her, one strong arm going around her waist, teasing the outer contour of her breasts as he too held onto the dispenser holder with his other hand. "I'm going in your cunt."

Feeling him plunge in, she held onto the curved soap holder for all she was worth. She wasn't in pain, but she was uncomfortable, trying to get used to the odd feeling of him entering from the 'wrong' direction.

With his ragged breath tickling her ear, he nudged her and she turned her face to receive his very thorough kiss.

"Relax, baby," he murmured, his harsh breathing fanning her face. "Close your eyes and relax."

Did he really enjoy doing it this way? She wondered, trying to do as he said even though it didn't make any sense. How could she relax and hold herself up at the same time? Or did he just enjoy the novelty of the position? Some men, she knew, just liked to be versatile.

"You don't like it, do you?" he asked, plunging in and holding it. "Be honest."

If ever there was a trick question that was it. She opened her eyes. "I'm getting used to it," she breathed, a bit theatrically.

"Don't try to fake an orgasm, Kayla. There are ways a woman reveals when she has one and when she doesn't. I know what to look for."

"It'll take some time to get used to the rhythm, okay? I'm trying. I really am."

Whipping his penis out, he picked her up, strode to the marble vanity, setting her on the edge and spreading her legs, he plunged into her again, rubbing her clitoris with gentle fingers.

"Oh, Bob!" she breathed, unable to stop herself, as she gave into the heady feeling she realized now she longed for, and laid back as he pumped her. "Oh, God! Yes!"

But despite his enthusiasm, he kept himself under control, going as slowly as he could, careful not to go in all the way. The purpose of this little exercise was to get her to enjoy sex with him again. He wasn't thrilled though he had to use her clitoris to get her excited, when before she'd trusted him enough to lose herself completely. But at least it was a start in the right direction.

Chapter Seven

"If I have to sign on one more dotted line, I'm going to scream," said Kayla, crossing one shapely leg over the other, as she fidgeted in the white leather arm chair. "The change of address form and car insurance, and taking out life insurance, I can understand. Even the application for the marriage license, I can see that. But this," she said, shaking the five page document, "isn't even legal. It'll never hold up in a court of law."

"It's just a rough draft," Bob said, sipping the worst tasting coffee he'd ever had, as he studied the make-shift contract on the computer screen.

He should've never let her make coffee.

But her lack of domestic skills was the least of his worries.

It was his loss of control last night that concerned him the most. While in the Army, he'd nearly killed his staff sergeant. Fortunately, he'd stopped, just as he raised the butt end of his rifle to knock the man down the stairs, after he had turned his back on him. He hadn't seen Bob raise it. Still, the shock that he was actually capable of killing another human being had never left him.

Kayla, however, was so tiny. He wouldn't have hurt her for the world. At least he hadn't believed he would. Until last night. He could've really hurt her. The thought sickened him. He'd never hurt a woman in his life. Until then.

He'd tried to make it up to her this morning. When they'd first woken up, he'd been surprised at her still being in his bed. But he'd recovered quickly, even telling her to use his shower. But the only reason she hadn't tried getting out of it was because she was afraid of a repeat performance of last night.

His main problem was somehow getting her to understand that she didn't have real rights like other women did when they married. That, he decided, was the main stumbling block in her thinking.

Getting wed was going to be just a technicality to satisfy the lawyers, nothing more. The vows they were going to say were simply words without substance. He'd hired her only so he could get his hands on his rightful inheritance. He'd engineered, and was producing this little act, and after he got the money, was going to get a divorce. But he didn't want Kayla to be scared of him in the meantime, counting the days until he filed for divorce. Conversely, he didn't want her heart broken by their divorce because she'd confused his act with reality.

He'd come a long way since he'd been under the control of first his parents, then the Army, then his professors. He had no intention of relinquishing his hard-won freedom now. He hoped this contract, such as it was, would help her understand.

"Do you really expect me to sign this? 'Two million dollars plus bonuses for quote, 'cohabitating' end quote, with you, and having your, quote, 'legal heir,' which you'll provide for, quote 'subject to the following paragraphs?'" What, exactly, does that mean?" Bob steeled his sigh. Part of Kayla's problem was not understanding finances. Anything with math, in fact, seemed to throw her. "I'll admit it's not perfect. But I don't see it as a major problem. No one'll see it if you're a good girl and do what we've already verbally agreed to."

"I don't suppose I could hire an attorney to look this over before I sign, could I?"

Bob stood up and stretched, deciding to make some fresh coffee. "It wouldn't be a good idea, considering the subject matter. Attorneys tend to be stuffy when it comes to this type of thing. Think of it as a personal form of protection. In case I don't fulfill my part of the bargain, you have this to fall back on, just like I do. Maybe we can blackmail each other with it, if worse comes to worst."

Kayla smiled at his weak joke, but studied him through the open door as he walked into the kitchen. He'd done a ninety degree turn since last night and, except for concocting this weird contract, was trying to make it up to her.

But she couldn't forget last night. Not completely. Even though he hadn't scolded her or mentioned her cleaning up her area upstairs, and had even encouraged her to make coffee this morning, he was just too unpredictable. She couldn't trust him again like she had at first.

She knew without asking he still expected her to sleep upstairs. While she now eagerly embraced the idea, it wasn't because that was what he wanted her to do; it was simply safer for her to keep her distance. She needed to check while she was cleaning up today, too, to make sure both rooms and the bathroom had locks on them; just in case. If they didn't, she'd push the top of one of the chairs underneath the doorknob to keep it from turning, and keep him out that way.

Reluctantly, she signed her name to the contract. It was better than arguing about it, which she knew they'd do if she refused. Even though she didn't see the reason for having something they'd probably never use. "Happy now?" she asked, handing it to him, as she padded into the kitchen.

"Thank you," he smiled, taking it from her before she could change her mind. "Did you understand most of it?"

"More or less."

"Did you understand the basic tenants, everything that was in bold? Those were the main ideas." She nodded, feigning disinterest. The truth was, Kayla understood most of it. But she wasn't about to admit it. She did think it was stupid, and knew it wouldn't hold up in a court of law. But the content itself, though worded with a lot of confusing lawyer-speak, clearly showed his mercenary attitude and his intent to micro-manage her and their baby's future, far beyond the time she'd be married to him. And that she didn't like. It made her more distrustful of him than ever.

Locking the contract in his desk drawer in the den, out of the corner of his eye Bob watched her little hips sway through the open door, as she strode across the kitchen, helping herself to the fresh pot of coffee he'd made. He had a hell of a lot to do to get ready for their wedding tomorrow. And so did she. But she looked so damned sexy, standing there barefoot with her nipples poking against the thin cotton tee-shirt he'd given her to wear that morning, with nothing underneath. He snuck up behind her and impulsively kissed her, holding her close, letting her feel his growing erection.

"You don't know what you do to me, babe," he whispered hoarsely, coming up for air, running his hand under her shirt and cupping a firm breast, as he deepened the kiss. "You have no idea." Kayla instantly stiffened. It wasn't because she was afraid, exactly. It just took her by surprise, especially his physical need that was almost savage in its intensity. She'd hoped last night had been a fluke, brought about by mental exhaustion. But she could again hear desire in his pleading voice. She felt his full-scale erection that pushed through his crisp white running shorts, poking the flimsy fabric of her cotton tee-shirt.

"Relax," he ordered, looking into her eyes, rubbing her back; which felt like heated satin. "I'm not going to hurt you anymore. You know that." She knew, all right. He'd been telling her all morning. But, while she wanted to relax and enjoy sex with him as much as she once had, she just couldn't banish her fear. Not completely.

He hugged her tighter. "I could be wrong," he whispered, kissing her hair, "but I think part of our not getting along is sexual tension. I've never wanted another woman the way I want you. Usually, after I take a woman to bed, I'm satisfied. But with you, I can't seem to get enough."

Was that because she was so young and alluring, with her innocent physical attraction? He wondered, as he absently continued to pet her, reveling in the touch of her soft skin. Or was it that he sensed he could control her if he showed enough power? He didn't know.

Studying her speculatively, he sighed heavily, then released her. One thing was clear. She wasn't ready for sex with him again. Not this soon.

"I have some errands to do," he murmured, turning away while he still could. "I need some groceries and have to see some friends about our marriage license, so we can tie the knot tomorrow."

"Tomorrow," she croaked. *So soon?* While she'd agreed to it, and had known it was bound to happen, she wasn't elated by the prospect. It was so different from the type of marriage she'd dreamed about since she was a little girl. In that regard she supposed, she'd never grown up.

Bob nodded as he took a sip of the fresh coffee he'd made. "I slipped some friends of mine a few hundred to push some things through for me in a hurry when the time came. This way, we can get it over with, right after I drop off my plans for my new client in the morning.

We have to get to the judge's chambers early though, to get our blood work done by a friend who'll meet us there, so you'll need to be ready to go no later than ten-forty-five, when I get back."

"Wonderful," she said, trying hard to sound enthused. "I should wear a nice dress, I guess, right? But nothing elaborate?" *Like a long white satin gown with a veil, suitable for a wedding where she'd walk down the aisle of a church?* She was being unrealistic, she knew. But, dammit all, life was so unfair. She'd been dreaming about having a big church wedding for years.

He nodded. Why did she look like he'd told her they were going to be executed, instead of going to be married? Granted, it wasn't motivated by true love, whatever that was, but she could at least pretend she was okay with it. "It's not a life sentence, Kayla."

"I'm just...surprised," she lied. "It's so soon."

"It's part of our agreement, Kayla," he said, trying to stem his growing impatience. "I have to have a legitimate kid to get my inheritance."

"I know that. But...I mean; marriage doesn't give you the right to own me or anything like that, right? We agree on that, don't we?"

"Yeah, sure. I won't own you. I'm just renting you."

"I'm serious! Don't mock me. I just want to make sure you understand that marriage doesn't give you the right to treat me anyway you want."

"You're referring to last night, I take it?"

She nodded. *As well as your need this morning, which almost caused you to do the same damn thing.* "I won't be mistreated, Bob. I mean it!"

"You do know that in this state, it's legal for a man to rape his wife, don't you? It's an outdated law, but it's still on the books, so it's still permissible."

"That's terrible! It should be repealed!"

"Maybe. My point is that, technically though, according to the laws of this state, I didn't do anything illegal last night, so don't try to emotionally blackmail me with that. I said I'm sorry, and I've promised you it won't happen again. But be aware that I didn't break the law."

"If I had been your wife, *technically* I guess you didn't, but we're not married yet."

"You're forgetting Common Law. There are a lot of Common Law marriages down here, babe. A man and a woman voluntarily living together, intending to set up housekeeping together, with the intent of having a family, is also recognized as a legal marriage. And since you'd already moved in last night, and we do intend for you to get pregnant, I was still legally within my rights." There was a little more to it than that, but he wasn't about to elaborate, since it also mentioned the wife's rights such as sharing her husband's money.

"I don't intend to file charges against you, dammit. I was trying to ensure you...you don't...you can't mistreat people, Bob. Law or no law!"

"I agree. I was too rough with you last night, but I've already apologized. I'm not going to grovel."

"I don't want you to grovel. I wasn't asking you to."

"Not in so many words, you didn't, but you still want my assurances I won't mistreat you. But you don't need my constant reassurance for that, Kayla. I'm not a barbarian. I did get carried away. I admit that. I was wrong. It won't happen again, all right? Believe it or not, I do care about you. I admit I got a little too rough last night. But I wouldn't actually hurt you." He smiled gently. "Okay?"

Kayla nodded. He was at least trying to make her feel better, and maybe, in time, he'd come to terms with what his problems were when it came to her.

"It's getting late, " he smiled, "and I have errands to do and you still have to get situated upstairs and get whatever you're going to wear tomorrow ready." He took hold of her chin, forcing her eyes to meet his. "All right? I'll be back in three, maybe three and a half hours at the most. Will you be okay while I'm gone?"

Hesitating for a minute, she finally nodded.

He hugged her, feeling like he was dealing with a child, trying to ignore the allure of her body. "Good girl. Now, about groceries. Anything you can't eat?"

"I'm lactose intolerant, but as long as I remember to take my enzymes with it, I'm okay with most things. Except spinach. I hate spinach."

"I'll pick up some multivitamins. I want you to be healthy, so our kid's in good health and develops right. I expect you to be a good mother, and part of that is eating right from here on, which, from the looks of your kitchen last night, you haven't done. Having a kid's a big responsibility."

Kayla stilled, absently kissing him good-bye when he pulled her close. But long after Bob's jeep disappeared, Kayla stood at the kitchen window, lost in thought. Why did she keep forgetting about the little thing which might be growing inside her this very minute? She'd once read that a pregnant woman shouldn't have arguments, not only because of the harmful by-products anger produced, but because the baby's brain cells started recording everything it heard from the moment of conception. Enough arguments, the article stated, could cause the baby to feel unloved.

Was she ready for motherhood? She'd adored her own mother and had been with her through the whole ordeal of specialists, tests and chemo, trying to be strong for her. But then she'd *had* to be strong. She didn't have any brothers or sisters. And her father had crumbled when his wife was diagnosed with breast cancer, drinking himself into an early grave, only six months after her mother had died.

The thing that'd really astounded her about her mother, was she'd kept her sunny disposition. Never once had she complained...about losing her hair...or the nausea after each chemo treatment...or the terrible pain. Earlier, she hadn't gotten upset when she'd miscarried when Kayla was ten, despite her wanting another child so desperately. And she hadn't even gotten angry with her father's drinking when things got hard. Nor about him losing jobs for several years when he'd been unable to stop.

Could she be like her mother if she had a child? Could she put up with Bob the way her mother had put up with her father? Despite her mother's feminine ways, she was the strongest woman she'd ever known, in every way.

She herself was a coward, and felt mortally injured from just a paper cut. Whenever she'd gone without sleep for more than two days, she was cranky and irritable too. And every time she got a cold that lasted for more than three days tops, she just knew she was dying.

After she and Bob got a divorce, she'd be a single mother, raising her child all alone. Was she ready for that? Heck, she couldn't even boil water without burning the pan. Her coffee was always deplorable because she'd never gotten the knack of measuring it right. She even burned toast.

Refreshing her coffee from the pot Bob had made, she inhaled its steamy fragrance. It was so unlike her earlier pathetic attempt. Not only did he make better coffee than she did, he also cleaned much better than she did. Even this morning, when she knew he was still tired, he'd scoured his smelly kitchen in less than half an hour, putting everything in its rightful place. She'd never been that energetic in her life. Especially in the morning.

Truth be known, as far as organization and skill went, he was the one most capable of raising a baby. Not her. It was mortifying. But it was also a fact.

Sipping the coffee, she wandered into the master bedroom. *His* bedroom. Not hers. Not theirs. She wasn't allowed to even sleep through the night in here. Not that she minded, really, she assured herself. She was probably much safer upstairs. But it would've been nice to have shared it with him during the long hot summer nights ahead if he behaved himself and forgot his Conan the Barbarian act.

But here too, everything else was in its rightful place.

Engraved beige-toned stationery and a solitary big black pen sat in the middle of a spotless teak desk at the far end of the room. A straight-backed, uncomfortable-looking, black chair was beside it. A practical black phone sat on the nightstand, along with a traditional white glass lamp with a blue lampshade that matched his bedspread. A long, low, black wood dresser with not a speck of dust on it, adorned with only a black leather case, was in the center, for his many tie tacks and cuff links. Plain blue drapes and a beige, thick-worsted carpet completed the décor.

But why weren't there any pictures? Any knick-knacks? Any comfortable chairs?

Something to make it seem lived in and loved? Why was it so sterile? His white tiled bathroom had everything a person could want, from a Jacuzzi to a garden tub with six pulsating jets. Pity she'd only tried out the frosted glass shower earlier. Maybe someday, when he was in a good mood, she'd try out the Jacuzzi. But even though he'd spared no expense, there were no personal touches in there either.

Taking down the towels and wash cloth she'd used, she glanced into the adjacent room.

This large square area with a patio door was where he exercised, apparently. He had everything from weights of various sizes to a treadmill, to an exercise bike, to a rowing machine, to a scale like she'd seen in doctor's offices. Wooden horizontal mini-blinds adorned the patio door. All of it was clean and polished to a high sheen, even the hardwood floor. But despite it all, this room too was barren and cold.

Catching sight of herself in his full-length mirror, she pulled up her sheer cotton nightshirt and studied her stomach. Even if she was pregnant, she wouldn't be showing this early, but she smoothed her hand over her flat abdomen anyway. How odd that she'd found the man of her dreams to have a baby with, only for him to be her employer instead of her husband.

***

Aimlessly, Bob pushed his grocery cart down first one aisle, then another. But his mind wasn't on his task. Why'd he have to come down so hard on Kayla last night and then again this morning? He felt so damn guilty.

He'd been right to lay down the rules in his contract. She was with him to do a job. As her employer, it was his duty to acquaint her with her new situation, and all it entailed. But he'd seen the pain in her expressive brown eyes when she'd given him the signed contract back.

It reminded him of his father's look when, after he'd tried to correct the course of his doomed marriage, he realized he'd never be the kind of man his wife demanded. Bob had only been ten at the time. But he remembered his father's look as vividly, as he had on that balmy August day, when his father had finally given up. Somehow, he'd garnered the strength to stay alive until he'd gotten Bob safely out of the house and into the Army at seventeen. Then he'd given up. Bob had just completed his basic training when he had received the news that his father'd died of a massive coronary. He was only forty-seven, just twelve years older than Bob was now.

His purpose, though, wasn't to hurt Kayla; it was to save her from building false expectations about their relationship, and then being devastated by their divorce after their baby was born.

He knew too, he was set in his ways with a strong tendency to be a perfectionist, so maybe that scared her. Maybe she felt she couldn't measure up. It was true he never did anything without first thinking about it, and figuring how to best get it done. And usually he did it. He maintained control of his life, of his environment, that way.

Which was why his overpowering desire for Kayla scared him more than it did her. It sprung from some animalistic nature hidden deep inside of him he'd never known he possessed...until now.

Why hadn't it ever come out around other women? Hell, he'd bedded so many over the years, sometimes two at a time, in all states from total inebriation to stone cold sober, with quite a few of them having a better figure than Kayla...but he'd never had such a strong desire to possess a woman. Was it because she was the most inexperienced woman he'd ever had? Or because she was ten years younger than him? Or because she'd honestly seemed to enjoy having sex as much as he did? Until last night, of course.

She hadn't enjoyed it much since. And he didn't blame her. Why in the hell had he lost control? Why couldn't he figure it out? He had to get a handle on it.

And the thing was, he cared more about her than he had any other woman. In the short time they'd known each other, they'd somehow bonded. Until...

God dammit! Why had he done it? What in the hell had gotten into him?

He should've brought her with him today as a peace offering, to let her know he enjoyed things beside sex. They might've had fun. Her getting settled in could've waited. Besides, other than her problem with dairy, he didn't have the vaguest clue what she liked or didn't like, with the exception of spinach. But he needed to know. She was, after all, going to be his wife and the mother of his child.

How would she look pregnant? She didn't even look twenty-five. Was that because of her innocence and her honesty? She did seem to have a purity about her, but it was totally unaffected. Would their child take after her in that regard? He hoped to God it would. The last thing the world needed was a miniature clone of him.

Starting to bypass the aisle with cookies and snack crackers, he stopped and backed up, taking his time to browse and study all the different kinds. Usually, he passed by this aisle. He avoided eating things with lots of salt and sugar. But many women loved chocolate, and the experts were now saying a little every day was nutritious. Taking down a box of chocolate chip cookies, he scanned the ingredients. Then he looked at the price, and dropped it in his basket. What the hell? It was only three–fifty. If she didn't like them, he'd toss them.

But what about meals? Meat? Vegetables? Starches? She had to have preferences. But she hadn't told him what they were. Why? Was she afraid he wouldn't have listened to her if she had?

Damn his aunt! She was the real instigator of this little drama he'd brought Kayla into.

She and her strict requirements, worded so there were no loopholes, so he had to do everything according to her exacting methods.

Stopping at the meat counter, he got his usual kinds, a roast, some steaks for the grill, thick pork chops to stuff, and a whole chicken for baking. As a rule, he didn't get hamburger. But maybe Kayla liked meatloaf or homemade meat balls. He did make a mean dish of meatless spaghetti sauce occasionally. Maybe he'd treat her to it this week. He might even find the patience to teach her how to cook. Lord knew she needed coaching. She'd just rolled her eyes when he mentioned her cooking breakfast early this morning.

Although he usually bypassed frozen foods altogether, he eyed the pizzas as he went down the aisle. Most people liked them, and he needed to insure she ate. Despite the current fad of staying slim during pregnancy, Kayla was thin enough. If she got pregnant, he didn't want her to get anorexic on him. Grabbing one of the biggest pizzas he saw, he suspiciously studied the ingredients, then threw it in his cart. It didn't look all that bad. And it was easy to fix, so he'd let her do it to get used to how the oven worked. It'd be good practice for her.

***

Kayla sat down wearily on the small bed, and glanced at her watch. It had been a little over four hours since Bob had left, and she was only now nearing the half-way mark in straightening up. She was exhausted and sweaty from making so many trips up and down stairs, washing her things which had gotten soiled from their cars.

She hated the rooms up here. In this one, the closet was much too small, but since it was the first bedroom she'd come to, she'd carted most of her things in here. But the closet had filled up quickly. Even when she moved half her stuff to the adjoining bedroom's closet, they still looked cramped. Most of her clothes were wrinkled, and some even had grimy, gooey stains that would never come off. Those, she'd have to throw away.

What about her other clothes, though? She'd have to spend a lot of time ironing what she could, even though it was a chore which she loathed, hated and detested with every fiber of her being. Some of her dressier outfits, like her tailored silk suits and cocktail dresses would have to be sent to the cleaners. As far as giving any of it away ... *dang!* There might be some things she wouldn't use right away, but she'd bought them to wear eventually. Why couldn't he understand that?

Sipping her fresh mug of coffee, she studied the room's décor. The furniture was heavy, dark wood, highly polished, just like what she'd expect from a man's sense of style. The garish pink and hunter green patterned bedspread matched the bright pink carpeting that made her nauseous. The color scheme, she knew, was in vogue. But it wasn't her choice for colors of a bedroom. She liked yellows and whites with light wood furniture. She also liked large windows that let in lots of sun; not a single small one like this one. And she especially liked drapes that matched the bedspread. There weren't even any pictures to lighten it up; no little objects that made it feel like home. Not even a plant. Just a lone silver metal lamp, with a plain white shade, sitting on the bedside table.

The other bedroom up here wasn't any better. It was just as dark, just as stark, just as small. The only difference was the color scheme. It was dreary with a burnt orange bed spread and gray drapes and carpet.

She'd go crazy if she had to spend much time up here. Even the bathroom up here was small, only half the size of Bob's downstairs, and was done in beige; beige tile, beige walls, beige floor tiles. The vanity was in a lighter wood than those in the bedrooms, but it was so small it was practically useless. Not only would the cabinet underneath not hold more than two sets of towels, she'd never be able to fit her cosmetics, lotions and creams into the small rectangular cubicle set into the wall.

Aware of the silence that seemed to be mocking her now that she was quiet and still, she glanced at her watch again. Where was Bob? It seemed like he'd been gone longer than four hours. And the way she'd been working, she was starved.

Running down the hardwood stairs, she hoped she could find something to eat that was easy to fix. Like cereal. Or fruit bars. Or a TV dinner she could just throw in the oven. The dials on it hadn't looked too hard. Surely she could use it without breaking something. She sighed heavily, studying the refrigerator's contents. Not only didn't he have TV dinners in the freezer, he had nothing in there at all except ice cubes. The cabinets were just as bare. Where was the cereal? The fruit bars? The candy? Chips? What did the man eat? There was nothing, unless she wanted a glass of milk and some raw carrots and celery. *Yuk!* Even if she could find her enzymes for milk, she'd never liked raw vegetables unless they had some type of dip, which he didn't have either.

Think, Kayla! Lord only knew when he was really coming back. With traffic and the crowds out on pretty weather days on the weekend, he could've gotten delayed. Why, he might not return for several more hours.

Wait a minute! On her way here, she'd seen a McDonald's. It hadn't been too far, not more than a couple of miles. She could go through the drive-through and get herself some burgers. She'd even get some for Bob while she was at it. That way, dinner wouldn't be a problem.

Going upstairs to get her keys and billfold out of her purse, she stopped cold. How could she leave? Bob hadn't given her a key to the house. But she'd only be gone a few minutes. This was a nice neighborhood. She'd just leave the front door unlocked. No one would break in. Not in broad daylight.

Feeling better than she had felt since he'd left, she threw her large purse on the bed and raced out. He might get a little upset if he found out what she'd done, considering people didn't ordinarily leave their doors unlocked. But it wouldn't take her more than half-an-hour at the most. Maybe he wouldn't even care.

Chapter Eight

Taking his time driving home, listening to some light, classical jazz tapes, Bob felt much better about everything. Kayla had faults, yes, but she was intelligent enough to learn. She just needed a firm, gentle hand— his—to guide her in the right direction.

She'd had the chance to think about things, too. She probably realized by now he was simply nervous about all the changes happening so quickly in his life, and had just been letting off a little steam here lately. She didn't seem like the type to hold a grudge.

After he gave the flowers to her, they'd have a little wine, he'd fix her whatever she wanted for dinner, letting her help. Maybe they'd eat by candlelight and go out in the back yard afterwards. He often did that when he was alone. It was relaxing, lying on the lounge chairs on the patio, looking up at the stars, letting his thoughts drift. He could point out the constellations to her as they appeared in the night sky, teaching her how to recognize them. There was some interesting history behind them. Thinking about the wonderful night to come, he pulled up in the driveway, then went rigid. He glanced at the numbers on the spacious brick house. 8729. This was his home. He was on the right street. Riverdale.

So where the hell was Kayla's car? It should've been right there, where it'd been when he'd left.

Surely she hadn't moved out? She'd been upset and fearful, but not overly so. And she'd kissed him good-bye.

Had she put it in the garage? She was welcome to, of course, but she should've asked him first. He had some brand new exercise equipment in there he didn't want anyone to touch. Hopefully, she'd left it alone. But all women, he'd found, had an unnatural curiosity about everything that didn't concern them.

Taking a few bags of groceries out of the car, he took some deep breaths, trying to calm down. He wouldn't shout. He wouldn't threaten. He wouldn't hurt her feelings. He'd talk to her in a soft voice; trying to get to the bottom of why she was so determined to behave as though this was her house.

Then again, maybe the problem was she didn't feel at home here. He'd seen her apartment last night, and it was neat and clean, so she wasn't sloppy or a bad housekeeper. He'd talk to her this evening about what she could do here, as well as what she couldn't. Hell, he'd given her the whole upstairs…but it should be more than that. After all, she'd generously given him her plasma TV, and DVD and CD collection. Okay, they'd share the den. It would be both of theirs. He'd even redecorate it if she wanted, and let her decide how she wanted it to look. She didn't seem like the athletic type, but he'd be willing to share his exercising room too, if she wanted, putting in any special equipment she wanted, just for her.

Maybe she had a psychological problem of some kind. He hadn't seen any evidence of that, but he had to take that possibility into consideration. Or maybe she had a learning disability. Whatever the problem was, they'd talk about it calmly like two rational adults, and solve who was in charge of what, tonight.

Turning the knob as he inserted his key, he stilled as the door opened too easily. He'd locked both the dead bolt and regular lock when he'd left. He knew he had. He always did.

But then if Kayla'd been in and out, moving her car, that explained it. Still, it wasn't safe, leaving doors unlocked. Anyone could've just walked in and helped themselves to anything he had. Even in this neighborhood, they weren't immune to crime.

"Kayla," he shouted, putting his bags on the counter. "I'm home. Come down here and help me put up the groceries." He wouldn't jump to any conclusions, he assured himself. She'd probably moved her car without thinking. Maybe she'd been in a hurry, wanting to have things just the way he'd told her when he came home.

"Kayla?" he called again. Chances were, she was so busy upstairs, putting her things up, maybe putting out some of the many knick-knacks he'd seen in one of her boxes, she hadn't heard him. Stopping at the foot of the stairs, ready to get some more bags out of his car, he looked up. "I'm home," he repeated. "I want you to help me put up the groceries. You need to start learning where things go."

Why wasn't she answering him? Come to think of it, why wasn't she making noise of any kind? The house was as still as a tomb. His voice echoed. There were no footsteps overhead. No sounds of doors opening and closing. No music from her radio or CD player.

"Kayla?" he shouted, taking the steps two at a time. Had she slipped? Had she fallen? Had she collapsed for some reason? It'd been a while since she'd eaten. Maybe she had low blood sugar or something. But why hadn't she fixed a snack of the fresh veggies he always kept in the fridge? Surely she'd have felt it coming on.

Spotting a four-tiered plastic shoe bag laying on the floor of the hall, half filled with shoes of various types and colors, he sprinted past, opening the door of the first room. She'd definitely been working in here. The closet door was wide open. Dresses were scattered around, and two doors of the chest were partially open. But where was she? "Kayla!" he called again, racing down the hall to the open door of the next room, which was right over his room. This obviously had been the room she'd chosen for her own, judging from her open purse on the bed and clothes strewn around. Open, half-filled suitcases lined one wall. The door to the closet was wide open, filled with dresses hanging neatly, the top shelf crammed with open boxes of assorted books and leather bound album looking things.

But Kayla wasn't there. And one shoe bag was neatly hung up... but the other one... why was it out in the hall? Had she been rushing from the hall to her room, working hard, when something had interrupted her? *Or someone?*

Had a bored kid with nothing to do, or one of the bums that occasionally got off the train at the nearby track, noticed her going in and out and, realizing she was alone, snuck in? Why else would her purse still be here? Women always took their purse if they were going out.

Why hadn't he thought to warn her of the sporadic robberies before he'd left? Even though the news had been on the TV and carried in the paper, chances were she hadn't paid any attention. Why should she? It didn't affect her. *Until now!* Had the robbers branched out into rapes... and abductions?

"Kayla?" he shouted, racing to the garage. What the hell? Where was she? Where was her damn car?

Grabbing his cell phone from his pocket he dialed 911. "Hello? I've—"

"Due to an unusually high volume of calls, this circuit is busy," came the recorded voice. "Please hang up and try your call again later."

Bob slammed the phone down. They'd just had taxes raised to pay for the new communication emergency system, and had nothing but trouble with it.

To be sure he hadn't overlooked anything, *like her dead body hanging in the shower*, he raced back upstairs, as he automatically tried 911 again. But neither the sink nor the tub was wet, and the spotless white towels he'd placed there weeks earlier were neatly hanging from their ornate metal holders.

"Due to an unusually—"

Bob slammed the phone down. Again. Going down the stairs more slowly than he'd gone up, he was puzzled. The banister was still highly polished with no tell-tale handprints on it. The white carpet was untouched with no dirty footprints on it. If she'd been forced to leave against her will, there should've been signs of a struggle somewhere. But the house was just as he'd left it, with the exception of the unlocked door.

Had someone kidnapped her and stolen her car? But if that was the case, why hadn't they stolen anything else?

If she'd left for some dire emergency on her own, she should've written him a note, letting him know where she was and why she'd gone out. She had to've known he'd be worried when he came back and found her gone, with the damn door unlocked.

Then again, he'd been gone a lot longer than he'd anticipated. He should've called her to make sure everything was going okay. He should've given her his cell phone number, too. Why hadn't he thought about that? And what about a key? He'd meant to have an extra one made while he was out, but had forgotten about that too; damn!

Getting the flashlight from the garage, he stormed outside to look for clues. The front door didn't have bent metal around the door jam or chipped wood to indicate a break-in. Maybe someone, a professional, had broken in, disabling the alarm.

Hearing the sound of a car coming down the street, he ignored it. The alarm box didn't look like it had been tampered with. There were no indentations or scratch marks on it to indicate someone had fooled with it. Whoever it was who'd broken in was good. There wasn't a mark on it.

Dialing 911 again, he waited.

"Due to an unusually—" came the tinned voice.

Again, he slammed down the phone.

As headlights illuminated him, casting his shadow on the door, he spun around to face the unwelcome intruder. Had the crooks come back for more?

***

Kayla watched Bob warily, as she stopped her car beside his. His posture was rigid and his face was hardened into deeply etched planes. His expression changed quickly from hostility to relief, to puzzlement and back to hostility, all in the matter of a few seconds.

Was he mad at her? Now? The last thing in the world she wanted to do was argue with him. Not only was she starved, she was exhausted. Should she try to get him to back off by meeting him with anger of her own? Or should she try to brazen it out by being silent, refusing to take part in what was obviously his favorite sport?

She knew the reason why he was upset, of course. Maybe she *had* been a little too impulsive in leaving the door unlocked when she'd gone to get her food. In retrospect, that probably hadn't been such a bright idea. But she'd been hungry, and in a hurry to eat. She still was. And leaving the blasted door unlocked had seemed like the only solution at the time.

But why was he standing out here, and why had he been examining his house with his car door still ajar? She stilled, confused. Then it dawned on her. Had someone actually broken in and stolen something? Dear God! No wonder he looked so upset!

"Is everything okay?" she whispered, rushing toward him. "Is the robber still inside?"

Bob was so relieved to see her unharmed, he wanted to hug her. She was all right! But what was she talking about? And why was she whispering?

"You're all right, aren't you?" she continued. "You didn't surprise anyone in the act, did you?"

"In the act? The act of what? What're you talking about?"

He was so brave, bless his heart. He didn't seem the least bit frightened. "It's all my fault. It never occurred to me anyone would actually try the door, then go inside. This is such a nice, quiet neighborhood. It looks so safe!" "Bob put his hands on her shoulders. "Slow down, Kayla. Please!

Tell me what you're talking about." "Why, the break-in, of course. What'd they steal? There's no one still in there, is there? Have you called the police? Do you have homeowners insurance?"

He tensed. "Someone broke in?"

She nodded. "Apparently. But I take full responsibility. I'm so sorry."

"Why? What'd you do? How'd you manage to get out? Did you hear them when they broke in?"

"Of course not. If I'd been here, I would've tried to thwart them somehow. But I was so hungry, you see. I went to get some hamburgers."

*She went out? To get hamburgers…*while someone was robbing his house? Was she making this up? How'd she get out? By promising to bring them something back?

"At least we don't have to worry about dinner, so something good's come out of this," she continued. "I bought several big burgers, two large orders of fries and two chocolate shakes. When are the cops going to get here? Did they say low long they'd be?"

"You didn't call them?"

She stared at him as if he was a backward child. "How could I? I had no idea anyone had broken in."

"So…you were gone when it, the robbery, occurred?"

"Thank goodness I was. At least no one got hurt. But…you called the cops, didn't you? "

"For all the good it did. Their damn communication system's out again. But how'd you find out about the break-in if you weren't here?" *Surely it wasn't on the news this soon.*

He was really stressed out, poor thing. "You just told me, Bob. Don't you remember?"

He groaned. He was getting nowhere fast, and getting more confused with each question. "Let's try this again. When did you leave?"

"About a half-hour ago. Someone must've been watching this house, trying to time it when we were both gone. But, how, I wonder, did they know the door was going to be unlocked? Maybe they just were opportunists and got lucky?"

"You left the door unlocked?"

"I had to," she shrugged. "You didn't give me a key and I was starving. Good thing I remembered where the hamburger place was. I would've been gone much longer looking if I hadn't."

"What makes you think we were robbed?"

What was going on here? "Why else are you out here examining the door and burglar alarm box?"

Feeling drained, Bob sagged against the door. It was beginning to make sense. She'd left the door unlocked when she left to get food. And this was all his fault. He knew she'd be needing a key, and he'd tried to remember to get one made. But what good would that have done even if he'd remembered? He should have given her his before he'd left, but he'd needed it to get a duplicate made.

"No one broke in," he muttered. "I don't appreciate you leaving the door unlocked the way you did. It was a foolish thing to do. I mean, I'm glad you're okay. It's just…maybe I was wrong to drag you into this." He smiled ruefully, running a gentle hand over her cheek, which was as soft as the magnolia blossoms blooming in his garden. "But…being a wife, having a baby are huge responsibilities. I don't think you're ready for those roles."

"Excuse me?"

"I really wanted someone older, more mature. I told George that, but he insisted you were the best one for the job."

"I *am* the best one." Even though she hadn't been sure she herself wanted to stay, now that it looked like he was going to dismiss her, she was having second thoughts.

"I don't think so," he whispered, wearily pushing himself away from the door and getting the last bag of groceries out of his jeep. "I need someone more mature, more predictable. I foolishly assumed things would be okay and you'd quickly catch on and start fitting in. Unfortunately, you haven't."

Following after him with her sack of aromatic, delicious food, which now made her nauseous, she dumped it on the table and left it. "I was only gone a few minutes. Everything else you wanted me to do, I've done. But if you really feel I don't fit in, fine. I'll leave. Tonight."

Holding her head high, she stormed past him, racing up the stairs. Grabbing two of the empty boxes she'd stashed out in the hall, she started dumping her things in. She could always find a campground or a rest stop if she went out far enough from the city. She'd stay at one for tonight, then figure out what she wanted to do. She didn't need his crap.

"Kayla?" he whispered, catching up with her, his pain apparent in his hoarse voice as he walked into the room where she was haphazardly throwing her things randomly into her boxes. "I'm really sorry about this. But you don't have to leave tonight. I'm not throwing you out on the street. Maybe we can both come up with someplace where you'd be happy and would fit in."

Taking hold of one of her half-filled boxes, he forcefully took it away from her. "Why don't you just go on downstairs and eat your burgers? Then get a good night's sleep. After breakfast, you can still leave then, if that's what you want to do. But we're both exhausted now. Too exhausted to make an important decision. "

"I'm a misfit, am I, *Mister* McKnight?" she snapped, grabbing back the box, putting it on her other side, away from him so he couldn't grab it again. "Well, thanks for your offer, but no thanks. You may be too exhausted to think, but I'm not. Misfit or not, I'll come up with a plan on my own. Tonight. After I leave here." *Maybe I'll go on to Odessa, driving straight through. There won't be much traffic heading out I-45. I still know a few people up there who can probably put me up for one night, maybe two.*

"You're being childish, Kayla. You're mad, so you're taking your toys and leaving."

"So?" She continued to throw her things into the boxes, then bolted downstairs. "It's my stuff," she yelled over her shoulder. "I can do whatever I want with it. Then she stopped. "Speaking of which, would you like to buy my plasma TV and collections of DVDs and CDs? They're worth a hell of a lot, but I'll sell them to you cheap. Say a couple of hundred for it all?"

"Kayla, please, I…I'll have to think about it. Put those boxes down and we'll discuss it."

He smiled angelically.

"Forget it!" she snapped, rushing out. "I'll cram them in somehow, and sell them to someone else."

Watching her through the open door, he was tempted to strangle her pretty little neck. There was no way he was going to let her go to God-only-knew-where at this hour. They were both so exhausted, it was a wonder either of them could continue standing upright. And while Kayla was going on an adrenaline rush, she'd soon crash and realize she was too damn tired to think straight, let alone manage a big move.

Kayla tossed the boxes in her trunk, throwing her tire iron and jack further into it. She should have never left Odessa. After all, it was where she'd come from. Maybe that's where she belonged. Maybe she could try being a waitress. It wasn't her first choice for a job, considering she didn't have any experience in it, but if it paid her bills for a while, why not?

Watching her rush back in, Bob slammed the door after her and locked the dead bolt. Although she glanced back with a puzzled expression, she didn't stop.

Dear God, she was so drained, so frantic. She didn't need this crap. Not tonight. But she had to leave; the sooner the better. Dragging a larger box from the hall, she started taking down some of her many dresses. Maybe she'd been too hasty in throwing all her shoes into a box she'd just taken out. Shoes and dresses should go together, at least the dressier shoes. She wished she could pack her things properly though, in her suitcases.

But that would take too much time. Stifling a yawn, she continued throwing her things in the damn box.

She glanced at the bed. It looked so inviting. Could she take a nap? A short one? And maybe, like the tyrant downstairs had suggested, eat something too. Her stomach was starting to growl so loud it could wake the dead. Surely she had time for a quick bite. It might be just the thing to perk her up. She hated to take the time…but it might pay off if she did. And maybe, just maybe, Bob would come up with a decent price for her plasma TV and collections in the meantime. The ready cash would sure come in handy if, God forbid, she got stranded out on a long lonely stretch of highway. That was the only thing about driving at night, the highways always got deserted the later it got. Wearily, she dumped more damned dresses in her stupid box. She'd just take this sucker out to the car, then eat.   Sitting on the hard, cold floor with his back against the wall, Bob patiently continued his sentry position, listening to her moving around upstairs. There was no way he was letting her back out. She'd have to mow him down first.

Why hadn't it occurred to her she could be pregnant right now? Where would she go if she was pregnant? How would she survive? He hadn't seen Chadwick's sign yet, but then he hadn't looked for it, either. The pregnancy book he'd bought said it would show up two to three days after conception, but the bluish color was so faint, it could be easily missed. He had to keep her here at least two to three more days to see if it appeared. And, if she looked like she was *trying*, at least, to do her part, hell, she could stay. She'd need a lot of coaching, of course. But they'd made it a whole twenty-four hours without killing each other. Maybe they could make it until after she'd given birth.

Kayla groaned. With every muscle in her being tightening with pain, protesting movement of any kind, she lugged the large, heavy box out of her room, down the hall, and to the first step. The damn thing weighed a ton. Leaning against the wall, she knew she had to take some of her dresses out of it to get it downstairs. But dammit, she'd just put them in.

Sagging to the floor, she yawned, then closed her eyes. She needed to rest, just for a minute. After she rested her eyes, she'd be fine.

***

Sprawled on the floor, Kayla's eyes snapped open at the thumping, swishing noise close by. *Dear God, where…*now she remembered. She was moving out, leaving Bob and all his neurotic problems behind.

Springing upright, flinching from the sudden pain shooting down the back of her legs, she tried to focus her bleary eyes in the direction of the sound, rubbing her lower back. Then she wished she hadn't. The big heavy box she'd just packed continued to plop down the stairs, landing with a thud in the entry hall. All of her things, every single dress, was spread helter-skelter along all the stairs. She felt like crying. Not only was she more exhausted than she'd ever been, and in pain now, all her hard work had netted her nothing. Not a damn thing, except for the two small boxes in her car

"What the hell?" shouted Bob as a whomping noise sounded, followed by a loud crashing splat! "What's going on?"

In spite of her fatigue, Kayla laughed. Apparently the box had scored a bulls-eye. Good! He deserved it.

"Kayla?" he shouted, coming into her view. He felt relieved, then concerned as he looked up the stairs. She was pale, looking worse than she had before, with dark circles under her beautiful brown eyes which were so large he could see them from several feet away. "You okay up there?" he asked gently.

She nodded, watching him come up, stepping gingerly around her clothes "Just sore from using a wood floor as my mattress. I must have fallen asleep, then stretched out. When I did, I must've kicked the box and it fell down the stairs. Did it hurt you?"

He smiled. "Nah! I'm too tough for a cardboard monster to fight. It startled the hell out of me, though. I must've fallen asleep too."

For a moment, their eyes locked, all hostility forgotten. *Careful, McKnight,* Bob cautioned himself. Kayla had let down her guard. But she could easily raise it again, shutting him out all over again.

Picking up a few dresses several stairs below her, Bob extended them to her, then sat down, careful not to crowd her, and looked at his watch. "Holy shit! It's nearly midnight!"

Great! Thought Kayla. *Just great!* No one except me will be on the road at all, unless I luck out getting an occasional truck for company. Maybe I *should* postpone moving until tomorrow, or rather later today, after I get some sleep. If, of course, I can get Bob to treat me with some respect.

Bob studied her as she aimlessly fooled with the collar of a blue silk dress. "Would you like something to eat? I doubt if your burgers will be any good by now, but I've got the fixings for some tuna fish salad. Do you like rye bread?" She nodded. Actually, tuna sounded real good right now.

"Want to help me fix it? If you do, I'll help you pick up your dresses later."

Kayla hesitated, then took the hand he extended to help her up. "It's a deal," she smiled. "As it happens, I'm free the rest of the night. I'll probably stay here until after breakfast like you suggested."

Probably? At least she was entertaining the idea of staying a few hours longer on her own. It wasn't much, but it was something. But he sensed there was something she wanted, something important to her, but she was reluctant to bring it up.

Walking into the kitchen, Bob spotted all the untouched sacks of groceries, and muttered a curse under his breath. He'd forgotten to unpack them.

Catching sight of a large brown stain that seemed to be spreading on the bottom of one of the sacks, Kayla tore it open, as Bob headed toward the other sacks. Quickly taking out all the packages of spaghetti, noodles and rice, Kayla stacked them neatly on the counter. Did he always buy this much? He had enough for an army here, with two of everything. "I hate to tell you this, but half your ice cream's gone."

"Toss it, then. No sense taking any chances." Taking a large handful of paper towels, she gingerly lifted up the sack, molding the paper towels around the bottom and sides, then put it in the sink, washing the container with the liquid soap on the sink and hot water before she threw it away. "This is a trick I learned from my mom," she grinned in response to his puzzled frown. "Washing out things you're going to throw away will keep the bugs away."

"If you want to do it, that's fine. But I have an exterminator."

"So did we. But every now and then a bug would get in and drive mom nuts. She hated them. All kinds. After she got Dad and I into the habit of splashing a little soap and water like she did on food stuff we were going to toss, we rarely saw an insect inside."

He smiled. "Like I said, if you want to do it, have at it. I don't mind in the least. But you aren't afraid of bugs, are you?"

"It depends on the bug," she shrugged. "But I hate all flying insects and, if there's a man around, any man at all, I'll try to get him to kill them before they can get to me. I think it's because I was stung by a wasp on my lower lip when I was in first grade, and was on the playground. I've never forgotten the pain."

"Ouch! I can see why. Wasps are mean. They don't need a reason to sting."

"Yeah, well, this one thought he did, I think. I was eating an apple and I thought the thing flying around me was just a fly. I found out real quick he wasn't."

As exhausted as Kayla was, she started enjoying working alongside him. He was a good conversationalist, well read; liked some healthy practices, while ignoring others and preferred traditional art over modernistic, like she did. They were a good team, too, working in unison, and by example, Bob taught her where everything went. It seemed like they'd just started, when they were through.

"Go ahead and sit down," he ordered gently, "while I make our food. And Kayla? Thanks for helping. I appreciate that. I really mean it."

She smiled, too exhausted to do anything but nod, as she plopped in a chair by the breakfast table. Then she leaned back and stretched, determined this time not to fall asleep.

Getting out the mayonnaise, pickles, rye bread and tuna, Bob started chopping an onion. She'd surprised him by taking the initiative and helping him right away, without waiting for him to ask her. Was it because she was used to unloading groceries? Not that it took a brain scientist to do it.

But she seemed relaxed, and proved to be a quick study, more so than he'd originally thought. She was a lot more intelligent than he'd thought, too, very well read and knowledgeable about art, astronomy and history.

The one thing she hadn't known about was finances and anything to do with math. But he sensed a phobia there, rather than mental deficiency. Money, in fact anything to do with numbers, actually scared her. But he doubted she was aware of being honest-to-God afraid of them. She didn't evade the subject, didn't try to bluster her way through it; she just became very quiet with her eyes wide, clearly showing her fear.

She was very quiet now too, not moving a muscle. And she was slumped forward, her head on the table. And... she was...*snoring?*

Poor thing! Her clothes were badly wrinkled, but her shorts were riding high on her shapely thighs. And her blonde hair was mussed, part of it falling over her attractive face. She looked like a sex kitten. But there was more to her than that. A lot more.

She'd admitted she'd never gone to college, just to business school instead. But he'd quickly realized she was self-taught and was an eclectic reader, interested in biographies of world leaders of the past as well as the present. She'd read most of the Classics on her own, too. And she seemed to really be interested in human physiology, and conversed about it easily. She was also interested in art, and loved to go to museums, and regularly attended exhibits of up and coming painters. But it was Van Gogh's and Vega's art she loved the most.

Gently, Bob picked her up and headed toward the stairs. She needed someplace she could stretch out, someplace soft. She was a sound sleeper, just like she'd claimed, not moving a muscle as he carried her. She was as limp as a rag doll.

But the stairs were still covered by her dresses from the wayward box. He stiffened. It wasn't the damn dresses that bothered him, though. Instead, he found himself oddly uncertain.

He felt he should take her to her own bed in her own room. It was, after all, something he'd carefully written into their contract. But he didn't want to do that. He wanted her with him in his own bed, and not just for sex. *Sex.* Having it was out of the question tonight. They were both too exhausted to do anything except go right to sleep.

So why? Why this need to have her close? He didn't like anyone sleeping in his bed all night...usually. But there was no harm in letting her stay a few hours. Besides, he didn't feel like trudging up all those stairs and then clear down here again.

Relieved he'd come up with the perfect solution, he walked quickly into his darkened bedroom. Holding her close with one strong arm as he bent to pull back the covers, he gently eased her in, unlaced and slipped off her tennis shoes, and covered her up, tucking her in like a child.

But as he put them into his closet, then stripped for bed, he stilled, feeling like someone had punched him in the stomach. Tomorrow was Monday...and they were supposed to get married! But they sure couldn't now, not with Kayla still upset with him, to say the least. *Damn!* He'd gone to so much trouble and expense to arrange things so perfectly. And what was happening to his perfectly made and well-prepared plan? It had been shot all to hell. And it was his fault it had. Feeling his heartbeat race, he plopped down on the bed, trying to get himself under control. Maybe he could simply postpone it for a couple of days without a lot of hassles.

He tossed and turned, trying to get some sleep before he had to meet with that new client, whom he'd forgotten all about, too. He looked at the clock again. Four, on the dot. Fifteen minutes had passed since he'd looked at it the last time.

Then he drifted off to sleep and had nightmares about his mother finally breaking into his room. She'd been hiding under his bed that night, waiting like a spider for him. The minute he laid down, she sprung up on him, her two hundred pounds holding him in place as she kissed him all over, covering him with her slobber and her foul, rancid breath, which always smelled like rotten fish.

As if that wasn't unnerving enough, he didn't know if it was a nightmare or a memory he'd tried to suppress.

Chapter Nine

As the first gray light of dawn spilled through the sides of the closed drapes, Kayla yawned and stretched, her back arcing with her arms high over her head. Rolling over, she deeply inhaled the pillow next to hers. She loved this bed. It was so soft and warm, and always smelled like Bob's unique scent, mixed with his after-shave cologne.

Then she bolted upright. She was in Bob's bed? Again? Dear Lord, how had she gotten here? And why?

Scrambling up, she tottered, trying to get her balance, trying hard to remember last night. She remembered sitting down at the breakfast table, waiting for him to finish making her a sandwich. She'd closed her eyes, listening to the chopping sound of a knife against wood, and the clink of spoons against glass containers. She'd wondered why she viewed his noise as comforting, while her ex-roommate's had always irritated her. But that was the last thing she recalled.

She glanced at the clock. Six-fifteen. And today was Monday. And, oh, God, she was supposed to marry Bob. *Today.* No way! She was going to move out. Or was supposed to. But now she realized she was reluctant. Why? What had changed? Had her subconscious recorded something of which she was unaware which had changed her mind?

Weaving her way to the closed door, trying to force her eyes to focus, she opened it slowly and peeked out, immediately smelling the steaming fragrance of flavored coffee. Hazelnut! Her favorite. Easing into the living room, hearing the clink of a spoon on glass and the rustling of paper in the kitchen, she headed there, being as quiet as she could. She knew the noise had to be from Bob. And while she wasn't afraid of him, she was cautious and more on her guard than she'd been when she first came here

Craning her neck, she stood at the threshold. Only to be met by Bob's large green eyes. Looking quizzically at her over the rim of his glasses and his newspaper.

"Good morning," he said as she advanced into the darkened room, lit only by a small lamp by the breakfast table. With fairly steady steps, she headed toward the opposite side where the coffeemaker sat.

"Hope I didn't wake you. I was trying to be quiet." He smiled. "You know, I'm beginning to like this arrangement. But I'm nervous about it, too. I've never shared my house with anyone, never wanted to. Until," he whispered so low she had to strain to hear him, "you came along."

Just why he felt that way, however, eluded him. In addition to her physical charms, he actually liked her; he'd enjoyed talking to her last night. But there was something else, besides her gentle and kind manner, her sense of humor, and her expressive face, that revealed everything she thought and felt. Maybe it was her need to be loved and approved of, which made him feel strong and very protective of her. He knew he didn't feel love, since he didn't believe in it. Or did he? He was beginning to wonder if it did, in fact, exist, and he'd simply been too busy to notice it. But then, since she'd come, he was beginning to wonder about a lot of things he'd never questioned before.

Surprised and touched, Kayla quickly took her mug of steaming coffee and joined him at the table. He looked terrible, like he hadn't slept in months, with bags under his fantastic green eyes, and his face was unusually pale. But he smelled wonderful, as usual. He was dressed up in a starched white shirt, dark green silk tie and charcoal gray suit pants with a black leather belt. She was still in her scruffy outfit that she'd had on since yesterday. She smelled like sweat. Her tennis shoes however, were missing. Had Bob taken them off her?

"Are you feeling okay?" she asked gently.

He shrugged. "Not really. I've been sitting here feeling...well, guilty about what happened yesterday. I know I have a lot of faults." He folded the paper he'd been trying to read, but couldn't concentrate on, and set it aside. "I'm finding out I'm difficult to live with, which I never realized before. I also tend to go off the deep end, so to speak, talking before I've thought things through." He smiled ruefully. "But this morning, I've done nothing but think. Unfortunately, I don't apologize well. I never have, and probably never will, for that matter."

Impulsively, she took hold of his hand, massaging it gently, helping him unclench his tight fist, and held on. Surprising her, he didn't object, and when he realized his hand was clenched, relaxed it. "You have trouble expressing an apology? Or admitting you're wrong? Or...? Her voice trailed off."

He coughed nervously. "When I was growing up, I had to be strong to resist some things. My parents fought a lot, so I had to pretend their fights and screaming didn't really bother me. But also…my mother… she was…well, not the easiest person for me to be around. I didn't have anyone I felt I could confide in, so I had to trust my own judgment. Back then, child abuse wasn't even a term. So I made a few mistakes in dealing with her. And I learned quickly not to apologize for them because when I did, she only became more aggressive. I decided then apologies were for wimps, for losers. Anyway…" his voice trailed off.

Sensing there was more, Kayla waited patiently while he swallowed visibly, then took a sip of his coffee. The way his brows came together, the way the end of his perfectly shaped nose was pinched, the turning down of his lips and the terrible pain she saw clearly in his clouded green eyes when he finally looked up, made it clear that whatever it was that he was about to tell her, caused him a lot of pain.

"You see, I…my mother…she never loved my dad. I don't know why she even married him. It wasn't that she loved him. Or that he'd asked her. *She* asked *him*. After he refused, she got her wealthy father to offer him a job and coerce him into taking it; on the condition he married her.

They said I was born three months prematurely, but…give me a break! I don't think so. I think my mother was carrying me when they finally got hastily married in a private wedding chapel off I-45."

Kayla nodded. Her own parents fought a lot, too. They had been married in their church, and had given up hope of having a child when she came along. She was fairly certain she was one of the reasons they'd had so many fights. Not that they ever told her that. But it was just a feeling she got from so many references to bills piling up.

"I think if I'd turned out to be a girl," he continued, "there wouldn't have been a problem. But ever since I can remember, my mother was touching me everywhere, all the time. I even slept with her for a time, while my father slept on the couch. I was…I think four or five then. But I was kicked out of her bed when I started wetting the bed. I've slept alone ever since." He smiled and winked. "But I haven't wet a bed since."

"Cunning little devil, weren't you?" she murmured, returning his smile, still holding onto his hand, watching his smile vanish as quickly as it had appeared..

"Even after that, though, my mother continued to touch me even more often than before, and in the most inappropriate places. She held me at church and held me when she went shopping, careful to keep her fingers on my…private parts…insisting she needed to hold me long after I was too big to be held."

Kayla winced. "I'm sorry," she whispered, squeezing his hand. She wondered, though, if he was aware of it, because his eyes were clouded over again, looking at something she couldn't see.

"When she couldn't pick me up any more, she made sure she was sitting right next to me, hip to hip, when eating or watching TV or standing someplace in the house, hip to hip. Hell, I couldn't even take a shower without her coming in, pulling the shower curtain open and cautioning me to be sure I washed my penis properly…and then she would try to touch it.

She continued until I knocked the hell out of her. I must've been ten or eleven then. But that only lasted for so long, and then she was doing it again. Not that she tried to touch me again; she didn't dare. But she'd peek around the damn curtain, trying to get a look, until I told her I'd kill her if she tried it again." He sighed heavily.

"I locked the damn door, of course. For all the good it did. She found out how to pick the damn lock."

"I'm sorry," Kayla whispered again, holding onto his hand for dear life with both of hers. "I had no idea."

He laughed bitterly, a sound raw with so much agony, Kayla felt chilled to bone.

"Hell, honey, that wasn't half of it! When I was fifteen, she started coming into my room, picking the lock in there as easily as she'd picked the one in the bathroom, telling me how much she hated my father, saying I was the only man she'd ever loved, even when I was small. I tried putting a chair underneath the door knob so it wouldn't turn, until she took all the god damned chairs out of the frigging house. That lasted for…two, maybe three more weeks, until I saved enough from my part-time job as a soda jerk to finally buy a deadbolt lock. I installed it myself."

Blinking back her tears, Kayla briskly rubbed his hands, and he paused for so long, she thought he'd stopped.

"But…I…I'm pretty sure…I think…there was something else too," he continued in a ragged voice. "The thing is, I can't remember it that well…it's more like a nightmare, but I think something else happened too, but I just can't grasp it."

Dear Lord, there was *more?* Holding onto his hands so tightly her knuckles were white, she impulsively tugged them to her face and kissed them, rubbing her cheek over them. "I'm so sorry. So very sorry. But it's okay now. You're safe." But she wondered if he even knew she was in the same room, as he continued staring vacantly out into space.

Finally, his eyes focused again, and he looked surprised to see her face covered with tears, leaning so far over the table. But he didn't draw back. Instead he turned beet red with a sheepish look on his face.

"I promise you I will never, ever tell another soul what you told me just now," Kayla hastened to reassure him, continuing to hold onto his hands. "You have my solemn word! I vow on my very own mother's grave! I'll never repeat to anyone what you just said…not ever."

"I know you won't," he whispered. "I trust you. A lot more than you know."

"Thank you," she choked out, feeling a fresh wave of tears cascade down her face, as he stared intently into her eyes. But as their eyes held, Kayla knew something was happening to both of them underneath the surface. And whatever it was, it was important.

When the phone rang, they both jumped so high, Kayla bumped her elbows sharply on the table. "Do you want to get that?" Kayla asked, as Bob continued to sit there.

"Not really. But I guess I should. I just…I thought you should know that about me when I was growing up. I think it's why I have trouble apologizing. The bitch…er, my so-called mother, reacted so damn strangely when I did, I guess it just stuck with me."

"I understand," she whispered, as he finally reached over his shoulder and grabbed the receiver. And she understood, without him telling her, that there were a lot more painful details he'd skipped. His face had been covered with sweat as he'd talked, as if he was afraid that no-good, damn bitch that was his mom would storm into the room and start fondling him again. With his eyes glazed, she knew he hadn't seen her, but had instead been mentally transported back in time.

Listening to him absently as he answered whoever it was on the phone, she wondered what the other thing was he couldn't remember, and how he'd handle it when he did remember. He was traumatized now. Would he be pushed over the brink by remembering the missing memory?

"I have to go," Bob said, getting up. "That was Collins, my new client's assistant. They want to start the meeting early."

"All right," she said, standing uncertain for a minute, then rushing to hug him tight.

"About what's supposed to happen afterward," he said, nuzzling her hair. "Our wedding. I'll leave it up to you whether or not we go through with it. The house key and my cell phone number are on the bar, in case you need to get hold of me. But I don't think I'll be gone more than a couple of hours at the most. If you're ready, great. If not, I'll understand. But please don't leave me, Kayla. I think we can work things out."

She hesitated for only a minute. "Of course we can," she whispered, not certain at all, but her heart aching too much to refuse him.

But he'd caught her pause, and turned so white, and the pain in his eyes was so excruciating, she felt like a part of her was dying as he woodenly turned to go.

"Dammit," she muttered, rushing after him as he gathered his things and opened the door. "Wait!" Reaching up and putting her arms around his neck, she intended kiss him lightly good-bye, wanting to erase, if she could, some of his torment.

Surprised, Bob dropped his drawings and his brief case, and wrapped his arms tightly around her. But instead of a simple light kiss, he tasted every available inch of her, nibbling lightly, then running his lips over her throat, her neck and her shoulders, as her body took over her mind and she arched back, allowing him the access he so desperately needed.

"I know you still have doubts, and I probably don't have the right to ask, but would you please not leave while I'm gone? If I came home to find a note of good-bye from you, I'd..." his voice trailed off as the pain resurfaced in his eyes.

"I wouldn't do that!" Kayla protested, blinking back her tears. "Please believe me. I'd never hurt you like that."

But as she said the words, she didn't know if they could work things out at all. But after he'd just confided the nightmare of the childhood he'd endured, she was beginning to understand him a little more. Did that irrational need to possess and dominate her stem from something in his background? And if it did, did he have the strength to withstand it, and treat her decently, without her fearing for her safety? Never before had a man even raised his hand to her in anger, and she'd be damned if she'd put up with it.

"We need to talk this out, babe. I know that. Please give me, give us, the chance to do it. I realized last night I need you. I need you more than anyone I've ever known."

Remembering how she'd woken up in his bed, she believed him. The need was there; she didn't doubt that. But did he have the ability to work through his other problems without trying to control her every minute?

"Look," she sighed, "if, and it's a big *if,* you understand that under no circumstances will you treat me like you own me, then more than likely we can see if we can work things out. Not that I've completely made up my mind yet what to do about anything. I haven't. But I can't talk openly to you if I'm leery of you suddenly getting the urge to do whatever the hell you want with me. I have to have some freedom and rights without fear of repercussions."

"You may find this hard to believe, but I agree with you. I've never hurt another woman in my life. I think what happened with you was a fluke, resulting from a lot of stress, exhaustion, trying to get used to each other. Those things won't happen again."

"They better not."

"You have my word they won't."

"If something does happen," she continued, "which causes you to lose control again, I'm calling the cops, outdated laws notwithstanding. I know some things about law too, and the domestic abuse program that's been instituted within the police department is one of the most vocal and enthusiastic. All I have to do is call them. I don't even have to press charges. They have to automatically arrest you and hold you until you can go before a judge. But I will press charges, Bob, if you ever lay a hand on me in anger again." She raised her brows. "That goes for any kind of abuse, physical, mental, psychological, or emotional. "My father hit my mother once when they were down here visiting me. That's how I know about the program. In addition to spending two weeks in jail because my mother refused to raise bail for him, he was fined five thousand dollars."

"Dammit, Kayla! What do you want me to do to prove it won't happen again? Sign my name in blood? What?"

"I...I just want to make sure I can trust you again. Maybe we should go slower than we have...physically." She hadn't decided about that part yet, but she wanted to gauge his reaction. Was he willing, with his strong sex drive, to go along with it?

"You don't want to have sex forever?"

"I didn't say 'forever.'. I said slower."

Nervously, he ran his hand through his hair. "Oh, shit! I guess it won't hurt to try."

It wasn't much, but it was something. "I'll see you when you get home. Now go to your meeting. I have a lot of thinking to do."

"We can still kiss though, right?" he asked, picking up his papers and brief case. "Just a little?"

"Dammit! Of course. I'm not banning intimacy on all levels."

Kissing her quickly, as if he was afraid she'd change her mind, Bob turned to go, then got out his wallet, and extended a couple of hundred dollar bills to her. "Just in case you need something while I'm gone."

Before she could object, she watched him literally run out the door.

Was she making the right decision here? She wondered, as she absently stuffed the bills in the pocket of her shorts and retrieved her coffee. Could they work things out? They both had a lot of problems.

But they were alike in some ways. Both needed their personal space, and that was a point in their favor. Both would respect the need for each other's privacy. She'd found out last night he had a lot of intelligence, too, and was willing to listen to her opinions and discuss them on a variety of subjects. He was also as quiet as she was. She had yet to even see the TV on. So sharing the same house shouldn't present any major problems, especially in a home this large.

The problems he had, the need to control and possess, probably stemmed from his childhood, just like his trouble apologizing; which he'd just tackled. But just because he had trouble expressing an apology didn't mean he wasn't sorry when he got out of line. She'd seen his sincerity in his eyes when he'd finally been able to bring himself to apologize for hurting her.

It all boiled down to his ability to control himself when he felt the need to control her. And controlling her was linked to his need to possess her…as a substitute for what? The contract he'd drawn up was an example of that; it was a way of controlling her.

Did his need to control have anything to do with him being in the service? Chances were, it had enhanced, rather than instilled that need. She'd seen stories in the news of soldiers who couldn't control their wives, who ended up killing them. But those were soldiers in combat. Then again, had he seen action overseas? She didn't know.

He also had a problem with emotional intimacy. To him, emotional intimacy led to sex. There were bound to be times when she couldn't have sex, especially during the latter stages of pregnancy. Could he handle it? Again, she didn't know.

As for herself, sure she had faults. Who didn't? Sometimes she'd let housekeeping slide due to being engrossed in a romance novel.

And she favored the cleaners in favor of having to iron her clothes, although she had improved on that, some, and had even bought an iron and ironing board. But she detested the chore, even though it was expensive to keep sending things out.

As far as cooking went, her skills were non-existent, but she was willing to try; provided of course, he'd eat what she tried to fix while she was learning. Her mother, of course, had tried to teach her, and for a while there, it looked like she'd succeeded.

But...it was when her father started drinking that she'd stopped. Most of both her and her mother's time was then taken up with trying to drag him home from bars, and hiding, and finally locking up, all the booze he'd secreted throughout the house.

Then, when her mother got breast cancer, which had gone undiagnosed for so long it was incurable, she'd spent her time trying to care for her, as well as for her father, whose drinking problem only increased.

Unfortunately, when it came to budgeting and managing her finances, she failed miserably. She tried. Lord knew she tried hard to correct her deficiency. But she lacked an ability to deal with anything concerning money.

That's where he could balance her out. He could teach her how to do that. In fact, he could teach her a lot of things about the domestic arts. But he couldn't push her. She tended to be stubborn when someone pushed, especially when they got angry with her for learning so slowly.

She remembered Mrs. Arnold, clear back in third grade, who'd pushed her to write with her right hand instead of her left. One day, while sitting at her desk, writing upside down with her left hand, she looked up to see Mrs. Arnold beside her, scowling down, looking like an angry giant. "No, Kayla! How many times do I have to tell you, we write with our right hand." she said, taking her pencil and putting it in her right hand. "Now write correctly. I'm warning you, if I see you writing with your left hand again, I'll give you an 'F'". Wanting to avoid a direct confrontation, Kayla didn't object, and had bowed to pressure.

But when she wrote an essay with her right hand, which was unreadable, Mrs. Arnold had wisely let her go back to using her left hand.

Odd that she still remembered that. And…she still disliked direct confrontations. Her running away from Bob wasn't because she was afraid of him, but was instead because she was afraid of confronting him. Physically, he'd been rough, yes, but he hadn't hurt her.

Well, maybe she was improving. She was certainly gearing up to fight him now. At least she'd made one decision this morning. She'd stay, at least for a while, to see if they could work things out.

But as for getting married? *Today?* God, marriage was such a big step. She simply wasn't ready to commit to it. She might have to eventually if she was pregnant though. Still it would take time; at least a week, possibly two, after conceiving for a home pregnancy test to show results. If it showed she was pregnant, so be it. They'd go through with the ceremony shortly after she found out the results. No way did she want to be a single mom, trying to make it without some kind of monetary support.

So she'd stay for another week or so, which would give them time to see if they could work things out in the meantime. But the problem was, would Bob hold off on sex? He'd promised to go slow, but his idea of 'slow' and hers, might be different.

Chapter Ten

Bob poured himself a stiff drink as he listened to Kayla. It was a little early to start hitting the sauce, but what the hell? Not only had his new client made unreasonable demands, Kayla was doing the same damn thing. Angrily, he jerked off his tie and unbuttoned the top buttons of his starched white shirt.

"I know what I said, dammit, but I was hoping after you saw I was really trying to change, you'd trust me enough to go through with our wedding."

Holding onto the handle of the upright vacuum cleaner, Kayla let out a sigh. She was hoping that, by being dressed in slacks and a prim blue sleeveless shirt, he'd get the message right away when he came home. All she'd done in the way of looking better was take a hot shower and wash her hair.

"I do trust you." *A little.* "I'm sure I probably will go through with it…later. In a week or two. Please understand. It'll give us time to really work things out."

"Without sex? Be realistic! I'm a normal man. You're a normal woman. And we live together."

"I didn't say it would be easy."

"No, it damn sure won't. It'll be impossible!"

"Let's see how it goes. If we both start improving and see real progress in say, a week, then we can get married then. How's that? In the meantime, I'll try hard to learn to cook and, if you start being more considerate of my feelings, which you're not being now, we'll go through with it. It's not that long."

"You won't be able to sleep in my bed, Kayla. You know that, don't you? There's no way, with you right next to me, I won't have sex."

"I figured that."

"And that's fine with you? Why? You don't want to have sex with me anymore?" She was treading on dangerous ground here and she knew it.

"Of course I do, but I just—"

Bob had had it. He couldn't undo the bad morning he'd had with an irate client, but he damn well could make sure his plans with Kayla would go as planned. "Then get dressed now. We're going through with the damn ceremony. I promised I wouldn't hurt you again, and I meant it."

Could she trust him? It wasn't she was scared, just leery.

"I'll help you change clothes, if you want," he whispered softly, quickly backing her up against the wall, starting to unbutton her prim shirt with one hand, as he kissed her so gently she barely felt it, while cradling the back of her head with his other hand so she couldn't turn away. "I want to help you any way I can."

Like hell he was. But what harm would it do to kiss him back, she wondered as he kissed her more deeply, while running his hand gently underneath her shirt to softly rub her lace-covered nipples. She wasn't giving in, exactly. She was just reassuring him she still found him physically attractive. Maybe they wouldn't go all the way. *And maybe pigs fly.* Dammit, why was she so weak? Why was he so handsome and such a damn good lover? Why did she think she could help him change and deal with his problems? Hell, she even had trouble dealing with her own.

"Like it?" he murmured, feeling her nipples harden.

Kayla nodded as she stared into his huge green eyes, trying to will her watery knees not to cave in, as she wound her arms tightly around his neck

"Say it!"

Bastard! "You know I do," she breathed against his mouth.

"A lot?" he asked, kissing her again, as he unbuttoned her shirt the rest of the way, kissing the upper contours of her breasts

"Yes," she breathed, as he worked his soft lips underneath the lace of one cup of her bra, and lightly nibbled and flicked the sensitive bud with his tongue.

"Want me to stop?"

"God, no!"

"Good girl," he whispered, unclasping her bra, delving under the other lace cup giving her other breast the same lavish attention. "Now push down your slacks and panties and slide them off."

"We're going to do it here? Against the wall?"

"No, outside in the driveway. Of course here."

Doing what he said, Kayla had grave doubts. But she had to admit that, in spite of them, Bob's sexual knowledge and obvious experience impressed the hell out of her.

"Nice," he whispered, fingering her bare ass, then reaching down between them, he unzipped his fly. "Now put your arms around my shoulders and lift up on your toes. Then put first one leg around my waist then the other. Don't worry, I won't let you fall."

Hesitating only briefly, Kayla did what he said.

Cupping her bare bottom in one hand, he positioned his fully erected penis inside her. Pushing her back tighter against the wall, he took hold of her hips with both hands, tilting her pelvis further up.

"Okay, so far?"

She nodded against his chest, holding on for dear life.

"Relax, babe. You're doing fine. Just follow my lead." Easing one hand directly underneath her ass, he lightly pressed his index finger against the back lower edge of her clitoris and started slowly pumping.

At first, Kayla just felt odd. But, as she inhaled his scent and his cologne mixed with soap, and felt his body heat warming her, while he bent his head down and softly but thoroughly kissed her as she looked up, she forgot her fear and the strange feeling of such an unusual position.

Although she'd experimented with having sex with a couple of men, those relationships had been short-lived and not all that great. But Bob, most of the time, was affectionate when they had sex. He invariably made her feel that he cared about her and that her pleasure, for the most part, in spite of that one lapse, was as important to him as his was. In spite of his upbringing, he had a gentle streak that generally showed itself when they were making love. Was it manipulation? Sure. She knew it was. In a way. But it was done in such a tender, caring way, it was hard for her to resist.

As he increased their tempo, thoughts fled, as feelings of ecstatic sensation and piercing desire, spiraling continuously higher and stronger, took their place. Lost in their vortex, she crashed down to reality shouting his name as loudly as he shouted hers. Sliding to the floor, he continued to hold her.

"Miss Leigh," he wheezed, "will you do me the honor of marrying me?"

Kayla didn't know whether to scream or cry. "Yes," she answered, willingly receiving his kiss.

***

In spite of Bob's plea to hurry, Kayla took her time freshening up and changing. She knew she'd been manipulated by an expert, but there'd been no way she could refuse him. And she'd known, somehow, from the time when he'd confided that terrible time in his childhood, she'd do whatever it took to keep from causing him more pain and heartache.

Despite their differences and problems, they'd find a way to make their marriage work, at least for a while; with work being the operative word.

Slipping into her French-cut white lace bra, over which she slipped her white lace teddy, letting the silk slither down her perfumed, lotioned skin, she studied herself in the full-length mirror on the back of her closet door, then turned to the two suits she'd narrowed down for her choice. She held the navy blue silk up to her, looking at her reflection. If she wore it with her white silk, frilly blouse, she'd look feminine and demure. But the wheat-toned, silk suit highlighted her hair. It was more severe than the blue one, with its straight skirt and no collar or adornment at all, other than the large, square, amber silk covered buttons. The top wasn't roomy enough to wear it with a blouse to soften its severe lines.

But she had the perfect heels to wear with it, three-inch, spike-heeled ivory silk pumps, which would make her a little taller. With them on, she wouldn't have to arch her neck so much to look up at Bob when they took their vows. The one thing she'd learned from her many jobs was, if you made people look up to you by being tall, they invariably looked up to you in other ways as well. To heighten the effect, she pulled her hair back, putting it into a bun, softened by an off-white silk ribbon peeking over the top of her blonde head.

She frowned in the mirror. She still looked young, but more serious-minded than usual; a feminine woman who openly acknowledged her gender, but also one who didn't tolerate any nonsense. Quickly she added her large pearl earrings to soften the effect even more. Those, and her tiny gold watch were the only jewelry she'd need.

Still not completely satisfied, she rummaged around in her

overflowing suitcase and took out the small pair of wire-rimmed glasses she rarely wore, usually favoring contacts. She stood back, studying herself again.

Perfect! Liberally dousing herself with her favorite Givenchy cologne, she quickly transferred most of the contents of her large practical shoulder bag into her ivory clutch purse.

Taking a deep breath, she walked out of her room and slowly descended the stairs to join her fiancée who was pacing in front of the fireplace.

***

For the second time since Kayla came to live with him, Bob found himself wondering if he was in the right house. Instead of the girl he'd been expecting, a poised young woman wearing glasses took his hand, which he quickly extended. After kissing him, she didn't say a word. And her expression was unreadable as he proudly escorted her out the door.

In slightly less than an hour, she'd transformed herself into someone he didn't know. Somehow, that made him more excited about marrying her, and made him more anxious to please her and make her as proud of him as he was of her.

Although he'd been less than thrilled when he'd initially come home and found her reluctant to go through with their ceremony, he realized now she was worth whatever he had to go through to make her his. He loved challenges, and this woman was an enigma. The rushed phone calls to set everything back an hour, the promises to pay more, were minor problems he would willingly deal with, in order to win her hand.

Did he love her? He still didn't know. Because he didn't really know exactly what love was. But whatever it was that he felt for her, it was damn close.

***

"Do you, Kayla Leigh, take this man, Bob McKnight, for your lawfully wedded husband, to have and to hold, in sickness and in health, to love and to cherish, 'till death you do part?"

Kayla swallowed the lump in her throat as Bob slipped a wide gold wedding band on the ring finger of her left hand. "I do," she whispered shakily.

"And do you, Bob McKnight, take this woman, Kayla Leigh, for your lawfully wedded wife, to have and to hold, in sickness and in health, to love and to cherish, 'till death you do part?" "I do," he answered with a firm voice, standing tall and proud, as his attractive new bride put the gold band which he'd given her earlier onto the ring finger of his left hand.

"I now pronounce you man and wife. You may kiss your new bride now."

Squeezing her hand reassuringly, Bob pulled her into his arms, running his hands firmly over her upper back, pressing her close, taking his time, kissing her with abandon.

Kayla was surprised by the ardor with which Bob kissed her, steaming up her glasses. Leaning against him, she tried to steady herself. *What was that all about?* She'd expected a chaste, dry kiss, not a wet, lingering soul kiss that left her breathless.

He'd barely spoken to her after she'd descended the stairs. And he'd kept looking her over, making her feel self-conscious. In the car, he'd done the same thing. But he'd just kissed her as if she was the most priceless woman in the world, gently at first, then more forcefully, making her feel not just loved, but cherished.

"Thanks, Tom," grinned Bob, taking his new wife's elbow with one hand, while putting the other possessively low on her back as he started ushering her out. "I owe you one."

Very aware of the unfamiliar gold band on her finger, Kayla tried not to stare at it. It fit perfectly though. Had he stopped by a jeweler's, after secretly taking one of her rings from her jewelry box, yesterday on his errands, or today on his way home? Or had he simply gotten it when he'd first decided on his plan, hoping whoever he picked would wear a size five?

Trying to remind herself it wasn't a 'real' marriage in the traditional sense, she strove to be as sensible about it as Bob was. He seemed to take it in stride and remained perfectly calm. But the ceremony seemed so real, she didn't feel it was a business transaction at all. And that made her tense, trying not to get caught up in the romance of it all.

Even so, it was a big change. This morning she'd woken up as Kayla Leigh. Tonight, she'd go to sleep as Mrs. Robert McKnight. It would take some getting used to.

"Seems odd, doesn't it?" murmured Bob, taking her hand, walking through the dim tunnels underneath downtown Houston. "We woke up as single people. Now, we're married."

She nodded. "My parents were married for forty-eight years. They never got along that well, at least that I know of. My being born as late as I was in their marriage, I know caused some stress for them. My dad had been ready to retire when my mom announced she was pregnant. But despite all their problems, and they had a lot of them, they seemed to care about each other, even when they were angry. Even when Daddy hit Mama that one time at my place. I still think it was an accident. He never could hit anything well, a ball or whatever. He invariably missed."

He shrugged. "They probably started out feeling something which passes for love, then it mellowed out as their relationship subtly changed. My parents hated each other from day one. For the early part of my life, they fought all the time. I remember hiding under my bed when they shouted at each other, and my mother threw things at my dad."

Considering what he'd told her earlier, she wondered why, but decided not to ask, since it could lead to more unpleasant memories for him. "You were an only child?"

"Yeah. It shows, huh?"

She smiled. "Only because I'm an only child, too."

"No kidding?"

She nodded. "My parents were devout Catholics. I think they'd tried to have children, early in their marriage. Then they forgot about it, thinking Mama couldn't get pregnant. When I came along, it shot their dreams of an idyllic retirement all to hell."

Walking slowly, the tunnel disappeared from Kayla's view. In unison with Bob she stopped, lost in the intensity of his magnificent green eyes. His mood was as somber as hers as they continued to hold hands and looked at each other with a new awareness. It didn't feel like love to Kayla. Or affinity. It was as if she'd known him before…somewhere… at another time…which was ridiculous. She'd never seen him before in her life until a few days ago. Yet…the feeling persisted. Why? What did it mean? Was it simply a quirk of her imagination? But, if it was, why then did Bob look as confused as she felt, as if he'd experienced the same thing?

Bob recovered before Kayla did from the strange experience, and started walking faster than before. He wasn't sure he liked the feelings he'd just had. He didn't believe in love. Or in reincarnation. Or any other hocus-pocus that couldn't be explained by hard facts and cold logic. He was sure he'd never seen her before but…something had happened. What was it?

"We need to start thinking about something to eat tonight. I forgot to take anything out of the freezer for dinner."

She laughed. "It's only four. We can defrost something in the microwave, can't we?"

"Sure. We could. But I'd just as soon eat out. How does Trulux sound?"

Trulux? One of the best, not to mention one of the most expensive, places in the entire city for steaks? "Don't we need reservations?"

"As long as we get there before six, we won't have a problem with them seating us. Besides, this is a special occasion. We just got married and I feel like splurging and showing you off."

Kayla wasn't flattered so much as she was...well, touched. Was it the way she'd worn her hair? Making a mental note to see, she decided to wear her hair the same way tomorrow, too.

***

In the dark jeep for their ride home, Kayla studied the profile of the man she was beginning to love more and more. They'd just had a wonderful dinner in one of the best restaurants in the entire city, complete with leisurely drinks in the bar while the courteous staff got their table ready. She knew it had cost a small fortune, but didn't know how much, since her menu didn't show prices. And Bob couldn't have been more gallant or affable, giving her secret smiles across the candlelit table, winking at her every so often, touching his knees to hers as they ate. He'd even told the manager that tonight was their wedding night, and they'd received complimentary glasses of wine to go with their dinner as a result. Was he going to be like this all the time now? Had the wedding ceremony changed him that much? Was that all it took, a legal event, to make him more openly affectionate and caring?

Bob's heart broke a little as he caught her dreamy look out of the corner of his eye. But he winked at her because he knew that's what she expected, and put his hand on her knee, squeezing it. *Poor thing!* She was really buying his whole act. Going out in public, telling strangers they were married, looking at her as if she was the only woman in the world for him was simply insurance to make it look good, in case the lawyers started snooping around. Kayla should've realized what he was doing, from their earlier discussions. But she chose not to, dammit, making him feel like a louse inside. Not only had everyone else bought his act, she'd bought it too.

"We need to talk, babe," he said, turning into their subdivision.

"About what?" she asked, getting cold chills; knowing from his flat tone, so different from the way he'd been talking all night, that something was wrong.

"I know you like this...this feeling. And I like it too. But I'm, well, I'm not the best adjusted person in the world."

"Are there any truly well-adjusted people in the world, Bob?"

"I don't know, and I don't care. The point is, I haven't told you about my father yet, and how he dealt with Mom. It's...my father was a good-looking man in his day, and before Mom got her hooks into him, dated a different girl every week. I know this for a fact. He used to show me pictures of him when he was young, with different ladies. Pretty ladies."

"Dad and I went in the yard nearly every night, with Dad carrying a lit cigarette; not because he smoked, but because Mom never allowed cigarettes in the house, and made him go outside every time he lit one. This one night, I was about ten or so, I think. Right before Mom got her crazy ideas about me."

Stopping the car in the driveway, Bob's familiar home disappeared, morphing into the house he'd lived in as a boy, as he remembered back. Kayla grew still as he started telling her about his crazy father's belief.

"I still don't understand! If you don't love Mom, and she doesn't love you, why don't you get a divorce?"

Kayla grew still. He wasn't just telling this, she realized, he was re-living it. His voice was raw and harsh with his anguish.

"If I hadn't had to marry your mother, son, I'd have had to marry someone else," continued Bob, speaking so low Kayla had to strain to hear him. "Problem is, I can't keep my pants zipped. Take Sally, here," he said, pulling out a picture from his pocket. "I dated her for three years with no strings attached, because I told her right off I was married. And Donna," he grinned, "she's my latest conquest; as cute as a button, and would do anything for me, so I get away with having sex with her anyway I want, in whatever position I choose. She, too, knows I'm married, but what she doesn't know is I don't spend most of my time with my wife. I spend most of it with Sally. Do you see what I'm telling you, son?"

Bobby shook his head.

"It's simple. Why settle for pot roast every night, when you can have smorgasbord any time you feel like it? Both ladies know I'm never going to get a divorce, and they accept that. But the thing is, if I got one, I'd have to make a choice and have one lady or another, because they, unlike your mother, probably wouldn't be willing to turn a blind eye to what I do in my free time. So do yourself a favor, son. Play it smart. If you find yourself having to get married someday, do it the smart way. Have an understanding right from the very beginning, so you can do whatever the hell you want whenever you want, with whoever you want."

Slowly, Bob's eyes refocused on his brick house and Kayla knew he'd returned to the present. "How sick! Surely you don't buy that?"

"I don't know. I never thought I'd get married. And here I am."

"Correct me if I'm wrong, but aren't you the one who pushed this?"

"It's called taking care of business, Kayla. I want my inheritance. But I care about you too. And I don't want to hurt you. But I see how seriously you're taking this romantic stuff, and it worries me."

"Yes, well, it's got me a little worried too. Now, surely you're not thinking of having any hot dates while you try to get me pregnant, are you? If you are, I'll be more than happy to grant you an annulment."

"I'm not thinking of doing anything this very minute," he lied, determined not to look again at her silk clad legs. "I just don't want you hurt, that's all."

"How considerate! Why didn't you think of that before we got married?"

"I didn't think you'd take this romantic stuff this seriously."

"Correct me if I'm wrong, but I could've sworn you said you needed me. Was that needing me meant to be just to get you your damned inheritance?"

"No," he murmured, getting out of the car. And in a moment he leaned back in, "I'll show you how else I need you."

"Bastard!" she hissed, getting out of the car herself. "You can sleep by yourself tonight, until you figure things out better. I'm not sleeping with you again until you do."

"Dammit! I'm trying to do the honorable thing by leveling with you, to keep you from getting hurt. Why can't you accept that?" he asked, storming ahead of her and unlocking the door.

Spotting a light go out in the house next door, and spotting someone peeking out the window, Kayla quickly edged in front of him. Good Lord, they were attracting his neighbor's attention now.

"Kayla?" He took hold of her arm as he followed, pulling her around to face him.

"What?" she asked, jerking out of his grasp.

"Let's not argue. Not tonight. We'll work something out, okay?" he asked, putting his arms around her, kissing her neck. "Let's sleep on the idea for a few nights and see what we can come up with."

"You're kidding, right?"

"It's our wedding night! Yours *and* mine."

"Tell me the truth, how seriously did you think this thing out? Marriage is a damn big step. It's a commitment to each other to be faithful to each other. I honestly thought you cared about me, a little. You were so affectionate this morning, and that show you just put on when we were out tonight was priceless."

"I do care about you! That's why I don't want you to get carried away by an illusion."

"Forget it!" She forced a yawn. "I'm exhausted. I'm turning in." She stormed up the stairs. "Alone."

"Fine," he muttered, watching her little hips sway, as she quickly ascended the stairs, not at all sure if he was making the right decision in letting her go. "If you want to pout like a child, go right ahead."

Storming into his own room, he jerked off his suit as he strode to his exercise room. He needed a release and bad. What better way to get it than to work his muscles until they cried for mercy? Pulling on his short gym shorts, he got on his treadmill, setting it for walk first, then building up the speed until he was running. God, it felt good, with his heart pumping in sync with his legs. He'd be damned if he'd think of her wiggling hips right up there over him. "Who needs you?" he shouted as her image appeared in his mind, with her blonde hair falling around her like a halo as she laid down on the bed, spreading her legs and holding out her arms to welcome him into her tight little body.

"God dammit," he hissed, jumping off and squatting down on his rowing machine. Turning the speed on high, he stretched out then took hold of the 'oars,' and 'rowed,' working his legs, bending and straightening them as his biceps bulged, working in unison with his legs. He took pleasure in aching with the strain. Who needed a woman when he had all this…he looked around…all this steel and metal?

"Shit!" Jumping off the damn rower, he picked up his weights, lifting them up to his knees, further up, past his bare chest, now glistening with sweat, and finally up over his head.

Doing ten more sets, he quickly put on his protective gloves and started jumping around, punching his punching bag until his breath grew ragged and his sore, tight muscles refused to do any more.

He knew better than to rush through his exercising routine, but dammit, he'd needed a release in the worst way, and this was the best way he could get it. He sighed with pleasure. He'd finally dispelled her image!

Grabbing a towel, he wiped off the sweat and put it around his neck as he strode out to the den and poured himself a scotch. Downing it quickly, he promptly fixed himself another, then another one, trying hard to ignore her footsteps over him.

Hell! He should have taken her to bed when he had the chance, before he'd started playing the gentleman who was intent on being so damned honorable and giving her a lesson in reality.

Hearing her footsteps increase then suddenly stop, he discarded his glass for the bottle, taking a healthy slug as he headed for the couch. *What's she doing now? What's she wearing? Is she lying down yet?*

Propping his bare feet on the coffee table, he leaned back, his mind projecting an image of her on the ceiling. She was lying underneath him with those pert breasts gleaming with the sweat of her exertions.

He moaned, feeling those firm hips of hers against his as she strained to reach her climax, with her long shapely legs squeezing him tight. God damn her! She was his wife now, and he had every right to have sex with her. But he was a man, and he'd be damned if he'd beg. He could damn well do without her. Hell, he'd done without her for thirty-five years, and had done very well. Only he hadn't known she existed then. How could he love someone when he didn't know what love was?

Through the patio window, the dark void disappeared as he saw his father and him out in the back yard when he was still a boy. "Daddy, what's love?"

His dad had laughed. "You want to know what love is? It's a fantasy; a four-letter word that's a synonym for fuck. To a woman, fuck means love. But a man, a real man, knows fucking is having sex, plain and simple. Using the word love though, gets a woman in the mood to be fucked real fast. They can't resist it. But don't you be fooled by it. If you go looking for love, you'll be chasing a dream that doesn't exist. Always remember that son. Always!"

As the scene in the backyard disappeared, Bob took another slug from his bottle. Why couldn't Kayla accept what he'd told her about love? Hell, he was just trying to protect her, like his Dad had tried to protect him. Why'd she have to get angry about it? All he'd done was tell her the damn truth!

Tilting his bottle up, he drained it. Then stood up and weaved his way to the bar again, dragging out two more bottles. He made his way back to the couch, spreading out. Resting his head against the plump pillow in back, he propped his elbow on the side arm, jerked open a bottle and took a long swallow, trying hard to forget the woman upstairs. The woman he desperately needed, but didn't know why.

Chapter Eleven

Midnight. The witching hour. As the minutes ticked by on the silver digital clock by her bed, Kayla pulled out another tissue from the box she'd brought into bed with her, and dried her eyes. She was bewitched, all right. She'd just married a man who'd seduced the hell out of her, then told her outright he still didn't believe in love, and she shouldn't believe in it either...on their wedding night!

Listening to cabinet doors banging open and slamming closed, she knew he was still up. He'd turned on her plasma TV set too, and judging by the loud, heavy panting sounds coming from it, she knew he was watching an all-night X-rated movie channel. The least he could do was show some consideration and be a little more quiet. Even if she'd been able to fall asleep, she couldn't have with all the noise he was making.

Throwing off her covers, she jumped up. She'd had it! She'd feel a hell of a lot better having it out with him. Slipping on her floor-length white cotton gown that was part of a peignoir set her mother had given her when she'd moved into her elegant new apartment, she eased quietly to the landing and looked down. It was pitch black down there, except for the flickering shadows of the TV screen directly opposite the staircase. Why? She'd assumed with all the racket, he'd have some lights on.

Curious in spite of her better instincts, she quietly descended the stairs. Stopping on the last step, she peeked around the corner. What were those three open liquor bottles doing on the coffee table, and why did it smell like a bar down here? Had he polished off all that booze by himself?

Glancing back over her shoulder to make sure she wouldn't be taken by surprise from the direction of the dark kitchen, she crept further into the living room.

Easing forward, she sniffed the air suspiciously. It reeked of both alcohol and sweat. Then she saw him sprawled on the couch, drinking yet another bottle, holding its glass neck with a finger hooked around it.

He looked terrible. His hair was askew, and he was wearing only a towel around his neck and some scrungy looking shorts.

"Ah, my little wife has decided to join me," he purred, his green eyes glittering brightly in the glare from the TV screen, his eyes boldly raking her from head to foot. "Couldn't sleep after all, huh? Was it the sounds of the X-rated movie which lured you down here? You get hot by watching other people fuck, too?"

Damn! She hadn't wanted him to see her. In the condition he was in, she didn't trust him. But now that he'd spotted her, she had no choice but to brazen it out.

He was drunk. She could tell by the way he spoke. He was speaking slowly, very distinctly pronouncing each word. Crossing her arms underneath her breasts, she advanced a few steps and peered into each open bottle. They were all empty, every single one. Except for the one he was still drinking from "We need to talk."

"Why? Because I haven't gotten around to naming you as beneficiary on my life insurance policy yet?"

"What a terrible thing to say! I'm your wife! I love y…" she caught herself. What was she saying? Surely she didn't mean it, especially with him sprawled out, drunk, still refusing to believe love existed. "What I mean is—"

But he was faster drunk than she was sober, and, before she could make up a plausible excuse, he'd jumped up with surprising speed, and cradling her head in his large hand, forced her lips up to his. "You love me?" he breathed, kissing her roughly, picking her up bodily, and striding into his bedroom. "Prove it."

Bracing herself, trying to wiggle out of his grasp, she futilely struggled against him as he burrowed underneath the low neckline of her gown and skimpy robe, licking each breast.

"You're drunk!" she scoffed. "I can't talk to—"

"You're right. We're through talking, lady."

Pressing her down on the bed with his weight, he followed her as she fell backward, her long blonde hair fanning out behind her. Before she could recover enough to escape, he jerked down her gown and robe, revealing her luscious little body.

Looking into her huge brown eyes, he wished to God he could fall in love, like she wanted. But he couldn't. Not after he'd seen his father have sex with the girl he'd been dating steadily throughout high school.

As he held her down, Kayla's face turned into Joan's, the girl he'd dated throughout high school. Although it had been prearranged, with his father as a test for Joan to show Bob how fickle women were, even when they claimed to be in love, Bob had never thought he'd actually have sex with her. But he should've known his father wouldn't stop until he'd gotten what he really wanted. Joan was, after all, a beautiful blonde with huge implants her doting father had gotten her for her eighteenth birthday. Bob's father had claimed she was a slut, already pregnant with another boy's baby. That was why, Bob's father said, she claimed she loved Bob and wanted to marry him; to keep from having an illegitimate child.

Following his father's plan, Bob dropped by his house with Joan while his mother was out at her weekly Bridge game. The pretense had been that he needed to get a sweater on that chilly October evening. Watching from his bedroom window upstairs, Bob saw his father stroll out to the side of the house, whistling, looking surprised when he'd spotted Joan. He couldn't hear what his father had said to get her to join him; something about the dying plants near the garage he supposed.

As his father lured Joan inside their detached garage, Bob slipped back outside and watched from the window in the rear. Like his dad had promised, he'd lit a candle so Bob could see for himself how easily she could be laid by any man who tried.

He was surprised Joan hadn't bolted the moment his father accidentally-on-purpose bumped into her, spilling some of his beer on her pretty pink sweater, then insisting he wipe it off. Although Joan did look surprised at first, she quickly calmed down as his father slowly stroked her breasts, edging one finger into her sweater-covered bra to stroke her nipple, which poked against the knit fabric in response. Judging by her slow wicked smile, she seemed to be enjoying the hell out of it.

"Are you always this naughty, Mr. McKnight?"

Bob's father returned her smile. "Call me Leonard," he corrected. "I'm only like this when I know a young woman wants me to be. Do you like this, Joan?" he asked, as he edged his finger beneath the knit covered bra, stroking her other breast. "You're an experienced man, Mr. McKnight. You tell me. Am I enjoying it?"

"Leonard, please." Putting his hands gently around Joan's waist, he ignored her question, and lightly kissed her. Then, when she stared calmly into his eyes and didn't back away he pulled her closer, kissing her more thoroughly, clearly running his tongue deep into her mouth, backing her up to the window more so Bob could easily see what was going on.

"What if Bob comes back?" she asked.

"He won't. Chances are he's gone to bed. He wasn't feeling too good after dinner. Besides, what do you care? Bob's a boy. What you want is a man. That's what you deserve; a man who knows what he's doing. As it happens, I'm very unhappy with my wife and have been thinking about leaving her," he lied smoothly. "I'd make a hell of a good catch for some young lady who'd be willing to give me what I want."

Bob nearly burst out laughing. Had Joan thought to check his father's wallet, she'd find two twenty dollar bills. His wife made sure he never had more than that at any one time.

Smiling wickedly again, Joan crossed her hands over her breasts and slowly lifted her sweater up over her head, her long blonde hair leisurely cascading downward. Wasting no time, his father gently slid down the straps of her unclasped bra, and fondled each full breast, sucking them in turn.

Standing there, Bob grew numb, watching his father bend her backwards over the hood of their old Ford. Following her, his father got his erect penis out of his jeans, letting Joan stroke it as he jerked off her jeans and panties, throwing them in a heap on the dirt floor.

Feeling like he was watching from far away, Bob continued his silent vigil outside the dirty rear window as his father entered her, banging her hips noisily on the metal hood of their Ford.

After they'd left, Bob remained staring into the now dark garage, unable to move, unable to think, unable to feel.

***

Kayla was growing frantic. For the past several minutes, Bob had been staring vacantly into her eyes. She tried to twist first this way and that, hoping to get away, only to have him continue to stare at her, automatically pushing her down harder.

"Bob!" she hissed. "Bob! You're scaring me. What's wrong? What're you looking at? Bob? Dammit, answer me!"

How strange, Bob thought, coming back to the present. He'd forgotten all about Joan and his father until now. But he'd learned his lesson well. Love didn't exist…for anyone…just like his father claimed.

Blinking his eyes, Bob looked around slowly, dazed, surprised to see Kayla underneath him. Did Kayla really love him, like she claimed?

Or was she like Joan, who claimed to love him only to spread her legs wide for his damn father? Would she hurt him like Joan had? Dear God, he didn't know. He just knew he needed her now, in the most elemental way known to man, and by God, he was going to have her.

Kayla stiffened, studying him. Had he remembered *another* tragic event from his past? Her heart went out to him. "Bob," she whispered. "It's all right. I'm here. You're safe."

He reared back looking at her as if she'd gone stark raving mad. Then he laughed, a high-pitched, bitter sound that sent chills down Kayla's spine.

"Get off me," she commanded, trying to keep her voice from shaking. "You're drunk and I'm tired. We need to get some sleep."

"Tsk, tsk, tsk. Patience, babe. All in due time."

"Now, Bob. Off!"

"You're more drunk than I am if you actually believe I'll get up. Hell, it took long enough for you to get down here. No way I'm letting you up now."

"Dammit, Bob, I'm serious!"

He put his fingers gently but firmly over her soft lips. "You're beautiful," he whispered, cradling her head, holding her still as he softly kissed the tip of each nipple, which peaked instantly at his touch. "So responsive. So sweet. I'm going to be gentle, babe," he murmured against her. "I promise. I need you, dammit. You'll never know how much. Stop trying to push me away."

He sounded cold-stone sober now. And needy. Still wary, she started to relax to see if he was on the level, or if this was just a ploy. She could withhold her body from him forever. But not her heart. Sensing her change of mood, Bob let go of her and stated trailing kisses down to her pubis, seeking and finding her already pulsating clitoris.

Kayla tried to steel herself. But never had a man thrilled her this way. Never had she known she could need a man this desperately.

Squeezing her hips, Bob kissed her sweet nub as if it was her tongue, laving it, blowing on it gently, inflaming her even more. Her clitoris slowly grew, pushing against his tongue with its gentle pulsating rhythm. Kicking away the remnants of her bed clothes, he unzipped his pants, shrugged off his shirt and wedged a knee between her legs which willingly parted.

"Open for me, sweetheart," he urged, his fingers finding her vagina, pressing his penis inside as he spread out on top of her, bracing himself on his elbows. "God, yes! Squeeze me tight, baby," he begged as her vagina tightened instinctively around him as he surged deeper into her welcoming warmth. "Give me what we both want, baby! Tighter!" Throwing caution to the wind, Kayla spread her legs wider, admitting his full length, squeezing it hard as her hips started bucking against him.

"Relax, babe," he breathed raggedly, setting a slow rhythm. "Follow my lead."
Bob was amazed he could make love at all, he was so damn drunk. But he had to try. He had to show her how much he needed her, and, damn it all, this was the only way he knew to get his message across.

Trying to go slow to prolong her pleasure, he finally gave up and let his penis take control. Letting it plunge deeply inside her, setting its own escalating tempo, he felt her tighten against him even more, massaging his penis from end to end. Her responsiveness inflamed him and he pushed her deeper into the mattress with each forceful thrust.

***

Aware of another person in his bed, Bob woke up with a start. He'd slept what? He looked at the clock radio on the bedside table. An hour. Propping himself up on his elbow, he watched Kayla sleep, oddly reluctant to wake her. With her hair strewn over half her pretty face, she was curled up in a ball on her side, facing him, the deep, even breathing of a peaceful sleep the only sound in the room. Careful not to wake her, he slid the covers down underneath her, then covered her up.

He stared at her in awe. She was his wife. And she'd proved herself an excellent match for him; her innocent enthusiasm exciting and inflaming him more than any other women he'd ever bedded. If they kept up at this pace, he'd get her pregnant in record time. That would be okay, of course. It was the whole purpose of this charade. Except it didn't seem like a charade when he was making love to her. It seemed like honest-to-God love. *How bizarre!*

Easing out of bed, he grabbed his robe off its hook on the back of the bathroom door and padded silently out to the living room, to indulge his secret passion for cigars. Only after having sex did he allow himself the luxury. And even then, he did it only after he'd lit the scented candles to dissipate the smoke. Opening the patio door to diminish the smell combined with that of stale liquor, he stood there in the near-dark, enjoying the light spring breeze, as he deeply inhaled.

With a luminous full moon high overhead and not a cloud in sight to obscure the numerous stars, it was clearly a night made for love. The problem was, he didn't believe in it. Love was for romantics, for the poets and great artists of the past. It had no place in the real world of today, with all the racing around and the hectic pace of everyday life.

Sure, men and women needed each other, but it was a physical need, and easily satisfied. He'd never seen his parents kiss, or even hug. They'd professed love for each other, but it was clear they didn't feel it. Certainly his father hadn't. All his running around with every woman he saw proved time and time again he didn't love his mother.

Staring into the dark lawn, it disappeared as he remembered one night, when he was about eight, his mother had caught his father trying to sneak in after he'd thought she'd gone to bed. Bob had been going to get a glass of water, when he saw his father tip-toe through the hall, holding his shoes, reeking of cheap cologne, his tie half-thrown over his shoulder, his shirt undone; but even in the dark, Bob could clearly see baby pink lipstick stains on the open collar. Since his mother never wore any shade except cherry red, Bob, ever precocious and curious as hell about everything under the sun, quietly followed his dad to find out what was going on.

Through the partially open door, Bob saw his mother pop straight up. "Why, dammit," she hissed, turning on the lamp, flooding the room with bright light, "do you have to do this night after night? It's our anniversary, for God's sake! Don't you have any decency? Don't you care how I feel, knowing you have sex every damned night with other women?"

Squinting and shielding his eyes with his hand over his brows like a strange salute, Leonard looked surprised. Our anniversary's today?" he asked slurring his words. "You sure?"

"April first ended at midnight, but technically yes. It would've been nice to share it with my husband." "I'm sorry," he shrugged, clearly not meaning it. "What do you want? A box of chocolates; to enhance your already-grotesque figure with another pound? That'd make you weigh, what? Two hundred and two? Two hundred and three?"

"What a terrible thing to say!"

"It's the truth," sighed Leonard, sitting down on the chair, shrugging out of his shirt.

Hearing his mother burst into hysterical tears as she plopped down, Bob ran back into his room just in time to escape his father, who was taking a blanket and a pillow downstairs to sleep on the couch yet again. But he hadn't gone fast enough to escape seeing the horrible pain on his mother's face, and he'd wondered then how two people could hurt each other so much.

Bob vowed it would never happen to him. And the best way to ensure it was never to fool himself into thinking he loved anyone, and to never get married. His marriage to Kayla, however, didn't count. He and Kayla both knew it was only a temporary business relationship, designed by him, void of romantic illusions, engineered for a logical reason.

Speaking of business ... he had to rush some more drawings over to Collins by nine. Writing her a quick note, so he wouldn't forget in the morning, he left it by the clock, along with another hundred and his house key, so she'd see it when she first woke up and not worry about where he was.

Slipping off his robe, he started easing back the covers. But as he did so, he realized his mistake. Revealing more of her than he'd intended, he stared at those beautiful breasts peaking high as the cool air assaulted them. As if his hand had a mind of its own, he reached out and cupped one, testing its weight. Bending his head to taste, wanting to indulge himself for just a brief few seconds, he wasn't aware her eyes had fluttered open and were watching him as he drank his fill.

"Oh, God!" Kayla whispered huskily, pulling him closer, edging under him. "Please, baby, please. Don't stop!" she pleaded, as he looked up.

With his senses dulled by her sweet scent and the sight of those pert nipples so close arousing him beyond reason, he quickly positioned himself over her to continue his husbandly duty. At the rate they were going, he could get rid of his exercise equipment any time he wanted.

He was getting enough exercise with Kayla to keep him in damn good shape without having to leave the comfort of his own bed.

***

Stretching her arms over her head, feeling more relaxed, more sated then she'd ever felt before, Kayla slowly opened her eyes, confused at first by the morning sun streaming in the edges of the large windows, and even more puzzled by the huge, comfortable bed she was in.

Slowly sitting up, she tried to clear the fuzzy cobwebs of sleep from her mind. She felt like she'd run a marathon, tired and relaxed, but exhilarated too in a strange way. Not only that… she was nude! She sniffed the air suspiciously, inhaling Bob's fragrant after-shave.

Then she felt her face grow hot. Good God! Had she really done all those things she'd thought she'd merely dreamed about? Had she really been that brazen … she swallowed nervously… begging for more time?

Hearing a loud clanking noise outside the closed bedroom door, she stiffened as she caught sight of the tiny silver clock off to the far left and Bob's note. Ten o'clock. But the note said he'd be back around one. Had he returned early…or had someone broken in?

She could call nine-one-one on her cell phone. It was right there in her purse, and no one could listen in if they'd picked up the extension. But what if the cops came and it was Bob out there? She'd feel like a fool.

Sliding out of bed as quietly as she could, she bypassed her gown, folded neatly on the recliner, and headed toward the closet. Taking down the first shirt she came to, careful not to let the hangers clang, she slipped on Bob's crisp white dress shirt. It hung clear to her knees, and the starch made it impossible to see her shape. Good! If someone had broken in, maybe they'd think she was much bigger than she was.

Rolling up the stiff sleeves as quickly as she was able, she eased into the bathroom, looking for a suitable weapon … just in case. Grabbing the first thing she came to, a large clear glass bottle of blue shampoo for dandruff, she hid it behind her with one hand, while carefully opening the door to the living room with the other. She peeked out cautiously. *So far, so good.* Gathering her courage, what little there was of it, she tip-toed stealthily further out, careful not to shut the bedroom door completely in case she needed to make a hasty retreat. She'd have given half-ownership in her Volvo for the fireplace poker or little shovel, but they were clear on the other side of the room.

Hearing something bang shut, followed by heavy footsteps, she froze. Whoever it was, was coming closer! It sounded like they were the kitchen now, making their way further inside.

Rushing the short distance to the bar in the opposite direction, she exchanged the bottle of shampoo for a large sturdy looking bottle of vodka that would pack a good punch, and tip-toed forward. Chances were, Bob wouldn't be slamming doors, knowing she was asleep down here. But an intruder might.

Flattening herself against the wall like she'd seen cops do in TV shows, she took a deep breath. "Freeze, Sucker!" she shouted, jumping into the doorway of the kitchen. "The place's surrounded!"

"What the …" she muttered. Where'd he go? The kitchen was deserted. But that was impossible. She knew the sound had been coming from here. It was unmistakable.

"Kayla?" boomed a familiar voice behind her. "What the hell do you think you're doing?"

Whirling around, Kayla's heart skipped a few beats. Then she sagged against the wall in relief. "Thank God!" she sighed, walking slowly towards him, trying to keep upright on her shaky knees, as he negligently leaned against the doorway leading to the garage. He was looking at her as if she wasn't quite right in the head.

"I thought you were an intruder," she whispered, putting her arms around his waist, hugging him tightly, laying her head against his broad chest. "I was scared half to death."

Plucking the bottle of vodka from her shaking hand, Bob held her against him. "You were going to confront someone with a bottle of vodka? What'd you plan to do? Get him so drunk he'd pass out?"

"I was going to hit him over the head with it. Or at least try. I guess it would've depended on how tall he was. I hadn't figured out the details." Taking her hands from around his waist, he took hold of her shoulders, steering her toward the bedroom. "I've got a much better plan. If there ever is a break-in, number one, keep in mind the alarm system will alert the police. They'll be here within three to five minutes. That leaves a small window when you'll be alone with whoever it is. But I have a loaded gun right here," he said, opening the small drawer in the bedside table. "Have you ever used one?"

She shook her head. "Not really."

Bob sighed. "It's a simple question, Kayla. Calm down. Either you've used a gun or not. Which is it? Yes or no?"

"No. But then I've never needed to."

He'd figured as much. "Okay, this is kind of a big gun; a Smith & Wesson .45, but I think you could handle it in an emergency. All you have to do is take off the safety mechanism, which is right here, and aim it fairly straight. Usually, people back off when they're looking down the barrel of a gun. But I don't want you to pull the trigger unless you're sure you have to use it to save your life. This is not a toy. Do you understand?"

She nodded. "I'd only use it as a last resort."

"That's right. That's the only reason I have one. If someone breaks into my house, I know I can stop them if I have to. Now, hold it. Test its weight. Don't worry; I have the safety latch on. Try to aim it over there, at the window."

"Like this?" she asked, bringing it up to her nose, squinting her eyes. "Would that do it?"

The way she was standing with her legs spread apart, her complexion as pale as if she'd just seen a ghost, was laughable. But this was serious.

She needed to know what to do in case someone broke in.

"Relax, okay? Try to stay with me on this. You don't need to emulate the cops you see on TV. They aren't real. All you have to do is aim the barrel at chest level. One bullet will stop a person. But it rarely comes to that. Most people who break in are looking for things easily taken, that can be quickly pawned, then they get the hell out. The last thing they want is to be shot. Looking down the barrel of a loaded gun will usually scare them off. And remember, the law of averages is on your side. The cops are quick here. They know exactly what to do. All you have to do is keep yourself safe for three to five minutes. A loaded gun will generally do it if they know the person holding it isn't afraid to shoot it."

"Do I need to take off the safety mechanism?"

"Yes. Usually. That would help when the time comes. But I think for now, just knowing where it is and how to point the barrel straight is all you need to know."

Holding it straight out in front of her, she aimed at the window. "How's this?"

Bob shook his head. God help her if she ever did have to confront an intruder. The only hope she had was if the guy laughed himself to death watching her. "Bend your arm at the elbow. Don't be so stiff. You don't want to extend the gun so far someone can grab it. Hold it closer to your chest."

"Like this?" she asked, aiming again.

Going behind her, putting his arms around her, positioning his hands over hers, he bent her elbow ever more, so her hand was nearly touching her breast. "Because you're so short, you've got to aim the barrel up a little. You're going for his heart, but don't worry about the exact location for now. Just aim high."

"Is this okay?" Again, she pointed, aiming the barrel more carefully.

"Don't fight me on this. Relax. Let me guide your hands."

Taking a deep breath, she went limp. "Is this better?"

"A little. See where I'm pointing? You've got to aim up. Even if you get him in the throat or face, that's okay. The important thing is to intimidate someone enough so they'll run."

Trying yet again, she held onto the gun, as Bob loosened his hands, letting her get the feel of it. "Am I getting close?" "Close enough," he said, taking the gun. "But that's enough for your first lesson. Next time I go to the shooting range. I'll take you with me. You need to get used to the kick when it goes off, and how to handle it."

"I think I'll get the hang of it eventually. It'll just take a little time."

"You didn't do bad. But remember, it's only to be used for emergencies. I don't want you imagining things and using it for every little noise."

"I understand. It's only for emergencies. I won't touch it otherwise."

"Good girl," he smiled, getting a good look at his shirt on her as he sat down on the bed, pulling her to him. "What gave you the idea of wearing this?"

Nervously, she smoothed her hair. "It was the first thing I came to in your closet. I didn't want to confront anyone in my robe and nightgown. But I was in a hurry, so I slipped this on and grabbed a bottle of shampoo from your bathroom."

"Shampoo?" he echoed, deftly unbuttoning the few buttons she'd done of his shirt. "I could've sworn you had a bottle of vodka."

"I did. But after I realized whoever it was, was in the kitchen and I had time, I ran to the bar and exchanged the shampoo for something larger. The vodka bottle was the first thing I saw."

He kissed her neck as he slid off the huge shirt. "Pretty gutsy, aren't you?"

"Pretty stupid, you mean. But I had to do something."

"Well, I won't tell anyone if you won't," he murmured, lying down, pulling her down beside him. "It'll be our secret."

"Are you good at keeping secrets?"

"Maybe," he said, kissing one firm breast then another. "But that's enough talking for now. I've got some other things for us to do. Last night was only a preview."

She sighed contentedly. He had no idea how much she loved him. And it was just as well. If he'd known, he'd be so scared he'd probably divorce her right away, inheritance or not.

"Ever fucked doggie style?"

"Excuse me?"

"Turn over."

She stiffened. "You're kidding, right?"

"Do I look like I'm kidding? Turn over."

"Maybe we should think this over."

"I already have. Now, turn!"

Before she could protest more, Bob bodily lifted her up so high, she put down her feet and hands. "That's a little better. Now get down on your elbows and knees." She really didn't like this. Not only was it new to her, it seemed kinky.

"Damn, Bob! I don't think this'll work."

"Sure it will. I've done it before."

"Oh?" she asked archly; trying, but failing to keep the jealously she felt from her voice.

"It was before I knew you, okay?" he asked jerking off his clothes and positioning himself on his hands and knees up over her.

"Sure," she said, with what she hoped was a negligent tone, striving to squelch her rising anger. "It doesn't matter to me how often you've done it, or with who."

"Glad to hear it," he said, lightly biting the back of her neck. "Now bend lower."

Before she could protest more, she felt his hand go between her legs, finding her opening, plunging his penis in, holding it.

"Get used to the feel. I know it feels strange, but just relax. It's one of my favorite fantasies. Now bend your arms more so your breasts fill my hands."

She really didn't like this. But she obviously had no choice. He was bound and determined to teach her this one, come hell or high water. Doing like he said, it felt awkward and she was more than just a little apprehensive. "Like this?" she asked, feeling the palms of his hands against her nipples, his gentle fingers stroking her breasts as his weight came down on her back more.

"Perfect," he murmured, nestling his head over her shoulder, looking into the space between them. "Just relax."

Instinctively she stiffened as he slowly withdrew, then entered again. But as he continued, she realized it wasn't so bad, especially with him kissing her neck and his fingers caressing her nipples which were quickly hardening into tight buds with her growing excitement. Damn, he was skilled!

Before she knew it, her body found his rhythm, and together they rocked faster and faster, until she didn't know whether it was just them or the entire bed that was shaking so hard. Feeling herself spiraling out of control, the force of her climax matched his, taking her to new heights of ecstasy.

Exhausted, they collapsed in each other's arms, with her nestled against him, hoping the closeness between them now would last forever.

***

Bob woke up two hours later with his arm around Kayla. He was uncharacteristically stiff and knew how he'd gotten that way. But why? What was there about her that caused his libido to soar out of control every time he saw her? Gently, he kissed her soft neck as he sat up. Sure, he wanted to indulge his fantasies with her. But he shouldn't care about her this much after they'd had sex. He'd never opened up to anyone the way he had to her. He'd never confided so much of his past to anyone before. Why?

And here it was, nearly two, and he had yet to get anything done. He'd thought he'd get a lot done when the meeting with Collins was cut so short. But he hadn't accomplished anything yet.

Was it like this for all newly married couples? He'd never really taken an interest in knowing before, but he guessed it was. There was just something about knowing there was a shapely young thing in a man's bed, ready to do whatever the hell he wanted. And Kayla was so warm, so sweet, so understanding, it was damn hard to resist her.

Chapter Twelve

At first, Kayla tried to ignore a familiar sounding man shouting in the other room. But, as he continued, she opened her eyes reluctantly, stretched, and sat up. Despite her exhaustion, she felt euphoric, and knew it was caused by her new husband and the magical things he'd introduced her to. She'd never known indulging in his fantasies could be so wonderful, so warm, and bring them so close.

"What?" he asked the caller on the phone. "Tonight? No man. This is a bad time for me really. I can't swing it, sorry." He listened. "Oh, hell, are you sure? Have you tried Larry?" He listened again. "What about Fred? I heard he was separated from his wife. Oh, really? No I hadn't heard. Well, damn, I don't know what to tell you. But count me out. No, Jim! Not tonight. That's not a good idea. Jim? Jim? Are you there? Shit!"

Using his speed dial to call Jim back, Bob was frantic. Jim was on his way over, bound and determined to have a private party with him and his two expensive call girls. Bob was a last minute substitute for Steve, who had to bow out due to a stomach virus. And now Jim wasn't answering his phone. *Great!*

He had yet to tell any of his friends he was married. They'd be angry as hell he hadn't invited them to the ceremony, so he'd planned to tell them later he'd eloped or something. But he didn't want to tell them this soon. Not until he'd planned it out.

Now, he'd have to tell Jim when he got here. But he needed to prepare Jim *privately* for the good news. No way was he going to tell him the truth about his unconventional arrangement. No one in his circle would understand.

Striding into his bedroom, Bob forced a smile. "Good, you're up. How'd you sleep?"

"Wonderful!" she said, bending her knees putting her arms around them as she received Bob's soft kiss. "How'd you sleep?"

"Terrific." He sat down on the bed, searching her eyes. "But something's come up."

"Bad news?"

"You could say that. I haven't told any of my friends about our marriage yet."

Why wasn't she surprised? Was it the fact he'd received very few phone calls and hadn't mentioned anyone, like people usually do when talking and getting acquainted? Just why he was so secretive about their marriage, she couldn't figure out. Surely, he didn't consider it bad news? "When do you plan to tell them?"

"I'm telling Jim, one of my best friends, tonight."

"Here? Or are we going out to meet him?"

His heart broke. Of course she'd assumed she'd be with him. "I'm telling him alone, babe. He's coming here with a, um…a couple of other friends."

"Why do you want to tell them alone? If you're going to tell them about me, shouldn't I be with you?"

He shook his head. "I'd just rather do it alone. I don't plan on telling him everything, just the bare necessities. But I'll feel more comfortable doing it without you."

"You plan on telling one of your friends who's coming, not all of them?"

He nodded. "It'll be faster that way. As soon as they get here, I'll take Jim aside. Then they'll leave, I promise. But you need to go upstairs."

"Are you ashamed of me?"

"Don't be ridiculous! Of course not."

"So introduce me."

"I can't! It's not the right time."

Kayla smelled a rat. Something was going on…something he wasn't telling her. "Spill it! What's going on?"

"Look, just go upstairs, okay? You can use the time to straighten out your room or get some reading done. Maybe take a nice long bubble bath."

"That should be fun. I don't take bubble baths. I take showers."

"Oh no, babe. No showers. They could hear the water if it runs too long and ask embarrassing questions." He forced a salacious grin. "Maybe we can take a shower together later."

"Don't try to placate me, Bob. Tell me what the hell's going on. Now!"

In spite of his best intentions, he was getting angry. "Have you forgotten our agreement?"

"I'm very aware of our marriage vows, but it seems you could use a refresher course."

"I'm not talking about that, dammit. You signed a contract with me. Please, Kayla, honor it, okay? Just this once! I'll get rid of them as soon as I can."

"How soon?"

"You're pinning me down to a time table, now?" He gritted his teeth. "I don't know how long. Maybe an hour. Maybe less. Maybe more. I just don't know right now."

"Are any of your friends who are coming women?" Like ex-girlfriends?

"I...what does that have to do with it?"

"Answer me!"

"It doesn't matter, Kayla. I'll get rid of them as soon as I can. I promise you. Just don't give me a hard time about this, okay?" "So they *are* women," she muttered. "Ex-girlfriends?"

"God, no! They're..." He caught himself just in time. She'd really get the wrong idea if she knew they were whores. "Look, I'd like nothing better than to strangle Jim right now. He's never had a brain in his head. But just let me handle it my way, okay? I'll get rid of them quickly."

Kayla arched a brow. Did he really think she'd let this slide? What kind of a fool did he take her for? He had a friend coming all right. Who was bringing a couple of damn whores! Of all the nerve! Well, dammit, it was high time his friends, or whatever the hell they were, found out about her; from her, herself, if necessary. "I'll give you thirty minutes, Bob. That's it. If they aren't gone by that time," *which they won't be* "I'm coming down, ready or not."

"Kayla, please!" he begged, watching her take her damn robe and gown off the chair and sashay out of his room, buck naked, her little ass wiggling like a bowl of jello. "God damn it!" Was she trying to control him now?

Catching up with her, he grabbed her arm, spinning her around. But the sight of those breasts so close to him, her tiny waist and those hips and small ass which drove him wild, blanked out his thoughts. Without thinking, he pulled her roughly into his arms, holding her still as he kissed her face, her throat, those pert breasts and responsive nipples, and bent down in front of her, his tongue delving into the crevices of her cunt, stroking her clitoris, burying his face in her mons. "Oh, God, babe!" he breathed raggedly against her, unzipping his shorts, taking out his erect penis, plunging it into her as she stood, slowly lowering her underneath him. "You don't know what you do to me. You just don't know!" Taken by surprise, there wasn't time for Kayla to think. All she could do was react to the onslaught of his skilled lips and tongue as they worked their magic. She mindlessly gave into the building excitement; the feel of his penis surging deep inside of her, slowly escalating its rhythm, going faster, taking her higher, until she shouted his name in triumph as she reached one of the most intense climaxes she'd ever had.

As Bob slowly lifted himself off her, he took a tissue from the breast pocket of his white knit shirt, and wiped off his penis, which started rising again at the sight of her nude body, glistening with sweat, smelling of the sickly sweet aroma of their sex, which smelled to him like an aphrodisiac. Whatever else she was, thank God she wasn't a prim and proper miss when it came to sex. No matter how angry they were, they came together quickly, hot and lustful, to screw, both of them needing it like air.

But his thirty-five-year-old body was beginning to feel the strain. He grinned as he stood shakily, not caring a damn bit. Extending a hand to her, pulling her up, he took his time kissing her, pulling her close enough to feel his rising penis.

Kayla arched back, looking at him. "I thought older men, Sir, slowed down?"

"You aren't calling me old, are you?" he asked, lightly squeezing her firm hips. "If the shoe fits…" she taunted.

"Keep that up, and I'll have to spank you."

"Promises, promises," she theatrically sighed. Hugging her close, he kissed her again. "Just bear with me on this, okay?" he asked, turning serious. "This is something I have to do alone."

"Fine, but I'm not backing down, Bob. If they haven't left in half an hour, I'm coming down to introduce myself. You're a married man now. It's time you acted like it."

Oh, shit! "You're right, babe. I will. I'll get rid of 'em in ten minutes, tops."

Ten? She doubted it. But going up to her damn room, Kayla showered in record time. Curious however, in spite of her better instincts, she eyed the home pregnancy tests Bob had placed in her bathroom. Chances were, it'd show up negative this soon, but what did she have to lose? Doing what it said, she quickly rummaged through her closet while waiting the obligatory ten minutes for the pink or blue lines to appear on the test.

Hearing the door bell, she slipped into her sheerest white cotton summer dress with the tiny spaghetti straps, nylons, and matching low-heeled white pumps.

Glancing at the test results as she dabbed on her most provocative cologne, she dropped the bottle, almost fainting. "Dear God!" she muttered, feeling numb, leaning wearily against the wall. *What next?*

***

Smoothing his wayward hair back, Bob glanced at his reflection as the doorbell rang, then straightened the dove gray light weight sweater he'd put on, with freshly pressed black Dockers. He was looking forward to this with all the eagerness of getting a root canal, but for some reason he didn't bother to analyze, he wanted to look nice when he refused Jim's generous offer of the broad.

"Hey, Jim!" he forced a smile as he opened the door wide. "Long time no see, man. How've you been?"

"Great! And you?"

"Can't complain…" his voice trailed off as he watched the tall, redheaded beauty next to Jim calmly unbutton her blouse, revealing the most perfectly shaped breasts he'd ever seen.

"It's warm in here," she complained as Jim's arm went around her and he openly fondled her large tits, running his thumb up around her dusky nipple, which peaked into a tight little bud.

"It's gonna' get a lot hotter too," he smirked, quickly kissing the tips of her breasts. With a wicked grin, he turned to Bob. "This is Lola. And this pretty little thing," he said, reaching behind him, pulling an attractive little blonde forward as she untied the spaghetti straps of her sundress and unzipped the back, "is Susan. Say hi to Bob, Susan. Bob's a real friendly guy."

But Susan, Bob realized, wasn't quite as brazen as Lola. Although she was ready to play with her dress unfastened, she surveyed him with practiced green eyes, not making a move to undress further. But the ever-resourceful Jim quickly jerked her dress down from behind, showing him her huge tits with the prettiest pink nipples he'd ever seen.

Well, hell, he had to show some appreciation of the lady's charms, so he kissed her, not prepared for the feel of her large tits crushing against his chest. But he was still bound and determined to try and get rid of them.

"This is great, girls, Jim," he said, but…" his voice trailed off as Susan bent and stepped completely out of her dress, those fabulous bare tits of hers, swaying. Totally nude, wearing only spike heels, she held his eyes challengingly as she again stretched her perfect body against him. *God, how much could he stand? He was a normal man, for Christsake, not a goddamn machine.*

"Look, girls," he tried again, only to have Susan's lips capture his as she took his hand and placed it over a breast, its ripe nipple tightening quickly, teasing the middle of his palm. Of their own accord, his fingers moved slowly at first, then more restlessly over Susan's breast as he returned her kiss while his erecting penis struggled to get out of his painfully tight pants.

What harm was there in having a quick one? Having sex with a well-built broad didn't interfere with the way he felt about Kayla. He cared about Kayla. A lot.

But he couldn't think about her now, not with Susan so tantalizingly close. Taking her hand, he led her into his bedroom, locking the door behind him. Kayla had given him thirty minutes. With luck, he'd be through in twenty. It wasn't as much of a concession as he wanted, but it was something.

***

Kayla glanced at her watch. Nearly seven. Bob had been downstairs for thirty-five minutes now. And while she couldn't hear anything, she could well imagine it. Dammit! She was pregnant and anxious to share the news with him. Where was his sense of decency, after he'd promised he make them leave right away?

In the past two days, he'd given her three hundred in cash. Not nearly enough to enable her to start over with a new baby on the way. But she had to do something.

Storming downstairs, she stiffened, seeing a strange woman on the couch with her legs spread wide as a blonde headed man she'd never seen her life had his head between her legs, hungrily licking her crotch. Well, she'd show him! Texas was a community property state, and whether Bob liked it or not, this house was half hers.

Rushing to the utility closet, she got the broom out, and without warning, started hitting the man over the head with it. "I don't allow trash in my house!" she screamed as he yelled, trying to evade her as she hit him again, as the woman grabbed her dress and fled out the door. "I'll kill you, you son-of-a-bitch! I'll run this broom handle up your ass if you ever try anything like that in here again!

Hearing the commotion, Bob threw open the door. Drained but oddly euphoric a moment ago, he watched in horror as his best friend got pounded yet again over the head with a damned broom. "Kayla! Stop it!"

Kayla spun on him. "You!" she screamed, spying the nude girl behind him, calmly sitting on his bed smoking a damn cigarette. "You bastard! How could you do this to me? How could you fuck your brains out? I just found out I'm pregnant! And here you'd promised me you'd get rid of them, and nothing would happen! I'll kill you! I'll make you regret it with your last dying breath. I've had it with you!"

Shit! Bob froze as her words sunk in. "You're pregnant?"

"Yeah, and you're going to make me a merry widow, you no-good louse," she hissed, swinging the broom high over her head, catching the blonde tramp's hair in the broom bristles as she tried to make a run for it. Snatching the broom back, Kayla nearly got what she was after; a bald spot that she hoped would ruin her for life.

"Dammit, Kayla!"

"Don't, 'dammit, Kayla' me, you low lying piece of shit!" she hissed, swinging her broom high over her head and as she edged toward him, watching him like a hawk, adjusting her aim, lowering her arms, then raising them as he bobbed to the right. "I'll teach you to fool around on me. I'm going to turn you from a rooster to a hen."

Standing still, spreading his legs aggressively, balling his hands into fists and planning them on his hips, he held his ground for two minutes, until the broom came crashing down so close to him he got damned splinters from the resounding crash of the stiff bristles.

"Kayla!" he roared. "For God's sake stop it! If you don't care about me, or even yourself going to jail if you succeed in killing me, think what you're doing to our child inside you."

"I'm teaching her self defense," she hissed, raising her broom again, swinging it over her head. "And I'm teaching you not to ever, ever, humiliate me again."

Clenching his jaw, dodging another glancing blow, he held his arms up. "I'm sorry, okay? I promise you it won't happen again."

"Damn right it won't!" Raising her broom again, she started brandishing it like a crazed sword over her head.

But she was tiring, Bob realized. She was breathing more heavily and wasn't swinging it as fast as she had been. All he had to do was keep dodging her damned make-shift weapon until she finally wore herself out, and hope no one was calling out the cavalry in the meantime.

But, as he watched her edge toward him, he wondered if he shouldn't just let her strike him like she wanted. Lord knew he deserved it, and more.

He hadn't wanted to hurt her. And although he'd tried initially to resist the allure of having sex with a strange woman, he hadn't been strong enough. *How ironic. And they called women the weaker sex.*

Somehow, he didn't know how, he was going to make it up to her. He *had* to. For such a little thing, she had a lot of spunk, ready to take on the world with that damn broom!

Chapter Thirteen

Ensconced in her room upstairs with the door locked, Kayla ignored Bob's frantic knocking and refused to come out and talk to him. He should have gotten the message loud and clear that she loathed, despised and detested him when she'd bodily thrown the entire broom at him before she'd rushed upstairs. But, judging from his impassioned pleas, he hadn't. If she'd been able to grab anything else, she would've thrown it *all* at him before she'd raced up here. Maybe that would've made an impression. But somehow she doubted it. And *he* was the father of her child? Good Lord! How could she have been such a jerk? And to think, once, she'd actually loved the son-of-a-bitch! "At least eat, Kayla," Bob pleaded, as china plates clattered outside her door. "I've fixed you tuna fish sandwiches, potato chips, pickles, and a dish of vanilla ice cream. I've got some hot tea brewing downstairs. When it's ready, I'll bring it up, too."

Tea? What she wanted was a good stiff drink; in fact several good stiff drinks. But she was hungry and hadn't realized it until now. Except for the pickles and ice cream, what he'd fixed sounded great. Pressing her ear against the door, she waited until she heard the faint sound of his retreating footsteps on the stairs, then opened the door slowly, peeking out.

Had he put the tiny magnolia blossom in water on her tray to soften her up? *How sweet, the bastard!* Angrily, she took it off, and placed it back outside the door. It was gonna take a hell of a lot more than a damn flower to soften her...like his head on the platter. That would've been good to start with.

Sooner or later, she'd have to face him. But right now she knew she'd kill him if she did. Leaning back against her headboard, absently watching the tiny old black and white TV she'd forgotten she even had, she tore off a bite of her sandwich.

He obviously didn't give a damn about her, and that was fine. She could live with it. He'd never cared about her, anyway. Tonight proved it. A person couldn't pretend feelings they didn't have for very long, although he'd fooled her earlier, before his whore had arrived. She'd actually thought he cared about her. But to him, she was just a brood mare, good for having his child and nothing more. Fine! So be it. She'd deal with it somehow.

God! She was so tired! Setting down her tray on the floor, no longer hungry, she leaned back against her headboard again, absently twirling her wedding band. She looked at it. It was beautiful, gleaming in the dim light of her lamp. *Too bad!*

Taking it off, she dropped it in the bowl of ice cream. If he wasn't going to honor their wedding vows, she damn well wasn't either. What was the use of pretending? But before she could think anymore, she felt herself drifting off, still fully dressed, and was immediately immersed in troubled dreams.

***

Bob looked up at the ceiling as he turned off the vacuum cleaner, trying to get up all the broom bristles which had flown all over. It was still deathly quiet up there. Closing the patio door, which he'd opened to get some much needed air, he lit a few scented candles.

For the past two hours, he'd tried to get Kayla to come out to talk to him. But she'd refused. Feeling lower than dirt, he understood, though. She hated him, and dammit, he hated himself for having hurt her like he had. Was he really that weak? Why the hell couldn't he resist women who made it clear they were only interested in his body? There was no substance there. And it wasn't like Kayla didn't want sex. Hell, she was more gung-ho and ready for it than any other woman he knew. And she was young and shapely...and now pregnant with their child.

She must've taken one of those home pregnancy tests he'd gotten at CVS. He'd bought six, in case it took a while to get her pregnant. He'd bought the brand the pharmacist had recommended, so he didn't doubt the results for a minute. And what had he been doing while she was so conscientiously performing that chore? Fucking. Screwing some damn paid call girl he'd never seen before in his life. And for what? A few minutes of illicit pleasure, thinking Kayla wouldn't find out. Only she had.

How could he make it up to her? He had a full bottle of Valium the doctor had given him a couple of years ago which he'd never used. Taking them with alcohol was supposed to be lethal. Should he do it and get it over with? Lord knew he felt like it.

Pouring himself a scotch and soda, he wandered out to the back yard and looked up at the stars. Did Kayla have any idea how much history was behind the constellations? Did she know how to identify the major stars? Did she know the difference between stars and planets and how to tell them apart?

Maybe they could build a relationship by starting off small, sharing their favorite interests. People who were friends as well as lovers often had the best chance of succeeding in marriage. At least according to Dr. Phil dot com. Why not? At least it was worth trying.

Taking his telescope from his work shed, he settled back in his favorite lawn chair, found the Northern Star, and settled in for a night of star gazing.

***

As the sun started making its slow way over the horizon, Kayla woke up with a start. Had she slept this way all night? Fully clothed and sitting partially up? No wonder she was cold and her back and neck were killing her.

Getting up, she stretched, trying to get the kinks out. But her tense muscles wouldn't relax. As quickly as she could manage, she changed into a pair of jeans and her favorite light blue pullover. She was going to have to get a portable heater. If she kept waking up this cold, her muscles would continue to stay knotted, no matter what she did.

Spotting her wedding band floating in the bowl of melted ice cream, the pain and humiliation she'd suffered yesterday came flooding back. Why had she married such a jerk? She'd actually believed him, dammit, when he'd said he was going to get rid of those tramps. And what had he done with her trust? Thrown it in her face!

Leaving her ring where it was, she squared her shoulders proudly, and with her head held high, she descended the stairs with her tray. She dreaded facing Bob, but she had to sooner or later. Why not just get it over with? It was even colder down here than upstairs. And she now saw why.

The patio door was wide open, the breeze blowing the drapes wildly. Where in heck was the thermostat?

Setting her tray down on the coffee table, she'd halfway closed the door when she spotted Bob. Snoring loudly, he was sprawled in a lawn chair, wearing the same clothes he'd had on when she last saw him, with a half-empty glass on the ground beside a telescope.

Deciding to let him stay put, she continued shutting the door. Maybe if he got pneumonia it would slow down his whoring some. Picking up her tray, she went on into the kitchen. What she needed was coffee; the hotter, the better.

Getting the paper from the front yard, she dropped it on the breakfast table. Bob wasn't the only one who read the newspaper in the morning; she did it too, whenever she had time. But today she was more interested in the want ads than sales going on. Humming to herself, she hurriedly made a strong pot and rinsed out her dishes, setting her wedding band on the counter.

She needed to find a job and a place to live, and soon. Spreading the paper out, she sat down, scanning the help-wanted section. "Good morning!" boomed a familiar voice directly in back of her, scaring her so bad she nearly overturned the table as she jumped. "Glad you decided to *honor* me with your presence. We have to talk."

Helping herself to the coffee which beeped, she narrowed her eyes as she eased past him.

"There's nothing to talk about. I'm getting a job and moving out. We can stay married if you want, technically, until you get your hands on all that precious money, but I don't want any of it." She paused as she took her seat again, and resumed reading. "You look like hell, by the way. Now leave me alone. I'm busy."

"Dammit! I admit I was wrong. I do have a problem. But you'd better realize you have problems of your own. Running away from them, for instance. At the first sign of trouble, you're always ready to bolt. I'm sure that's why you had so many jobs. Instead of staying and trying to tough it out, you ran. Just like you want to run now." Helping himself to the fresh pot of coffee, he sipped it and shuddered with distaste. But fixing a new pot wasn't high on his list of priorities. "I finally figured it out last night while I was looking at the stars," he said, taking a seat across from her. "You never stayed at your jobs until you were actually fired, did you?"

"A couple, I did," she lied as she continued scanning the paper. "Besides, that's none of your business."

"That's where you're wrong. As my wife and the mother of my

child, everything you do is my business. I think we can work things out together though, if we work at it. Believe it or not, I do care for you an awful lot. And I won't sleep with another woman as long as we're married. I wish I could tell you I'd be true forever, but I can't. I'm very sorry for what I put you through. I realize I should've told my friends about you earlier. We can even throw a party, if you want, and invite them to a cook-out in the back yard, and I'll introduce you to them then. I…" his voice trailed off as he stared at her bare hands. "What the hell did you do with your wedding ring? Why aren't you wearing it?"

"Unlike you, I'm not a hypocrite. Why pretend to be married when you keep playing musical beds? Our marriage is a farce, and you know it."

He felt his heart break, but was determined to hide it. "You agreed to go through with it a few days ago."

"That was before I knew you had a problem keeping your plants zipped. I told you though, I'll stay with you until you get your precious money. But a wedding band symbolizes eternity I'm not going to wear it."

Dear God, he didn't want to fight with her! He'd done nothing but think last night while outside. He deserved to be shot. But if he took his own life that would be running from his problems like she did, and that he refused to do.

"Let's get one thing straight, *Mrs. McKnight*, I've never cared a damn about any woman I ever took to bed. You're the only woman who made sex special, instead of a need to be assuaged. I know I'm messed up, big-time. Hell, I was sexually abused by my mother and my father kept trying to sleep with my girlfriends. Those he seduced, he told me weren't good enough for me. But that didn't stop *him* from sleeping with them. So sure, I have problems in that area. Big problems. But I'm going to try hard to be the kind of husband you want me to be."

"At least for a while?"

He nodded. "That's the best I can do. For now."

She didn't know if she could stand being hurt any more by him. Maybe he would improve in time. But there were bound to be times when he slipped. Life was full of temptations. Did she want to act as his warden, his confessor, his pillar of strength when he had lapses?

"Not good enough. What you're asking of me is impossible. I can't take it anymore."

She looked so fragile, so angelic; with her fresh scrubbed face and no make-up, so sad despite her angry words, he wanted to take her in his arms and kiss her and assure her everything would be all right. But he didn't dare. In the mood she was in now, God only knew how she'd take it.

"Let's table it for now," he muttered; trying to keep her from seeing his own pain. "Regardless of what you do, you've got to eat. Let me fix you some oatmeal." "I'll fix some toast later. How healthy is that? You've got to start eating healthy foods."

"Healthy? You want to talk healthy? How healthy is sleeping with every woman you see? You don't know what diseases strange women have. By sleeping with them, and then sleeping with me, you're exposing me and our baby growing inside me, to God-only-knows-what."

"I'm not a complete ass, dammit! I usually wear a condom."

"You don't with me."

"I don't have long enough to put one on when we have sex."

"If you're that way with me, you're that way with other women. And besides, condoms don't protect against any kind of VD, much less HIV, which you can also get from kissing, and...and..."

Her voice cracked as she tried to bat away her threatening tears, imagining him kissing that slut he'd been with yesterday. Had he been as gentle with her? Had he kissed her as he whispered sweet nothings into her ear, too? Had he reassured her he cared about her, dammit? Had he made her feel loved, too?

Jumping up, she flung her coffee in his face and threw her cup against the cabinet beside the sink as hard as she could, ignoring the shards of glass that came raining down as she tore out of the kitchen, ran up the stairs and bolted herself in her room.

Throwing herself on her bed, unable to stop the tears, she openly sobbed. She'd never hated anyone in her life as much as she did him. She had to leave to save her and her baby from being contaminated by him.

It couldn't be in Houston, where he could easily track her down. She had to move to another city, another state. Maybe Little Rock or Santa Fe. She'd get an unlisted number and rent a post office box using her mother's maiden name for her mail. She'd never been to either city, but if she bought newspapers and brought them here, that would give her secret away, so she couldn't do that. But libraries always had out-of-state newspapers.

Feeling better now that she'd made some plans, she dialed information on her cell phone to get the library closest to her, when her stomach suddenly lurched and what little she'd eaten in the past twenty-four hours all came up. Struggling back to her bed, she laid down, exhausted.

Maybe she should go to the doctor first though, before she planned the details of her move.

***

For a long time Bob continued to sit where he was, feeling numb. He'd give anything to undo the pain he'd caused Kayla, which he'd seen clearly in her widened, anguished eyes. Why had he made such a goddamned stupid mistake, having sex with a woman when Kayla was right upstairs? How could he be that heartless?

Hell, he couldn't even remember what the woman looked like now. But he'd bet his last dollar Kayla did. From here on in, the whore's image would be branded in her memory. As would the memory of Kayla's eyes when she'd looked at him, right before she'd thrown her coffee.

Getting up slowly, absently brushing the shards of glass out of his hair, he spotted Kayla's wedding band. Picking it up, he ran it over his cheeks. And for the first time in his life, Bob wept.

***

For the next few days, Kayla was as carefully polite to him as he was to her, content to go her own way, careful to avoid a room when he was in it. Although she knew he wondered where she went every morning, he hadn't questioned her, apparently content she hadn't openly read a newspaper or mentioned moving out again.

He had, however, made sure she ate, by getting up early and leaving a bowl of oatmeal at her door, along with a full pot of steaming tea. To keep him from complaining, she ate as much as she could of the gooey stuff, and flushed the rest down the commode. When she asked him once why not coffee instead of tea, he told her he'd read that a pregnant woman shouldn't have either coffee or cola. She'd let it slide, and had started getting her java from a Starbucks close to the library.

At least she was starting to feel a little less nauseous now, but with her doctor's appointment next week, she knew she should probably tell him about it. But as busy as he was with exercising every morning then conferencing with various people about his new client's demands, she hoped he was too occupied to try to horn his way in. The last thing she wanted was him going to the doctor with her.

Chapter Fourteen

For what seemed like the hundredth time, Kayla looked at the luminous dial of her digital radio clock. She still felt nauseous, despite having thrown up what little she'd eaten for dinner several hours earlier. With her doctor's appointment the day after tomorrow, she didn't want to call her and ask her about it. But maybe some seltzer or something would help settle her stomach so she could sleep. The pink stuff she'd bought earlier hadn't done any good.

She knew Bob was still up. He never went to bed before midnight, working from early morning to late at night on his client's changes. Maybe he had something in his medicine cabinet that would help her. As much as she dreaded asking anything of him, she was desperate.

Slipping on her blue quilted robe and her furry white slippers, she dragged herself downstairs.

"Kayla?" he asked, sitting at his drawing table with only the lamp lit over it, in the otherwise dim room. "What's wrong? I thought you'd be asleep by now."

With his glasses on, he looked intellectual; his green eyes magnified by his thick lenses. He hadn't bothered to change clothes when he'd rushed in nearly two hours ago from yet another meeting with Collins, his arms loaded with rolled up blue prints, fresh off the presses, smelling to high heaven, reeking of what she now knew was acetone, a smelly drying agent.. But with his shirt sleeves rolled up and his shirt partially open, showing several inches of his furry chest, he looked so masculine, so strong, she wanted to rush into his arms and get some much needed comfort. But she didn't dare, afraid he'd misinterpret her need for sex.

Keeping to the shadows, she plopped wearily on the couch. "I just… I'm not feeling all that great. Do you have any seltzer or something for an upset stomach?"

"Sure, I…" his voice trailed off. "How long have you been nauseous?"

"Just an hour," she lied. "I tried some pink stuff I'd bought earlier at the drug store, but it didn't do any good."

"Is this the first time you've been nauseous?"

"Not really," she hedged. "But do you have anything or not?" "Have you tried eating some crackers?" She shuddered with distaste. Just the mere idea of food made her nausea worse.

"How about Coke without the fizz?"

"I was thinking more along the lines of a pill or seltzer."

"Kayla, dear, you're pregnant," he smiled sympathetically, getting up, extending his hand, leading her reluctantly to the kitchen. "You shouldn't try self-medicating with drugs of any kind. Only your doctor can prescribe for you now. Speaking of which, shouldn't you be going soon?"

What was this, Twenty Questions? "Yes, but about my nausea, you really think Coke's going to help?"

"Without the fizz, yes," he said, getting it out of the refrigerator, slowly pouring her a tall glass, watching the fizz slowly go down. "It's an old home remedy without drug interaction that really works. But about the doctor, I assume you've made an appointment?"

Kayla stifled her sigh. *Here it comes. He's going to insist he comes along.* "I'm going Tuesday morning. But I know how busy as you are. You don't have to come. She's in the Woodlands, so I won't be gone long." "What if I *want* to come?" "It's not necessary." "I'm the baby's father, dear. Sooner or later, I'm going to get involved in this."

"Can I have the Coke now? Or do you want to fight about your rights?" Stifling his sigh, he held the glass too high for her to reach and eyed it. "I'm waiting until the fizz goes down. You don't need gas bubbles." He cleared his throat. "You're going to wear your wedding ring to the doctor, I assume? I put it on your dresser the following day after you took it off."

"I saw it. But I'm waiting to see if you can start being faithful to me." "Haven't I been so far?"

"Since the last whore was here? You've been faithful for five whole days, yes. Let's see if you can make it an entire week." Giving her the Coke, he took off his glasses and rubbed his eyes. He was getting a headache. Again. They couldn't even talk for two minutes without getting into an argument.

"I already apologized for that, remember?"

She nodded, sipping the Coke, then making a grimace, got some ice.

"You do plan on telling the doctor I'm the father, right?"

"I already told her nurse. When she started asking a bunch of questions, I also told her about our marriage, such as it is."

"I see," he muttered, stiffening visibly. He could just imagine what all she'd told her. Well damn, if she wanted to argue, okay. "Where have you been going every day?" he snapped. "Don't tell me it's none of my business, because it is. You're my wife for the next nine months, like it or not."

"Fine. Someday I might tell you. But not before I'm good and ready, and the more you push, the longer it'll be."

"You're still playing that card about me having a momentary lapse with that girl, whose face I can't even remember, aren't you? Admit it!"

"Fine. I admit it. I still can't understand why, when I'm ready and willing to have sex with you regardless of how you want to do it, or the time you choose, you go to another woman for it."

"It's over, Kayla. I've already apologized. It was a mistake and won't happen again. Do you want my apology in blood? Why won't you give me the chance to redeem myself?"

What he was asking for was difficult. What if he made the same mistake again when the next temptation came along? She couldn't go through another night like that. "It's too soon. I can't forget it. I wish I could. I really do. But I can't."

"I can *show* you better then *tell* you how sorry I am."

"You want to have *sex*? With me ready to throw up? That should be fun."

"I didn't mean right this minute. But what's wrong with cuddling? You look like you could use some. I could do with some too."

"That's not what you have in mind, and you know it. You'll try to seduce me at the first opportunity. But it won't work, Bob. I wish to God, I could forget! But you have no idea what you put me through."

"Yes I do," he murmured as she disappeared from his sight. In his mind's eye he saw his father having sex with Joan, the love of his life, when he'd been a senior in high school. He could still see her long blonde hair billowing out behind her as his father got on top of her. Her blue eyes became heavy lidded with desire as his father lovingly sucked her pert breasts as he ran his hands all over her hips, her mons, her clitoris as he stripped her and spread her legs wide, then entered her and smirked, while looking Bob straight in the eye through the window. Unfortunately, that had only been the first of many times his father'd had sex with her. He'd even started picking her up from school every day, taking his lunch hour late and parking just a block away from the school, where he fucked her in the back seat. Everyone in school knew what was happening, making Bob's mortification complete.

Desperate to leave, Bob threatened to tell his grandfather about his son-in-law's hobby, unless his father signed the necessary papers to let Bob get into the Army two months before his eighteenth birthday.

Kayla was watching him warily as he stood against the counter, not moving a muscle, his eyes glazed, looking at something only he could see. He had no idea where he really was.

Feeling her anger dissipate a little, she felt sorry for him, as he stared with horror at something only he could see. She wished there was some way to erase the terrible pain she saw revealed in his sad eyes. But whatever he was seeing, and whatever problem he had with it, he had to work through it himself, she decided. All she could do was stand by helplessly until it passed.

The seconds stretched to minutes as he stared vacantly at her.

"Oh, dang it, I guess wearing your ring couldn't hurt," she muttered, hoping he'd somehow hear her, wherever he was mentally. "I'll put in on when I go back upstairs."

Sitting down to finish her Coke, she continued to watch him, then glanced at her watch. Three minutes passed by. Then five. Then another five.

Finally, Bob blinked his eyes as he returned to the present. "Kayla?"

"I'm here," she whispered.

"I'm…I'm sorry. I was just thinking about something which I thought I'd forgotten. What were we talking about?"

She decided to skip the details, since it might have been one of them which had sent him into his trance-like state. "I decided to wear my wedding ring," she hedged.

Closing his eyes, Bob massaged his temples, trying to get his headache to abate. "Why?" he asked, sounding drained.

"It's a woman's prerogative to change her mind," she shrugged.

He opened his eyes. "You feel okay?"

"Yes, Bob. I haven't taken leave of my senses. I just decided I'd wear

it, if it's okay with you?" *Considering you were the one who originally
brought it up.*

"Fine," he murmured, getting up. "I'll see you in the morning, then."

Watching him turn off the light despite her still being in there, she
was puzzled. Although he was functioning, he still hadn't fully returned
to the present. Listening to him in the den, she waited a few more
minutes. When she came out, he was prone on the couch, sound asleep.
Hesitating briefly, she returned to her room upstairs.

***

Kayla wasn't sure how long she'd slept when she felt Bob start to
ease into her bed. From the dim light of the bathroom shining in her
room, she could see he was dressed the same way he'd been when she'd
last seen him. At first she ignored him, managing to doze off again. But
she came awake abruptly when she felt him rise over her and push away
the low neckline of her gown to suck her bare breast.

"Bob," she murmured, pushing futilely against him, "Dammit, stop!"

"Why?" he whispered against her, his breath fanning her breast, his
voice slurred with sleep. "You feel so good, babe," he breathed, tracing
slow, lazy circles on her other breast with gentle fingers, teasing her
nipple into a tight, excited bud. "Your beautiful little body likes it too,"
he laughed throatily, moving directly on top of her, letting her feel his
erection against her silk-covered thigh.

"My body doesn't have any sense!" she snapped, trying to scramble
away from him, all too aware of the traitorous response of her breasts.

"I love you, honey. Let me show you how much."

Like he'd showed the whore? "Get off," she hissed, as he edged further
over her, his strong leg encasing both of hers, his hand leaving her breast
to hold her arm tight against the mattress as he sucked her other breast.

"You like this, babe. Admit it," he urged, sliding the hem of her gown
up, massaging her thigh and her hip, easing his fingers in between them,
seeking and finding her clitoris.

While it felt physically good, Kayla realized there was something
missing. Was she still so angry at him that she couldn't feel pleasure
with him? Or was it caused by the bond of trust she'd once felt that
was irreparably severed?

"Relax," he urged, his fingers lightly teasing her clitoris that, while
beginning to enlarge, was slow to do so, not giving her the thrill she'd
usually felt right down to her toes.

"I know you want this," he whispered, moving down her, trailing kisses down her abdomen, to her mons, capturing her clitoris between his lips.

Glancing briefly into her eyes, Bob momentarily stiffened. Something was very wrong here. Her eyes didn't have that drugged-with-desire look they usually had. In fact, she looked unusually alert, watching him silently, not giving into the intense pleasure he knew she had to be physically feeling. She should've already lost the ability to think. But she hadn't. *Why?*

Intensifying his efforts, he braced himself on his elbows and started circling both her luscious breasts with his thumbs while kissing her clitoris passionately. But she wasn't responding like she had in the past. While her clitoris was wet, it used to be soaked by now, matching his desire, which was running rampant with need. He didn't know how much longer he could hold out, but he had to try to give her as much pleasure as she was giving him.

Spreading her silken legs wide, he propped her thighs over his shoulders, then scooted lower, turning her ass up, and encircling her cervix with his tongue while stroking her clitoris. That got a little more moisture out of her. But not much. Frantic he wasn't making the progress he'd hoped, he eased his hand between her legs and his fingers found her wet erogenous zone at the base of her cervix and stroked with a firm but gentle touch. Finally, he felt her pelvis tense and mounted her. But just as he entered her, she relaxed.

Bending his head down to taste her nipples again, he tried to re-awaken her desire. But, despite the costly effort to his self-restraint, he couldn't get her beyond the level she'd already reached; semi-aroused. Unable to control himself any longer, he surged deeply into her, ejaculating again and again, fucking her more thoroughly than he ever had and shouted her name as he reached an earth-shattering climax.

But as he slid off her, he saw she was already half-asleep, her eyelids fluttering closed, then opening again briefly, only to close again and stay that way. Had she realized, at some point, he was trying his damnedest to show her how much he loved her? It wasn't like her to not respond to affection. She'd been such an enthusiastic sex partner before…before he'd slept with that damned whore. Was that what this was about? Dammit! Why the hell couldn't she forget that?

He'd hoped that by coming up here, she'd know how much he cared, showing her, in the best way he knew, how much he cared about her.

He caught sight of her stomach and stared at in wonder. Inside, right now, his child was growing. Was it boy? Or a girl? He knew from having read everything he could about pregnancy on line that it was still forming.

But he also believed the theory its little memory started recording sensory data almost from the moment of conception. Not only that, but it could feel the emotions of the mother through the chemicals she released in her blood. When she was happy, it was happy. When she was angry, it, bless its heart, was angry too.

And when she was sad... *Oh, God!* He'd hurt Kayla so much. But... it was unintentional, both times. But Kayla seemed focused on the most recent, the emotional abuse of having seen proof that her husband had been cheating on her. How could he have been so stupid? So thoughtless? He knew she'd been right upstairs. He knew that the chances of him getting caught by her were great. Why in God's name had he done it? Was he that weak? And she'd been devastated! He'd thought that by making love to her, he could undo the pain and restore her to her former self and re-establish their relationship to where it had been. But he'd failed. Kayla's scars were too deep. Scars he'd inflicted recklessly. How could he have hurt her like that? She'd trusted him once. But he had a sinking feeling she never would again. The way she'd just responded when he made love to her was proof. She'd enjoyed it a little. But it was far from the total release he'd hope to give her.

Was it just habit? He was used to doing whatever he felt like. All his adult life, he'd entertained whoever he wanted, whenever the mood struck. Was he doing it to get back at his mother, where it seemed laughter and happiness of any kind was banned? He remembered when he once laughed out loud while watching TV, only to have her storm in and turn it off, taking the knob to turn it back on with her.

Or was he doing it to get back at his father, proving he too could take any woman he wanted to bed?

But his parents were both dead now. How much longer was he going to try to get back at them? Hell, they no longer existed. *Dear God!* He'd been shadow-boxing with his memories of them for a little over ten years now. Why? What was the point?

Hadn't he hurt himself enough, exposing his body to all types of diseases, just like Kayla claimed? Building up a reputation of being a lady-killer who was a sucker for any woman with a great pair of legs. But, during the past year, he'd had trouble remembering any of their faces after they'd left, and had started envying his friends who'd settled down. He'd had what they had, and what he wanted, with Kayla. Until he'd thrown it all away.

Feeling worse than he ever had, he staggered downstairs. Glancing at his worktable still piled high with half-finished plans, he bypassed it and headed into the kitchen to make a fresh pot of coffee. He'd get no more sleep tonight.

***

For the past few minutes, Kayla had put off waking up. When she finally did, she groaned, remembering last night when he'd gotten into her bed. At first she'd been startled, then angry. Had he actually thought that by waking her up, she'd respond to him sexually? Even if they'd been on the best of terms, it would have been difficult. It always took her a couple of good hours to become alert in the mornings.

But she missed the closeness they once had, the intimacy of two people who could always forgive and forget by getting close and lost in their own private world. And she had tried. At least for a while. She hadn't been able to respond to him like she normally did, although she'd tried hard. She used to love having sex with him. Whereas, last night, she'd been getting a little bored with his attempts to inflame her.

Heading downstairs to make some coffee while she took her shower, she made it halfway to the kitchen when her stomach lurched. *Dear God! Again?* Rushing past Bob in a blur, she hoped she'd reach his bathroom in time.

"Kayla?" he yelled, running after her. His heart stopped for a moment, at the sight of her hanging her head over the toilet bowl, throwing up spit, gagging unmercifully. Grabbing a washcloth, wetting it, he knelt down beside her, wiping off her heavily perspiring face, then pressing the cool wet cloth lightly to her throat. She was as meek as a child, shaking like a leaf, looking at him with widened eyes, her panic showing clearly in them

"It'll be okay, babe. Don't try to talk now. I'm going to ask you a couple of questions, so just nod or shake your head. "Do you have any cramps?"

She shook her head.

"Good. What about any bleeding? Spotting? Discharge?"

Again, she shook her head.

Thank God. She wasn't having a miscarriage like he'd been afraid of. "I know you don't want me to call your doctor, but she has to be informed about this. I don't think it's anything to worry about now, but it will be if it continues. You can't afford to lose weight. Okay?"

She nodded. But instead of telling him the doctor's phone number, she just leaned against his broad chest, huddling close to him to get warm as her eyes fluttered closed. God, she'd never felt worse! Not only was she nauseous almost constantly, she had trouble lately keeping her eyes open.

"Kayla!" he barked, worried. "You're not going to pass out, are you? Do you feel faint?"

She shook her head. "Just…tired…sleepy."

Relieved, he scooped her up, getting her into his bed, tucking her in. "Honey, what's your doctor's number?" he asked, grabbing the phone, sitting close beside her.

"Baldwin, six-one-eight-three."

Dialing, he hoped to God him having sex with her last night had nothing to do with her condition now. Everything he'd read on line stated women could have sex, sometimes up until the eighth or even ninth month. Had he been too rough, maybe? He'd tried to be gentle, but there at the end, he'd lost it when having his climax. Or maybe he'd worn her out, trying to get her excited when she was physically incapable of it, with her body being more concerned with the baby than with him.

Then it dawned on him. Maybe that had been it! That was why she hadn't responded more to him last night. Damn his hide! If he'd only paid more attention to her instead of being so wrapped up in himself, and so preoccupied with his damn ego, he might've seen what was going on then, before it got out of control. It broke his heart to have seen her hanging on for dear life to that blasted commode.

"Doctor Marsh, please," he spoke into the receiver as a woman with a clipped British accent answered. "I'm Bob McKnight, Kayla's new husband. She has an appointment tomorrow with the doctor." He gritted his teeth. "No, I'm not sure of the time, but the reason I'm calling is she's been throwing up a lot and can't seem to open her eyes. Is there something the doctor can send out to stop the nausea? I'm afraid she might start throwing up in the car in the morning if she keeps this up."

Looking in at Kayla, assuring himself she was still dozing, he went back out in the hall. "No, no cramping or discharge. She didn't feel warm, so I doubt if there's a fever but she was shivering." He drummed his fingers on the cell. "Yes, I'll hold. Thank you."

Why was it that doctors were so damn slow when answering their patient's calls? You'd think they'd be better organized, and limit their practice to the number of patients they could adequately handle. But every single one of them invariably took on more than they should.

"Yes, I'm here," he spoke into the phone. "I see, okay and…my pharmacy number?" How long had it been since he'd even seen a doctor, let alone had a prescription filled? The last time he could remember was several years ago when his doctor prescribed Valium, which he decided not to use. He'd used the pharmacy in the doctor's building to have it filled, but that was way across town.

"I usually use CVS on West Twenty-Third, but I don't know their number. Okay, fine. You think it should be ready in half an hour?" He raised his brows.

"Two hours? Why so long? Why can't she call it in right away?" Sighing, he listened as the woman explained the doctor was making rounds, but she would page her at the hospital. "I see," he muttered, hanging up, hating doctors and their snooty, overworked nurses.

Touching Kayla's forehead again, and assured she wasn't running a fever, he eased close beside her to wait. Although he hated to leave Kayla all alone for half an hour while he got the prescription, he had no choice. But surely she'd be okay for that time. He was irked, though, that the doctor was sending out only enough pills to see her through the rest of tonight and early in the morning. Didn't she trust her patients?

And why was Kayla having so much trouble? Had she caught a virus maybe that was unrelated to her pregnancy? He'd read pregnant women got sick from time to time like everyone else. But then again, she was so tiny, his instincts told him it had something to do with her pregnancy, but what?

The nurse said she could eat if she felt like it, after she started taking the pills she'd be calling in. But lightly. Clear soups and crackers.

Did she like chicken soup? Homemade or canned? Canned, he decided. Making it from scratch would take forever and keep him in the kitchen instead of in here. Fortunately, he had several cans of it already. He wouldn't have to go by the grocery store, which could tie him up for longer than he already had to be.

He wished he could talk her into moving down here to his room permanently. Sure, he'd made a big damn deal about it at first, hating the idea of sharing his personal space. But he couldn't see her living in those cramped quarters for another nine months.

Chapter Fifteen

"Wear whatever you're comfortable in," Bob smiled, leaning against the door jamb. "You look good in everything."

Kayla sighed as she eyed her twenty pairs of jeans and slacks in various colors, styles, and materials. Thanks to Bob, she was feeling worlds better. Not only had he called the doctor for her, he'd gotten her prescription and stayed with her all yesterday and last night. Except for the brief time he'd been gone to get her medicine. Every time she opened her eyes, he was right here, straightening a blanket he'd placed around her, tucking her in more securely, wiping her face with fresh-smelling damp washcloths.

But the way he was constantly hovering was beginning to make her edgy. And he was adamant about driving her to the doctor's too, seeming afraid that, if left her for longer than five minutes, she'd disappear into thin air or meet with some terrible tragedy, for which he'd blame himself.

Letting him take her upstairs this morning to get dressed had been a bad mistake. She hadn't realized he was going to stay with her constantly.

Taking out her newest pantsuit in a bright yellow cotton blend, she held it up to her chin, studying her reflection in the mirror.

"That's nice," he murmured.

She nodded. "I think you're right. I'll wear this." She raised her brows, hoping he'd leave while she dressed. "Do you want to help me?"

"Sure. Tell me what you want me to do."

"Leaving me alone while I dress would really help. Besides, I'd love some hot tea," she lied to soften her irritated tone.

He grinned. "Hot tea it is. I'll be right back."

"Take your time," she murmured, immediately feeling more relaxed as he disappeared down the hall. She knew she made a terrible patient, never wanting anyone around when she was sick, except vary rarely when she was unable to walk by herself, like yesterday when Bob found her hugging the commode. She'd been petrified when she tried to get up, but couldn't. But now that she was feeling stronger after having rested and having drunk several cups of the hot chicken soup Bob coaxed her into having, she wanted some time to herself.

Deciding to forgo nylons, she stepped into her yellow pants, foolishly thinking they'd be tight, as if her stomach had started swelling already. But not only weren't they tight, they were loose. Had she been losing weight by too many skipped meals? *Dang!* They'd fit perfectly at the store two months ago. Now, they were just hanging limply on her.

Slipping off her gown and sliding her yellow lace camisole over her head, she rotated her stiff shoulders. What she'd like to do was lie out on the patio this afternoon and soak up the sun after they came back from the doctor's. She was so pale, she looked like a ghost. Her usually healthy glow had disappeared.

Bob let out a low whistle as he carried in her tea, still with the bag in the water. "I love that top," he grinned, unable to tear his eyes off her lace teddy. "And I love the way you fill it out. You're really built, babe." Hesitating briefly, she went into his arms as he encircled her waist with his arms. He did care about her. In his own way. And he took care of her with a surprising gentleness.

"I'd better finish getting dressed," she sighed, disengaging his hold, very aware of his hurt look. "Don't want to be late for our appointment."

But Bob wasn't about to be so easily appeased. "Are you still mad about what happened last week?" he asked, sitting in the chair he'd occupied all day yesterday. "I've detected a growing chill in the air ever since then."

Christ! He wanted to fight? Now? Her pregnancy exam wasn't going to be hard enough? Even in the best of times, she hated pelvic exams. She could just imagine what she was in for, with her fighting the urge to throw up.

"I have no idea what you're talking about," she snapped, jerking on the top of her pantsuit.

"Don't lie to me, Kayla. We might as well get it out in the open so we can settle it once and for all."

"*Settle* it? We can't *ever* settle it! We think too differently. I want you to be faithful for the year I'm here. But you obviously think taking care of your dick and its instant gratification is more important than caring about me, about the hurt and humiliation."

"That's over with! I'll never see her again. Hell, I've even forgotten what she looks like.

"I haven't slept with anyone but you since then."

"It's only been one week! You think one week is some kind of record?"

He'd been trying to be patient with her, trying to solve their problem, but instead of her cooperation, he was the target of her temper. Well, two could play at that game! "Maybe. You don't know me, Kayla, and at the rate you're going, you never will. I thought I'd finally found someone I could trust enough to just be myself with. I know I have a lot of problems. It'll take a strong woman to get me turned around. I thought I'd found that woman. You. But I was sorely mistaken."

"I guess so!"

"You *admit* you're not strong enough?"

"I...I didn't mean it that, way...not exactly."

"Good glad to hear it. But I'm still taking you to the doctor. Picking her up, he let her kick and pummel him all she wanted, as he sprinted down the stairs and threw her in the car. He was taking her to the doctor, and there was nothing she could do about it.

"And if you dare to interrupt me while I'm driving, Kayla, remember it's your baby, too, that might die," he warned.

She stilled immediately. She hadn't thought about that. Buckling herself in as he sped out the driveway, she remained quieter than she'd been since he'd met her. It wasn't just that she didn't trust him, not exactly. It was just like he'd claimed. She didn't know him and how easily he could get distracted on the road. And she wasn't taking any chances.

Kayla had been right. It hadn't taken long to get to the doctor's office. He made it inside of half an hour, a record in the sprawling metropolis of Houston. But he was surprised by the serenity of the office, hidden so deep in the trees, it hadn't looked like anything was back in there. It was much smaller, too, than he'd expected, and old-fashioned; looking more like a large house than an office, surrounded by a huge veranda, surrounded by lush plants and tall marshy grasses blowing in the breeze.

"You're the husband, correct?" asked the silver-haired receptionist sitting at the huge custom-made maple desk, lit by lamps instead of overhead fluorescent lights. Bright Early American couches were strewn around the room, separated by large maple tables and bright, deep red and white chairs on a surprisingly plush deep red carpet.

"Yes. Bob McKnight."

"Nice to meet you. You can go in with Kayla if you want, while the doctor examines her, but would you mind filling out these forms? You can give them to the nurse when you're finished."

"Are you sure this woman's professional?" he whispered to Kayla as he started filling out the forms as they waited to be called. "She isn't some sort of quack, is she?"

"Shh! She'll hear you. Just be patient. I think you'll be pleasantly surprised."

Five minutes later, as they walked down the wide hall, covered in soothing blue patterned wallpaper with a darker blue carpet, Bob relaxed. A little. This area looked a little more like what he'd expected, but not much. "Kayla," smiled the elderly, motherly looking nurse, as the receptionist showed them into a large examination room with hardwood flooring and paneled oak walls. "Not feeling all that great, I take it?"

As the two exchanged pleasantries and the nurse took her vital signs, Bob looked around, much relieved. One entire wall was plate glass, which looked out into the vast forest beyond. This was more like it! Lit by fluorescent lights, the room was dominated by a large examination table, covered with a long blue leather cushion and stirrups, while beside it was a functional wooden desk made of roughhewn oak.

"Kayla's normal temp is ninety-seven-point-one," the nurse announced to Bob. "Today, it's ninety-nine-point-six. It's nothing to worry about, but it does possibly indicate an infection or something of the sort's going on. After her exam, the doctor will be able to tell you more." Turning away, she sat down on a stool and pumped up the blood pressure cuff while keeping her free hand on Kayla's pulse. "And her BP is one twenty over seventy-five," she continued. "A tad high for her; but well within normal range. I expect the rise is due to being pregnant. That happens a lot." Making a notation in Kayla's file, she turned to her and asked a few questions about her last period, as Bob again tuned her out. Smiling sweetly, the nurse walked over to Bob. "Don't worry, Dad. Everything will be fine," she assured him, patting his arm. "The doctor will be here after she finishes with her current patient, which shouldn't be too much longer."

Watching her go, Bob went behind the screen and watched Kayla try to tie the strings of her huge gown. Gently, he took hold of her hands, edging them away and tied the strings for her. "You doing okay?" he whispered, kissing her forehead, on which beads of perspiration glistened.

She nodded. "I guess."

"Still feel nauseous?"

"A little. But I always feel better after I throw up."

"Maybe you're just scared right now." Taking her hands in his, he rubbed them, trying to warm her as he walked her back to the examining table, then picked her up, setting her on it.

"I am. I hate pelvic exams."

He nodded. "You have to put your legs over these?" he asked, looking at the chrome stirrups.

"I put my feet in them with my knees bent and legs up in the air."

"Is it like this in every gynecologist's office? Or just this one?"

"Everyone's," she sighed. "Unfortunately."

"How long have you been coming here?"

"Two years now. She was recommended by Darlene, a girl I know here in town from a previous job. She took my place there."

Looking up as a knock sounded on the door, Bob watched the masculine looking Dr. Sandra Marsh enter. She was wearing low heeled gray leather pumps, no jewelry or make up, a stethoscope hung around her neck, and a starched white coat hung open in the front over a plain white blouse and gray slacks.

Nearly as tall as Bob, she looked him straight in the eye. "You're Bob, I take it? Kayla's new husband?"

He nodded as he extended his hand. Her handshake was firm, short-lived and no-nonsense; a reflection, he decided, of the woman herself. He trusted her immediately.

"Well, baby," she said to Kayla, jumping up and sitting beside her. "I understand you're not feeling too great. What's been going on?"

As Kayla recounted her symptoms, yawning heavily at times, the doctor was busy checking her pulse, listening to her heart and lungs with the stethoscope, and feeling her throat underneath her ears. She had a unique style, both chatty and professional at the same time. He wondered if she'd learned that someplace, or if it was her own invention.

"Okay, baby. You know the drill," she said, jumping off. "Lay down, scoot your tush to the end, right here," she instructed, patting the end of the table, "put your little cold toes on these already freezing stirrups and spread your legs wide. She winked at Bob. "It's kind of like having sex in the missionary position, but without all the fun."

As the gray-headed, motherly-looking nurse came in, seemingly on cue, she lined up the instruments the doctor would need as Dr. Marsh dilated Kayla's cervix and looked deep inside. Taking out a pen from her pocket, the nurse stood by to write in Kayla's file.

"Chadwick's sign present," muttered Dr. Marsh, going deeper. But Bob tuned her out as she sprouted other medical terms he wasn't familiar with. The doctor and her employees all seemed to work as a perfectly timed machine. And while the office was in a respectable upper-income location, her office was conspicuously void of accoutrements, which he'd expect in a doctor's office, especially in this part of town.

"Ah hah!" she gleefully crowed. "I think I've found the culprit of some of your problems." She turned to Bob with a smug look.

Halleluiah! But Bob kept his expression composed, merely raising his brows, showing only mild interest.

"Congratulations, Dad! You scored twice in one shot. Your wife's carrying twins."

Chapter Sixteen

For a moment, Bob thought he hadn't heard right. He coughed nervously. "Would you repeat that? I'm sure I misunderstood."

Dr. Marsh grinned. "You heard right. Think of it as a 'two-fer' deal. One delivery; two babies." She turned to Kayla. "I'm pretty sure that's why you're having a hard time right now. There's not a heck of a lot of room in your little body, and you can only stretch out so much. Your other organs have to rearrange themselves, and I believe your expanded uterus is pushing against other organs which are pushing against your stomach big-time. That's why you're so nauseous and can't keep down anything."

Taking off her rubber gloves, she snapped them playfully then wadded them up and threw a perfect pitch straight into the trash can, as she wheeled her stool close to Bob. "Get dressed, baby. I've got a whole bunch of rules for first-time parents-to-be of twins."

Bob got up, starting to follow his wife. "I need to help her."

With worried eyes, the doctor shook her head slightly. "Mary, help our new mom get dressed. And take your time," she whispered as Mary passed her.

Promptly Bob sat back down, his heart plunging into his own stomach. *Great!* Now he felt nauseous too.

"Have you noticed signs of excessive emotion?" Dr. Marsh whispered, lowering her voice even more. "Has she been, you know, unlike herself? Crying easily? Throwing things? Blue one minute, and all sunshine and smiles the next?"

"As a matter of fact, she has. But I just thought…well, I didn't tie it to her condition." "All new moms tend to be emotional. It's natural, considering her hormones are running rampant, and this is the first time her body has had to deal with so many of them. And don't forget, she's carrying twins, which means, basically, a whole lot of stuff she's not used to is being dumped into her bloodstream by the bucketful. Her future pregnancies will be a piece of cake compared to this one. But, this is very important —you're going to have to be her anchor in her stormy sea, if you catch my drift. You have to be gentle and understanding at all times, and above all, patient. Even if you don't agree with her, pretend you do; if the matter isn't serious and she's not planning on going to Hong Kong to celebrate her birthday or something like that, play along with her for a while. Humor her. And keep in mind, she'll eventually return to her even-tempered self once everything's over with. Mood swings are often a problem for first time dads, so if you need a support person, call me and I'll have Mary get you together with a dad who experienced the same thing with his wife last year. Any questions?"

"I understand about her uterus pushing things around, but can't anything be done to alleviate her nausea? She's too thin already to keep upchucking like she's been. Already she's losing weight."

"That's natural at first. Some women do lose weight, but they gain it all back and more. I'll give her a stronger pill to take; one which eventually will take hold. If she eats light, which I'm sure she already is, she'll be fine in a couple of weeks. In the meantime, she needs to take it easy. No lifting, only minimal housekeeping. After the nausea clears, she needs to take the prenatal vitamins. By then, the results of the blood I'm having Mary take will be back, and I'll know if she needs to take one or two vitamins a day."

"How are you feeling, babe?" Bob asked Kayla as she joined them, seating herself on a stool Mary slid over for her.

Kayla yawned. "Okay, I guess. I'm just tired."

Dr. Marsh nodded. "Perfectly natural to be that way. Lots of new mothers are like that. But the good news is, after a few weeks, that'll clear on its own. I'll have Mary give you the prescriptions I'm going to write. I'm putting you on a stronger medication to control what's euphemistically called 'morning sickness,' even though it can occur at any time. Eat light and take one of the pills I'm prescribing three times a day, whether you feel nausea or not. Once it goes away completely, and you're able to eat normal foods again, you'll be ready to start taking some pre-natal multivitamins I'll prescribe."

She paused. "Now, about sex. You can still have it. But no rough stuff, and not every night, okay? From this point on, your honeymoon is over. If you feel pain, Kayla, any pain at all, no matter how small, stop. If stopping doesn't take care of the pain, call me immediately. As you progress in your pregnancy, the missionary position may be uncomfortable. If that's the case, try having sex lying on your side. But don't try far-out unusual positions, okay? Any questions?"

"You are going to need a lot of rest," continued the doctor. Even after the natural sluggishness wears off. Take frequent breaks from whatever you're doing and put your feet up whenever you sit down, if you can."

Dr. Marsh looked from Kayla to Bob and back again. "And one more thing, if you have any cramping or discharge, call me, no matter what time of day or night."

"When's the due date?" asked Kayla.

"Ah, yes," smiled the doctor, glancing at the small calendar in the pocket of her white coat. I'm going to say the last week in December. But twins tend to come early, so you might go into labor in your eighth month, so I wouldn't be surprised if you'll have them by Thanksgiving."

"I know it's probably a little early," Bob said, "but can you tell now if we're having boys or girls?"

"Do twins tend to run in either one of your families?"

Bob and Kayla both shook their heads in unison.

"Then you're probably having what we call fraternal twins, meaning that two separate eggs were fertilized at the same time. You could have two boys, two girls, or one of each. And don't be surprised if they don't look alike. They're not identical twins; they're just like regular sisters or brothers."

Taking her prescription pad out of her other pocket, she started writing.

"Any more questions? If you think of something later you want to ask, don't hesitate to call the office. Oh, and Kayla, I want to see you again in six weeks. And before you leave today, Mary will take some blood." As the routine chores were performed, Bob tried to hide his excitement. Kayla was going to be just fine. And, if the doctor was correct, the babies would be born by the end of the year at the very latest. He sighed contentedly. He'd get that twenty million yet.

But he couldn't get over the fact they'd be getting twins! Man! They'd hit the damn jackpot!

***

Driving home, Kayla turned to Bob. "What do you think? Are you as excited as I am?"

"Sure. Are you?"

She nodded. "I'm excited, but there's an awful lot we have to do to prepare. Figure out where the nursery will be. Decorate it. Furnish it. Start putting in supplies, like diapers, baby lotion, some little gowns for them to wear, things like that."

"You want to nurse them?"

"Absolutely! Babies who nurse are healthier than babies who are on formula. That's what I've heard anyway."

Bob sighed, imagining Kayla having a baby at both of her beautiful breasts, with them loudly suckling. He'd give anything to nurse at her breast too. Would she allow him a small taste? Maybe later, he'd bring it up, when she was completely over the nausea and feeling exhausted part. Right now, she was excited, riding an adrenalin high. But once that was gone, she'd crash. "What do you think we should name them? Any ideas?"

"We'll have to get some books with names. I'd also like to get something about the stages of pregnancy. I got some things from Dr. Marsh's office, but they aren't very detailed."

"Start making a list of everything we'll need. When you're able, we'll start hitting the malls."

"This is going to be so much fun!' she grinned. But she sobered quickly. "I just hope I'm as good a mother as mine was. Do you plan on taking an active part in their lives? I mean, you've already said we'll get divorced after they're born, but they'll still need a father in their lives."

Damn! He hadn't thought about that when he'd first formulated his plan, other than providing for the kid financially. But rather than risk an argument with his lovely wife, who'd started thinking about motherhood even before she conceived and had even shied away from it that first night, after he'd asked her, he nodded confidently. "I plan to be around. I don't even want you moving out right away, not until you're confident you can handle two at the same age, at the same time. Of course, we can always hire a nanny to help you, if need be, I guess. But I want you to be the main caregiver."

Although, he reflected as he automatically turned into their subdivision and drove slowly to their house and parked, a mother being the main caregiver didn't ensure the best environment for the child. His own mother had been proof of that.

Looking in the rear view mirror, his mother's face appeared beside his as the years diminished, and he saw himself at seven, looking at her with adoration, before he realized she was in fact, a pedophile who liked young teenage boys.

As the houses in his neighborhood disappeared, they were slowly replaced by the old refrigerator, stove and kitchen sink he remembered from childhood.

"You must go to church on every holiday, Bobby," warned his mother. "And The Feast of the Blessed Virgin is one of our church's more important days."

"But why, Mom? All she did was give birth to Jesus, right? So why not have a holiday for you too? You gave me birth."

His mother looked startled for a moment, then arched a brow, smoothing back her black hair with a dreamy look in her gray-green eyes. "Why, yes, I did, didn't I?"

"Sure did, Mom. Why don't you talk to one of the priests about it and ask them? I'm sure he'd say yes."

"What a good idea," she giggled. "I just might do that. Yes," she nodded, wandering out to the living room. "Right after I rest, I'll do that. I'll go down and talk to Father Sorenson."

"But, Mom," he protested feebly as she disappeared into her bedroom, soundly closing the door. "You haven't cooked dinner yet. And besides, Father Sorenson died last year."

Knowing he wouldn't get dinner that night, Bobby got out the Rice Krispies and milk. This made the fourth time that week he'd go without his mom cooking dinner.

As his face slowly replaced that of him as a child, Bob frowned. He'd totally forgotten that, until now. *Why?* Kayla would never be like his own mother. She was too conscientious. Too sane.

"Bob?" Kayla asked, putting her hand gently on his shoulder, watching the impish smile on his face replaced by a look of disbelief; to one of extreme disappointment, to resignation, as if he'd accepted his fate. She knew he was remembering an event from his childhood. But it was better for him not to dwell on it so much. "You're safe now. Remember that. No one from your past can ever hurt you again."

For a moment, he looked blankly at her. Then, without a word, he got out of the car, went around it, and helped her out. But he didn't look at her again until after her nap, when she was helping him fix dinner.

***

Knowing that Bob expected her to learn to cook, she went downstairs when she heard the clanging of pots and pans.

"Do you feel like helping? You can always learn later."

"I took that stronger pill when you got the new prescription filled. That, and that five hour nap I took did me a lot of good. So did changing. I'm much more comfortable in shorts."

"Okay, if you're sure you feel like it," he said, getting his big apron from a hook inside the pantry door, looping the long strings around her tiny waist three times, and tying it in back with a big bow. "A good cook always starts off with a good wine."

"Hold it. You aren't wearing an apron. Why do I have to?"

"Because I'm the main cook. Main cook's never have to wear aprons unless they want to, which I don't."

Sighing theatrically, Kayla tried to look properly contrite.

"As I was saying, a good cook starts off with wine."

"What kind? Red or white?"

"It depends on what you're having. I personally prefer a robust Bordeaux with my steak cutlets."

Putting a little olive oil in a skillet, he turned on a low flame. "First we sauté two cloves of fresh garlic," he said, scooping up a handful, dropping them in. "Now, a half-cup of minced garlic," he continued. "Now you add this diced green pepper. Notice I sprinkle my ingredients, never pour."

"Why's that?"

"It gives it a better flavor," he lied.

Kayla, shrugged as she slowly did what he said. "I have a lot to learn, I guess. When does the wine go in?"

"It depends on what you cook. For this, which doesn't take long, I started drinking it, oh, about fifteen minutes or so ago."

"I see…and…*drinking* it? You don't add it to whatever you're cooking?"

"Not unless you want to. I rarely do."

"So I have to drink while I cook. Interesting. But what if I don't want wine?"

"You aren't having any. With your stomach, that's all you'd need. Notice I didn't get a glass for you. But you can have soy milk if you want. It's vanilla flavored."

"I'll pass," she murmured, adding the only remaining thing; fresh sliced mushrooms.

"But if you're going to drink it, what difference does it make if it's red or white?"

"A good cook is always proper. You don't want to be called 'gauche' do you? Or worse yet, 'tacky.'"

"So I have to learn about *drinking* wines? In order to cook?"

He nodded. "But don't worry, I'll teach you as we go. Now notice how I stir this," he said, getting a long wooden spoon out of a bright copper container. "It has to be done very slowly as it simmers." He handed her the spoon.

Doing as he instructed, she sighed contentedly. It felt so right being here like this, with this man. He could be charming when he wanted. And he had a gentle, teasing sort of humor which she liked a lot. She felt, oddly enough, like she'd come home. Of course the fact he was big and strong and handsome too didn't hurt.

"Why use a wooden spoon? Why not regular silverware?"

"Well, I suppose you could, if you wanted scratched pans. But I prefer keeping mine in good condition."

"Ah! Good point."

"Besides some silver you scratch off could get in your food. Why take that chance?"

"*Excellent* point. I see your reasoning."

He smiled, getting behind her, gently squeezing her shoulders, then kneading them with slow, practiced stokes. He liked her companionship. She was funny and gentle. Not mean or petty. She did have a temper that wasn't caused solely by her being pregnant. But he'd always preferred a woman who had some spunk and fire in her. It invariably made the relationship interesting and challenging enough to hold his interest. She was the first woman he could see spending the rest of his life with. Of course, there was a ten year gap in their ages. But she didn't seem to mind, so why should he?

But he was worried about her distrust of him, and the once great sex between them deteriorating. He could tell she was as attracted to him as he was to her by the way she looked at him, her readiness to get close to him, her occasional allusions to sex, and her subconscious grooming rituals; things like smoothing her hair and straightening her clothes, and standing up straight when he was around. But she no longer trusted him enough to give into the feelings he knew she wanted.

That disaster in bed a couple of nights ago was proof. She'd come close to losing herself, then catch herself and pull back repeatedly. She wasn't giving him the opportunity to make things right; to prove to her how wonderful he thought she was by making sure she enjoyed herself every bit as much as he did. That special intimate bond between them in bed was broken. How would he ever get it back the way it used to be? There had to be some way. If he could just figure it out.

"You sure do know how to rub," she whispered, half closing her eyes, her stirring and big spoon forgotten. "That feels so good. You don't do full body massages by any chance, do you?"

Working his way inward, the pads of his fingers soothingly getting the kinks out of her tight neck muscles, he seductively laughed. "I could learn how real quick, babe, if you're interested."

"Maybe I am," she murmured, rolling her head back against him, feeling a shiver of excitement all the way down to her toes as he lightly bit the sensitive tip of her spine. "I do feel better than I have been."

Squeezing her shoulders again reassuringly, he got beside her, slowly adding the wafer thin slices of beef to the sizzling skillet. "I'm not rushing it, Kayla. I want to wait until you stay better. Speaking of which, I hate to bring this up with you learning how to cook, but I just remembered the doctor wants you to eat light."

"I don't get any?"

"I don't want to chance it, Kayla. I don't want to take the chance you'll get sick again."

Watching him get out a silver bowl from the fridge, brimming with chopped lettuce, tomatoes and green peppers, she stared hungrily at it.

"Could I have just a little of it?"

"It's too early for you to eat this kind of food, babe. You'll just have to be patient."

"Fine. I'll stare at you while you eat then."

He clenched his teeth. "All right. But just a bite. That's all you get. One bite."

Beaming her brightest smile at him, she put her arms around his waist and tightly hugged him. "You're a good man, Bob McKnight."

"Why, thank you, Mrs. McKnight. Now set the table for me while I get out your crackers and heat up a can of chicken broth for you."

"Crackers?" she grimaced, letting go of him. "Are you serious?"

"You heard the doctor. But remember, you still get a bite of what I'm having."

"One lousy bite?"

He nodded and kissed her soft lips lightly. "Doctor's orders."

She sighed heavily. It was going to be a long night. A very long night.

***

With dinner over in record time, she helped Bob clean up the kitchen.

Thank goodness she hadn't married a slob or a male chauvinist who believed it was the 'little lady's' job to clean up by herself after meals.

Bob didn't seem to mind doing his share, and more, around the house. Maybe the fact it was his house had something to do with it, but she sensed that no matter where he lived, he'd be the same way.

Cuddling close to him on the couch as he clicked the remote to start a DVD on her plasma TV, she tried to keep from laughing. What was it about men and remotes? Ever since they'd moved the TV in, he'd taken control of it, securing the remote in his desk drawer after each time he'd watched it. Her father had been that way too, never once asking her mom if she'd like to control the channels. She still remembered the looks her mother had given him when she had been engrossed in an old movie, only to have him click to one sports station right after another to get all the scores. That had been years ago, before the days when he'd turned to drinking and everything had gone to hell, but she still remembered it as if it was yesterday.

Reaching over her to turn down the light, he grabbed a handful of the popcorn out of the big bowl on the coffee table and settled back, putting his arm around her again As she put her head on his broad shoulder, she wished they could go on forever just this way. Words weren't necessary. Neither were drinks. It was simply the quiet contented companionship of two like-minded people settling into the patterns of everyday domestic life.

"I've been thinking babe. I think you'd better start moving into my bedroom. I can't see you running up and down stairs in your condition. I'll start moving your things down in the morning."

"You think that's wise?" she asked, reluctant to give up what she'd begun to think of as her own personal space. "I know you value your privacy as much as I do mine. Maybe we should sleep on it for a few nights before we make a final decision."

He reared up, studying her. "You afraid I'll hassle you about sex?"

She laughed. "No. You're not the type of man to force yourself on any woman. I trust you implicitly in that regard." She grabbed some of the popcorn out of the bowl. "I just want to make sure we're doing the right thing."

"Has it occurred to you that you might get sick in the middle of the night? I won't be able to hear you clear up there if I'm asleep, no matter how loud you'd shout. So what'll you do? Just stay in the bathroom, waiting until it passes? That could take a long time, especially since every episode leaves you so tired you can barely sit up, let alone walk."

"You have a point. I hadn't thought about that."

"Too bad the beds up there are so small, otherwise you could share mine all night."

"I'm not buying larger beds for those rooms, Kayla. Especially since we'll probably end up turning most of that area into a nursery. And that's another thing. Your bedroom up there's liable to be one of the first we get rid of, considering it's the closest to the bathroom. The only other place for you to sleep is the couch, and I'm sure not going to let you do that."

"Actually, there is another room we could use for the nursery."

"Oh, no, you don't. Don't even go there!"

"But how often do you exercise?"

"A lot since we haven't been having sex. And before you came, I used it nearly every morning. I've spent a lot of money on that room, getting it the way I want it."

"You could always move it upstairs."

"And share that cramped area with the clothes we can't squeeze down here? Are you out of your mind?"

"How about the garage? There's a lot of space out there."

"It gets damp in the garage. My equipment might rust."

"You could always buy a dehumidifier."

"No way!"

"You're an architect, aren't you? You could design another room and build it for cheap. I'm sure you know some builders who'd give you a good deal."

"Do you have any idea how long it would take to do that? I can't spare the time right now. Have you forgotten I have Collins's things to tend to?"

"You'll be a millionaire soon. At the rate he complains, you'll have all that money way before he ever makes a final decision."

"I'm still going to continue my work, Kayla. I love what I do."

In spite of herself, she was impressed. "That's very sensible of you. But the thing is, you'll have the time to devote to adding another room. Think about it. You don't have to give me an answer right away."

"I have, and I won't. I'm not giving up my exercise room."

"You want me to move my things down here?"

"That's blackmail!"

She smiled brightly. "But it's for a good cause."

"All criminals think like that."

"It would just be temporary, if you want. You could make the extra room, theirs".

"And where do you suggest I store my equipment in the meantime?"

"That's up to you. This is your house."

"Thank you for remembering that."

She smiled seductively. "You're welcome. See how agreeable I can be?" *Let's find out and get one thing settled.* "So, you don't find me repulsive?"

"For God's sakes, no! You're one of the most desirable men I've ever known."

"You really think so?" he smiled, showing all his teeth. "As set as you are against moving into my room, I was beginning to wonder."

"It's a big move. It might not take one day to get all my things down here. It might take several to get everything set up the way I want without taking over your personal space."

"Trust me. I won't let you do that."

"Then we might have problems," she sighed.

"Of course we will. All married couples do. But I sense something more going on here. Are you afraid of yourself, that you'll want me sexually in spite of all your instincts not to?"

"My instincts? They don't tell me not to want you. I'm just...I don't know...I don't want our relationship to be platonic. That's the last thing I want. I want us to have a normal, healthy sexual relationship. On the other hand—"

Before she could say another word, he pulled her into his lap and kissed her parted lips with such exquisite tenderness it took her breath away. "Baby!" he murmured against her, lightly nibbling her soft pink lips. "You have no idea how much I wanted to hear that," he breathed, tasting her sweet mouth with gentle thrusts of his tongue. "I want you so damn much it hurts. I wish to God I could show you," he whispered, pulling her on top of his erection as he ran his hand under her tee-shirt, edging his fingers into the lace cup of her bra, gently rubbing her extending nipple with his thumb. "You don't know how much I'd love that. But... but, I don't think tonight is the right time," he sighed raggedly. "I don't want to take the chance on you getting sick again."

Withdrawing his fingers out of her bra reluctantly, he smoothed down her shirt and eased her off his lap. "I want you healthy and well before we have sex again," he whispered against her hair, kissing it, deeply inhaling its sweet fragrance as he pulled her close, putting his arm around her shoulders again. He sighed, hoping he wasn't being *too* theatrical. "We'll just have to wait until then." He looked at the screen with a puzzled frown. "So I guess we'll have to watch TV. Do you have any idea what this movie's about?"

First he was seducing the hell out of her, then he was worried about a damn movie? Was he trying to drive her crazy? Who the hell cared about a movie? She glared stonily at him.

Grabbing the remote, he clicked it off, and switched to the TV program selector, clicking the channels one by one "I think the early news is on."

"Back to the subject at hand," she said, putting her hands on his cheeks, turning him towards her. "If it means that much to you," *which I hope it does*, "I'll change rooms tonight."

He reared back. "Are you sure?"

Was he playing hard to get now? She nodded, searching his eyes which didn't reveal a blasted thing.

"Okay, then," he said casually." He grinned over the top of her head as she came into his arms. "Since you're so sure."

But as he held her, he mulled over their decision. He hoped he'd done the right thing by coercing her. But he had a feeling they were in for a bumpy adjustment period. Neither of them had ever had to learn to share anything before, except for that short period Kayla had had a roommate, and he had been in the Army. While neither was stingy when it came to sharing things, personal space was another thing entirely.

She'd shown her reluctance to share it this evening. Even though she was cramped upstairs, she'd started thinking of it as hers and didn't want to give it up. Maybe she sensed that he, too, wasn't thrilled about the idea of giving up his private space. Their styles of living were so different. She liked to spread her things out over the tops of every single thing; vanities, dressers, chests of drawers, even closet shelves and on the floor of closets, while he tended more toward the spartan way, taking pleasure in seeing the wood on top of furniture and the marble of bathroom vanities, and keeping them uncluttered.

He knew she'd watched TV in her room. He could hear it whenever he went up there. That was going to be contentious, too. No way would he let a TV in his room, much less let anyone watch it in bed.

As far as sleep went, he'd found out quickly she needed more sleep than he did, even before she conceived. When she didn't get enough at night, she took naps, messing up the bed to get under the covers.

Now that she was pregnant, she needed even more sleep. Just today, she'd taken a five hour nap! He didn't even need five hours of sleep at night, much less during the day, just to keep him going. The doctor said her overpowering need would pass in time. But he knew it wouldn't leave entirely. He had to give her some leeway. But he had limits.

He didn't have the vaguest idea how they'd reconcile their differences. But there had to a way. He just hoped they could do it without killing each other in the meantime.

***

"You aren't going on a world cruise, Kayla. You'll still have access to everything that's up here. I just want you to limit your nightgowns to two for starters because there's only room for two. My closet's stuffed enough as it is with your damn clothes. I measured the space. There's only four inches left on the pole."

She transferred her gowns from her suitcases to hangers, putting them in her closet up here, now that she had the space from him having taken half of her things downstairs. She was getting more irate with every passing second. It was his idea she move some of her things down there. Now he was being bossy. "Why are you rushing me? I hate it when you do that."

Frowning, she sat down on her bed and fingered her floor length purple chiffon gown with the flowing sleeves which she hadn't hung up yet. "I really like this. It's one of my favorites."

"But...? I sense hesitation there."

"It's just that it's awfully sheer. I'm afraid it's too chilly down there." Bob clenched his jaw. "Then pick something heavier. Like..." he picked up her bright orange cotton gown with long sleeves, "this. It's bright, like you claimed you wanted ten minutes ago, and it's sturdy."

"Orange makes my skin look green!"

Deciding not to ask her why she'd bought it then, he took hold of a demure looking pink gown with a high ruffed neck. "What about this? This color goes with your skin, doesn't it? It looks fine to me, and its wool."

"But look at the length. It's much too short. I'd freeze."

"What about pajamas instead? They're warm."

"Tell me the truth. Would you be attracted to a woman who wore pajamas to bed?"

"Maybe. Maybe not. It depends on who's wearing them."

"Excuse me?"

"You want me to be honest, right?"

What did he expect her to say, 'no'? "Of course," she lied. *Scratch the pajamas.*

"Whatever you're going to decide on, do it fast. I'm giving you five more minutes. If you don't make a decision in that time, you'll sleep nude like I do."

"But I'd freeze!"

"If you'd sleep nude, I promise you, you wouldn't freeze."

"I hate to seem prudish about this, but you do realize my shape will change, don't you? My waist's going to disappear."

"But your *breasts* will increase, *dear.*"

"I've never slept nude before."

"You've never been married before either."

"My mother never slept nude."

"How do you know what she slept in before you were born? Did you ever ask her?"

"Of course not. I just assumed she slept in her gowns."

"Because she wore them when you were around?"

She nodded.

"You have a lot to learn about sex and marriage, Kayla."

"You've never been married before either! What makes you an expert?"

"I know human nature. I'm not saying all wives sleep nude. I'm sure they don't. But I'd like the woman I marry for life, if I ever go that route, to be adventurous enough to at least try it."

Did he mean her? She wondered. "After we have sex, I don't get back in my gown. That counts, doesn't it?"

He sighed heavily. "Not really. But if the idea scares you so much, by all means wear something. Just be quick choosing it."

"It doesn't scare me. Not exactly."

"Do what you want, Kayla. I haven't got time to psychoanalyze you. I know you'd love to debate the idea, but I'm pressed for time."

"Fine! Taking out the dark blue gown with the high waist and long sleeves she'd been eying from the other side of the closet, she extended it to him. "I'll take this one for sure."

Pushing aside gowns she hadn't transferred to hangers yet, he plopped heavily on the bed. They'd been moving down her things, bit by bit, since nine and it was nearly time for lunch, with still more to go. Not only was he getting hungry, he was tired besides. And he still had to finish Collins's drawings by his ten a.m. meeting with him tomorrow.

Taking her floor length, off-white satin gown with the daringly low, plunging neckline out of her closet, she turned her back to Bob as she held it up to her. She'd only worn it once, deciding it was much too risqué for a single woman to wear to bed all alone. Whereas now...

Dammit! She still didn't know if she had the nerve to go nude like he wanted. But he'd made his preference known loud and clear. And he had been cavalier about not having sex with her for fear she'd get sick again. If he'd really been attracted, he wouldn't have given up so easily.

"I'm not saying if I'll wear these or not," she muttered.

Bob hid his grin. He'd turn her into the kind of wife he wanted yet.

Chapter Seventeen

Exhausted from their morning exertions, Kayla was ready to drop. Where, she wondered, did he get all his energy? Unfortunately, not all people, including her, could tap into it, and now he wanted her to *cook?* She'd already done that once.

"I wouldn't call heating up tomato soup and fixing grilled cheese sandwiches cooking exactly. All you need's a pan for the soup and a skillet for the sandwiches. They're fairly light too, so you should be able to tolerate them." Watching him get out the things to make them with, she took a stool out from the cooking isle and rested her head on her hand, trying to stifle a yawn. After she ate, she was going to crash for several hours.

"You do know how to heat up soup, right?"

"Yes," she hissed. "And I can do it without scorching the pan too."

"Then come over here and do it. We don't have all day."

"I'm a little tired, so give me a break, okay?" she said, reluctantly getting up and placing the can under the electric can opener and pouring it into the pan. "And I know you're tired too. But let's try to get along and not be too testy."

"I'm not testy, Kayla. Just busy. Unlike you, I can't spare the time to take a five-hour nap this afternoon, like you did yesterday."

"Who said my nap would be that long today? I never took that long of a nap before in my life until yesterday. Usually they're just a couple of hours, unless I'm sick."

"Are you sick now?" he challenged.

"No!"

"Then why are you moving so slow? Can't you fix sandwiches while the soup's heating?"

"I *could*, if I knew how."

"Damn, Kayla! I thought at least you had *some* basic cooking knowledge."

"I do. A little. But I've never cooked grilled cheese sandwiches in my life. They've never been high on my list of favorites." Bob stifled his groan as he angrily buttered the bread. He knew he was being hard on her. But he was already tired and while she'd be taking her nap, he'd have to make some headway on those drawings instead of taking one too. Then this evening, instead of kicking back and relaxing, he'd be helping her move some of her things from her bathroom. As indecisive as she'd been this morning, no telling how long it would take.

The problem this afternoon wouldn't be exertion, it'd be keeping her from moving so many cosmetics she'd clutter up his space.

"While I'm doing this, put a little oil in the skillet. Not much. Just enough to coat it, and turn it on low. I always add a little salt and pepper to the bread after I've buttered it. Some people don't, but to me, it tastes better that way. Then just add a couple of slices of cheese to each sandwich and start browning it. That's all there is to it."

"Do you always eat two sandwiches?"

"Most of the time. You can have two too, if you want. I just thought it'd be better to see how you do with one first."

"One's fine," she muttered, yawning. "I'm more sleepy than hungry anyway."

"Try not to sleep as long as you did yesterday, okay? I know the doctor said you need your rest, but she didn't say to sleep your life away."

"You think I like feeling like this? I'm not doing it on purpose."

"I'm not saying you did. But I think you could benefit from a little structure. Why don't you set the alarm today for say, two hours?"

"Why don't you go to hell?" she hissed, storming out. "And finish lunch today yourself. I'm taking a nap where I can sleep as late as I want. Upstairs!"

Watching her little hips wiggle in those alluringly short shorts, and the idea which wouldn't leave him of her sleeping nude all the time, got to him. Catching up with her easily, he picked her up as she went up the first step. "Oh, no, you don't! Your place is down here with me."

He carried her into the kitchen so fast she thought he was going to insist she finish the damn meal. But instead of setting her down, he reached down, still holding her fast, and turned off the burners.

"What are you doing? I don't like the gleam in your eye."

"I was going to be patient and try to work with you. But I've changed my mind. We've both gone without sex for too long. What we both need is a good long fuck."

"Absolutely not! It's daylight out. I'm tired. You're hungry. And we've still got a lot to do."

"You're a prude," he murmured, sitting down on the bed with her still in his arms, and falling backwards, keeping a firm hold on her as she tried to scramble away. "It's time someone loosened you up."

"If I was a prude, I wouldn't have agreed to marry you."

"All that shows is you were desperate. But there, for a while, you were showing signs of promise. It's time we get that potential back."

Before she could spew forth the retort he saw forming on her lips, he cradled her head in his hand so she couldn't turn away. Sticking his tongue between her parted lips, he thoroughly explored her sweet tasting mouth, then rolled over on her, landing her on her back. With her blonde hair billowing wildly out behind her and her lips swollen from his kiss, she looked like a wanton angel.

Taking hold of her wrists with one hand, he pushed them firmly over her head as she resisted with surprising strength. He arched a brow. "You want to fight?"

"Do I?"

"Hell, yes. You have for a while now. I just missed the signs."

"There's only one way to prove it."

He reared back. "Yes, there is," he murmured, pulling her to a sitting position. "Strip for me."

"Don't push it, McKnight."

"I'm not," he said, getting up, bringing her up with him, standing against the door, keeping it closed in case he'd miscalculated and she bolted.

Kayla swallowed nervously. He had read her right. She did want sex. But she'd never stripped for a man in her life.

"You've seen enough X-rated movies to wing it, I'm sure," he assured her, reading the doubts on her face.

Damn him! He wasn't going to make this easy for her. She turned her back, crossing her arms over her breasts, starting to pull up her T-shirt, only to have him take hold of her shoulders, turning her back around to face him.

"Stripping requires you to face your audience. No maidenly modesty's allowed."

Jerking her elbows up to rest lightly on her breasts, she reached further in back with her arms still crossed, and slowly pulled up her shirt. Bringing it up to her shoulders however in the back, she was forced to stop. She wasn't a contortionist and without that ability, it was impossible to continue.

"The idea's to show your breasts, Kayla. Not cover them with your damn elbows."

"I know that! Just be patient." Glaring at him, she snapped the drapes closed. "Maybe this'll be better. It sets the mood more."

He shrugged, his expression not giving a thing about how he felt. Dim or light, he could see her well enough. Shutting the damn drapes didn't make it dark.

Pulling her shirt down primly, she walked towards him, not taking her eyes off his, which were insolently raking her body. Stopping roughly two feet away from him as he slouched against the door with his arms crossed over his chest, she took a deep breath, determined to get it over with quickly. Crossing her arms over her shirt, she pulled up her shirt as swiftly as she could without seeming to rush.

Letting her hair stay mussed, she held her shirt in front of her breasts for a moment, then dropped it and reached around in back, unclasping her white lace bra. She glanced at his eyes as she dropped it. But he still didn't move. His eyes still didn't change, except they seemed to widen. But the movement was so faint, she couldn't tell for sure.

Taking a step backward, she unzipped her shorts and bent over to slide them down to puddle at her bare feet. She wanted him to say something, or do something to see if she was on the right track. But he didn't. He just continued to look at her, his eyes slowly roaming over her body, not revealing a thing.

Taking hold of the elastic of her white panties, she pushed them down to join her shorts, and stepped out of both. Walking close to him, she stood there, nude, hoping her expression didn't give her fear away and wishing to God he'd do something before she lost her nerve and ran into the bathroom, and locked herself in there for a week.

For a long moment, Bob stared at her in awe. She was so incredibly young and inexperienced, she had no idea of the power she had over him at this moment. If she'd asked for the damn house, he would've given it to her. And his car, and hell, the whole twenty million!

Her large breasts were perfectly formed, thrusting out proudly, her light tawny nipples already beading with excitement, knowing what her mind had yet to grasp. It was hard to envision two babies were taking shape within that slender, flat stomach, not more than twenty-four inches around. Within her perfectly shaped hips and womb, their babies nestled, calling it home for the next nine months. How he envied them, knowing that, after their birth, they'd suck their sweet young mother's nourishing milk 'till their heart's content. Taking gentle hold of her wrists, he held them at each side of her perfectly shaped thighs as he bent to lightly taste her sweet lips, then her even sweeter nipples which beaded tighter as he molded his lips around one, taking his time, flicking it lightly with the tip of his tongue.

Looking up into her eyes, over which her lashes were lowering, he bent to pay homage to her other breast, molding his lips to it with the same loving devotion.

Staring into her eyes, he walked her backwards until the back of her knees touched the bed, then took off his shirt and shrugged out of his shorts and briefs, letting her thigh feel his erection as he bent her back onto the bed. She looked up at him with widened eyes.

"You're so beautiful," he growled huskily, propping himself on his hands on each side of her, pinning her arms to her side. Lowering his body to thoroughly kiss her parted lips, his hairy chest lightly grazed her nipples, which peaked delightedly against him. "So damned beautiful."

Kayla didn't need to hear anymore. Hungrily, she returned his kiss, her tongue matching his, thrust for thrust, not able to get enough of him, wanting him to touch her more forcefully, arching against him in her need. Gone were personality clashes and moral issues, replaced by the purely instinctive animal need of a woman needing a man who knew how to tame her and inflame her body, dulling her senses, making her body need his more than she needed anything else.

"Impatient?" he purred, licking first one nipple then another.

"Shut up and fuck me," she ordered, arching against him again. "Let me feel you. All of you, dammit. Now."

"Is that anyway to talk to your lover, babe?" he whispered, running his tongue over her silken neck, her soft throat; laving her full breasts and the valley between them until they were wet. His saliva mixed with the sweat of her exertions as she struggled and writhed against him.

"I want you!" she snarled, yanking one of her hands free, grabbing his penis tightly, massaging it before he could stop her.

"Dammit! I want to make this special, babe. I...oh God, Kayla! You don't know what you're doing to me."

Following him as he reared up, she scrambled beside him, taking his penis between her lips, running her tongue on the sensitive underside, lightly sucking the pulsating quivering tip.

"I'm coming, babe!" he warned, unable to continue to endure her sweet torture.

Grabbing his bare ass, Kayla hung on, keeping her lips on his penis as he stiffened, then his body jack-knifed several times against her, thrusting repeatedly until he was spent.

"Oh, God!" he moaned hoarsely, collapsing backwards on the bed. "I don't know where the hell you learned that," he raggedly breathed, "but I'm so glad you did."

Deciding not to tell him he'd been right; that she had watched her share of X-rated movies, she scooted next to him, cuddling his face against her breasts.

"You're a wanton wench," he groaned, kissing her breasts, unable to resist them even now, though he was spent.

"Yes, well," she murmured, "after you get your strength back, it's your turn to do to me what I just did to you." "Turnabout's fair play?"

"You've got it!"

She grinned.

"You've gotten bold, Kayla Leigh McKnight."

"I've missed this," she said simply. "I've missed us getting together like this."

"Oh, babe, so have I!" Running his face over her breasts, he kissed every inch of them as he sat up and scooted her onto his lap. "Lie back," he ordered, grabbing some pillows, putting them under her head so she could watch as his face bent over her, continuing to kiss and lick her, running his lips over her ribs and flat stomach.

"I feel like I'm watching an X-rated movie," she sighed, watching his hands play lightly with the curls of her thatch, teasing her erecting clitoris.

"Hmm. Spread your legs for me, babe. Lift them high. Show me what you've got."

Feeling like a slut and reveling in the feeling, she raised one leg slowly, bending it at the knee, then the other, spreading them wide.

Bob didn't need an engraved invitation. Like a hungry rabbit, he burrowed down, tasting her every inch, licking her quivering clitoris, kissing those protective folds over it as they swelled with need, her cum pouring out of her sweet little body.

Watching the broad muscles of his shoulders and arms work as he wrought his magic, massaging her as he kissed and tasted every inch of her, Kayla felt swept away on her own little cloud. She needed this more than she realized. No man had ever made her feel this way before. Chances were, no other man ever could. His body read hers like a book, in perfect synchronization, matching her moves in perfect harmony.

Suddenly, she stiffened, and as he relentlessly continued his ministrations, she lost it, spiraling out of control in the highest most intense climax she'd ever had. Reaching the pinnacle, she screamed his name, then floated gently back to earth, staring into his magnificent green eyes.

In that magical instant, she knew she'd met her soul mate, and in total peace, closed her eyes and was instantly asleep.

***

Equally astute, Bob felt the magical moment at the same time she did, and knew somehow a bond of perfect union had been forged between them on some deep level. But, unlike her, he didn't attribute it to just having great sex again. It went deeper than that, multifaceted with meanings they could probably never completely grasp.

Spreading out beside her, he covered them both up with the ends of the bedspread to ward off the chill now that their physical exertions had ceased. Soon, he was fast asleep.

Chapter Eighteen

Stretching, Kayla smiled dreamily as she saw Bob close beside her in bed. But looking up at the drapes, she realized it was dark out. The last thing she remembered was them having terrific sex…this afternoon. Dragging herself up, she looked at the clock on Bob's side. Eight fifteen? They'd slept, what, seven hours straight?

She'd always believed people don't sleep unless they need it, so she was tempted not to wake him up. But knowing he didn't share her opinion, she leaned over him. "Bob? Honey, I think you might want to get up. It's after eight."

Opening his eyes, he stretched his arms high overhead, coming down and surrounding her; he pulled her down to him, giving her a breath-taking kiss. "You're still nude," he mumbled. "I want you to start sleeping like this always."

That was another thing they didn't quite agree on. But since she'd never done it, she could at least try it. If she found she didn't like it, she could always put something on later. "All right," she murmured, receiving another incredibly spectacular kiss as a reward. Nuzzling his neck, smelling his fragrant after shave lingering on his skin mixed with the after scent of their having sex, she would've been content to lie there forever with him. Contentedly, she closed her eyes.

"What time did you say it was?"

"A little after eight."

He opened his eyes wide. "At night?"

She nodded, winding her arms around his neck, knowing he was going to get up, despite her not wanting him to. "We haven't really had a honeymoon yet. Let's declare one and take a few days off for just us."

"Sure, babe," he said, disengaging her arms, sitting up. "As soon as I can free up some time."

"You could tell Collins to go to hell."

"Yeah, right," he laughed, throwing off the covers. "I could tell him you said so too. That should impress him."

"You *could*. But you won't."

He bent down to kiss her again. "You're right. And while I get working on his plans, you can practice cooking."

"You're hungry again? We just...oops, no we didn't. We forgot to eat lunch."

"And I'm famished."

"I'll have to toss what you took out earlier."

"Better than getting food poisoning."

"True...oh, dang, I forgot to bring down a robe. I don't feel like getting dressed this late."

Taking a tee-shirt out of his drawer, he threw one at her. 'No problem." She held it up to her. "This is sexy."

"On you it will be."

She shrugged, pulling it over her head and stood, feeling the lightweight cotton as it slid down to cover her thighs, while the sleeves came down to nearly her elbows. "How's this for chic?"

"Very nice," he grumbled sexily, pulling her to him, cupping a breast, rubbing his thumb over her nipple that pointed out, puckering the thin fabric. "You do have a way of filling out clothes."

"Think so?"

"I know so."

"But what are we going to have for dinner? Do you want anything special? Or should I wing it?"

God forbid. But rather than hurt her feelings and risk her anger after they'd just made up, he didn't say anything and swatted her ass instead as he padded after her into the kitchen.

"What did you do that for?"

"It's a love pat."

"Some people think spanking's sexy. Do you?"

"The way I do it, it is."

"Are you gentle?"

"Honey, sex isn't always gentle. Sometimes it gets a little rough. But I don't get carried away. I've never hurt anyone."

She wished he'd stop referring to his experiences with other women. She was well aware of his exploits. "Are you planning on trying it with me?"

"If you want."

"I do."

He shrugged. "Your choice."

"But you won't get carried away?"

"I heard the doctor, Kayla. I'm not going to risk hurting you and our sons."

Sons? "Dr. Marsh didn't say I was carrying boys."

"I've already decided."

"You could be wrong."

"I'll bet a hundred bucks. You say it's girls?"

"It could be. Or maybe it's both, a boy and a girl."

"You only get one choice for our bet. What do you think they are?"

"Both girls."

"You're on. Now," he said, looking in the freezer, "what can we have?"

"I can fix spaghetti."

"Sure, out of a jar."

"No, I'm talking about homemade. I know how. It was the one thing my mom was able to teach me before she went in the hospital with breast cancer."

Damn! Why'd he have to open his mouth? "She had breast cancer? Oh, honey, I'm so sorry. I had no idea." But Kayla, he realized, wasn't listening. She was blinking back tears with a far-away look in her huge brown eyes.

As the kitchen faded and Bob's face was replaced by her mother's, she remembered standing, bending over her in a hospital bed. Her mom had just called her in, preferring to tell her the bad news herself.

"Are they sure, Mama? Maybe they made a mistake."

Her mother shook her head, her curls shaking. "They're sure. But… Kayla, stop crying. You've got to be strong for your father. He took it bad enough as it was. If he knew how affected you were, he'd go on a binge and end up killing himself."

"I don't care about him! It's you I'm concerned about."

"Honey, I've been married to your father for forty-three years now. I love you both equally, but you're stronger than he is, Kayla. You always were. Show your strength. Let him lean on you."

"How long do you have?"

"Six months, maybe a year. They're going to try me on some experimental drugs. I've already consented, Kayla, so close your mouth. If you say anything, I swear, I'll take you over my knee and spank you. You're not too old for that, young lady." As her mother and the hospital room faded from view and she came back to the present, she was unaware she was crying and just barely aware of Bob taking her in his arms.

"I was just... I'm sorry," she whispered hoarsely. "I was just remembering my mom when she was first put in the hospital. I don't know what caused me to remember that. I thought I'd forgotten. It was the worst day of my life, ever. I'd never seen my mother so strong, so determined to try and fight her cancer. And I, who should've been strong for her, went to pieces."

Bob held her tighter, stroking her hair, trying to soothe her, letting her cry it out.

"Six months to the day later, she died," sniffed Kayla. "Daddy went on the biggest drinking binge of his life that day. So, in between planning Mama's funeral, I had to look for him, and didn't find him until the day after I'd buried her, when the police called and asked me to identify my dad's body. He'd been killed in a barroom brawl the day of Mama's funeral. I've never forgiven him for that."

"Alcoholism exists in a lot of families, Kayla. But don't worry about our kids. They won't become one. We'll work together and make sure of it."

"I hope so. From what little my mother told me about it, he'd had problems since he'd been sixteen. When he married Mama, his family was ecstatic, knowing if anyone could convince him to stop, it was her. They were right too, apparently. She got him a job and he stopped for nearly twenty years. But then I came along, and he started up again. He was secretive at first, she said. But when she found him passed out on the front porch when I was about three or four, she knew, and got him some help. But he kept falling off the wagon. He never did recover. Not completely."

Bob reared back, looking her square in the eye. "But Kayla, surely you don't think you were responsible for that? You weren't, honey. Don't let anyone ever tell you that. If he'd been drinking since such an early age, he'd have used any excuse to get started again."

"That's what Mama said. She never blamed me. But Daddy did. Not that he ever came right out and accused me. He just kept telling me, on the rare occasions when he saw me, what it was like before I was born and how happy he and Mama were then."

"He was looking for a scapegoat, honey, and you were close at hand. People like that can't take responsibility for anything they do. I'm sure he blamed other people for his other faults and failures too. You are not responsible for your parents' troubles, Kayla. They were already formed by the time you were born. You told me they had you late in life, right?"

She nodded. Mama was forty and Daddy was fifty-five. They were planning to take early retirement before I came along. I don't think he ever forgave me. Because of me, he had to continue working another ten years to pay all the additional expense of raising a child."

"There was a fifteen year age difference between your father and mother?"

She nodded. "He married Mama on her nineteenth birthday, right after she graduated from high school."

"Well, he's dead now, right?"

She nodded again. "He was killed in a barroom brawl the day of her funeral. They never found out who did it. But the bartender claimed Daddy started it, so I don't think the cops looked all that hard."

Too bad he died, thought Bob. He would have loved to kill him himself, slowly and painfully for the hurt he'd inflicted on his little girl.

"Forget him, Kayla. You're with me, and you're safe. He can't hurt you again."

She reared back. "He never raised a hand to me. Mama was in charge of disciplining me."

Bob sighed, holding her tightly. "He hurt you in other ways, Kayla, blaming you for his drinking, for one."

"Oh, I never really cared what he said," she shrugged. "Mama was the one who raised me, who loved me, who took care of me. I rarely saw him. Whatever he said never bothered me. It was Mama who counted, not him."

Despite her bravado, Bob sensed she did care; a lot more than she'd ever admit. Her adamant refusal was proof. He hugged her tighter. "Tell you what, let's go out to eat. What do you say? There's an all-night place not too far from here. It's too late for you to cook." "No, it's not. You have to work. I've kept you from it too long." She kissed him. "You just go back to your drawing board, and I'll whip up my famous spaghetti sauce."

"Famous?"

"Maybe I exaggerated. But Mama liked it."

"That's a ringing endorsement, if I ever heard one. But it's past eight, babe. How long's it going to take?"

"A half hour at the most."

"For spaghetti sauce? It's that fast?"

"The way I cook it, it is."

Bob forced a smile as he reluctantly left the kitchen. But why, he wondered, did he have a strong feeling he'd regret this?

Fifteen minutes later, Kayla emerged from the kitchen and ran up the stairs. "No sense in you getting my cosmetics," she smiled. "I'm not going to bring down a lot. You just go on with what you're doing. Dinner will be ready in a minute. I'll bring you out a cup of coffee too. I just fixed a fresh pot."

Was that what he'd smelled burning, the coffee? But he hid his distaste and forced another smile. No sense in hurting his new wife's feelings. She was bound and determined to make him a good wife. He just hoped his stomach could stand it.

He didn't look up when she passed him ten minutes later. Out of the corner of his eye, he saw she was carrying a box, but he didn't want to see what all she'd brought down. Later, after she was asleep, he'd go in his bathroom and inspect it. If it was too much, he'd just take it all right back.

Stretching wearily, he sighed. It was going to be a long night.

***

Sitting in bed, keeping the sheet discretely tucked over her bare breasts, Kayla smiled at her husband as he joined her. "Did you really enjoy dinner? You weren't just saying that?"

"For the tenth time, babe, I loved it. Not as much as I'm going to enjoy dessert, but it was good. But you need to temper your enthusiasm when it comes to making coffee. It's one measure of coffee for every two cups, not every cup. I think that's what's the problem is."

"I thought men liked it strong."

"It's good. It's very good. But…if I drink strong coffee before I go to bed, that makes it hard for me to get to sleep."

"You say that like it's a bad thing. It might be kind of fun to be up all night."

"Behave, Mrs. McKnight. Unless…" He got up and sat on the foot of the bed. "Come here."

"Now? We just got in bed."

"Come here," he repeated. "You've been a very naughty girl. I have to spank you."

"But I'm nude. And the light's still on. It's late, too. Don't you want to get to sleep?"

"All the better to see you; all of you. As for sleep, I couldn't care less about it right now. So come here. Don't make me come after you. I'm being serious now, Kayla. Come here."

Hesitating a moment more, she took a deep breath. "Remember I've never done this before," she said, reluctantly getting up, dragging the sheet still around her for several inches, until he got up and headed toward her, then she dropped it. "It feels a little strange with nothing on. It was hard enough when I wore that skirt you first saw me in, but I was wearing something at least. I guess it's natural to be a little nervous right now."

"I'm sure it is. But I promised you I'm going to be gentle and I will be."

"I wasn't just talking about that. I meant walking around nude."

"I know. But you've got a beautiful body. You should take pride in it."

"Thanks. But it kind of feels like, I don't know…like maybe I'm flaunting it or something."

"I'm your husband, Kayla. You shouldn't hesitate to show me everything about you," he growled, spreading his legs, positioning her between them. "Like these," he whispered, kissing her pert pink nipples. "They're spectacular. Incredibly soft, yet firm. I could barely eat, staring at them poking through my tee shirt. You should wear more of my things. I'm serious. Wear them around the house. It's okay to turn me on, just as long as you give me what I want."

He was already fully erect. The way it was pointed straight up at her, quivering, she could tell how anxious it was to get on with it.

"He likes you," he whispered hoarsely, following the path of her eyes. "But he can wait. Now bend over my knees."

Starting to do as he said, she stopped and straightened. "You're going to use your hand, right? No belts or anything."

"I'm going to use my teeth too."

He was going to bite her? She felt the blood drain from her face.

"I'm going to nibble you, Kayla. All over. Just relax and do as I tell you. Now bend over."

Putting his arms on her waist, he helped position her. "That's it. Comfortable?"

"Yes," she lied, tensing, squeezing her eyes closed, convinced she was going to hate this. Silently, she cursed herself for not only agreeing to it, but actually having asked him for it. Had she been insane? She should've thought this out more. Why'd she have to be so impulsive?

"Relax, Kayla!" he ordered, swatting her ass lightly. "Loosen your arms. Let them fall naturally. Bend your legs too. Stop bracing yourself on your fingers and toes." *Had she been doing that?* Taking a deep breath, she did as he told her.

She was still tense, but not quite as much as he'd been a moment ago.

"That's better. A little." He leaned down, peering at her face, his breath fanning her face. "But open your damn eyes. If you keep on like this, I'm going to call it off. There's not anything to be worried about."

"I'm not worried. It's just that I've never been spanked. Mama was always threatening to do it, but she never did. Just the threat alone was enough to keep me in line."

Running his hand over her smooth bottom, he decided to go slow with her. She probably had been a sweet, gentle kid. She still was. Immature as hell, but blessed, or cursed as the case may be, with one fantastic body that wouldn't quit. He didn't really want to go through with it while she was so tense. But there was one sure way to relax her.

"Stand up."

"Now?"

He lifted her up bodily. "Right now. You need to start getting comfortable with your body and your sexuality. Might as well start tonight."

"I've already gotten comfortable with it."

"Not to my satisfaction, you haven't. I want you to show me how much you like sex by masturbating for me." Taking gentle hold of her waist, he sat her down beside him and pushed her further up on the bed so she was lying down, with her blonde hair spreading around her on the bed and over part of her flushed face.

"You're kidding, right?"

He arched a brow. "Do I look like I am?"

"No…but I don't really think this is a good idea."

"The fact you're protesting shows me it is. Do you want me to start you off?" he asked, lying down beside her on his stomach.

"No. I just…" *Damn, he's going to think I'm a prude now.* "I can do it." Placing a finger on her clitoris, she spread her legs to get a good grip on it.

"Start here at the top," he instructed, placing his hand over hers, moving it. "Now rub, slowly, then work your way down."

His green eyes were glittering with a look she recognized. Already he was excited, and she hadn't even started yet.

Closing her eyes, she started rubbing.

"Open your eyes and look at me," he instructed, leaning over her, kissing her pretty little nipples, which were already tight with anticipation. "Lift up those hips and wiggle them against your fingers," he coaxed, sliding his hand underneath her, pushing up. "That's it! Now wiggle more. Great, babe! You're doing fine."

She *was* getting hot by doing what he said. For a man, he knew a heck of a lot about a woman's body. He was getting hot too. The way he'd started perspiring, with the smell of his sweat mingling with hers and her cum, which started pouring out of her, was oddly intoxicating, inflaming her more.

"Now spread these pretty little folds of yours with your other hand. That's it," he purred, gently touching her quivering clitoris as it was fully exposed to the air. "Now, rub it, babe. Let me see it grow. Feel it harden? Look down at it, babe. Does it feel as good as it looks?"

She nodded, feeling out of breath, watching it grow, feeling it harden as her excitement escalated.

"Oh, that's beautiful, babe. *You're* beautiful." Putting his hand over hers to keep up the pressure, he kissed the sides of her clitoris and ran the tip of his tongue over the ridged rim.

"Perfect," he murmured, going lower, spreading her legs, continuing to lick her as he lifted up her ass. "You have no idea what you do to me, babe," he whispered fervently, continuing to lick her, pressing his face to her mons, sticking his tongue into her vagina as far as it would reach. "You're driving me out of my mind."

Stiffening quickly, Kayla held it for as long as she could, then her body took over, spiraling out of control as she convulsed over and over, surprised to find Bob crawling on top of her, plunging deeply into her, pumping her for all he was worth.

"Yeah, babe!" he sobbed raggedly as her cervix instinctively clenched his stiff penis as he mounted her more securely with his knees on both sides of her waist, his ass high in the air as he pumped, bracing himself up on his elbows. "You know what I like. Give it to me, babe. Give me all of it!"

Kayla stiffened again, then soared away as another earth-shattering climax overtook her, shaking the bed vigorously, the springs protesting squeakily.

"You okay?" he whispered, as they both finally came to.

Breathing hard, it was all she could do to summon the energy to nod.

"Good. Then tomorrow we'll do spanking." He winked as they crawled into bed and he turned out the light. "Oh, and before I forget, while you were cleaning up in the kitchen, I rearranged a few things."

"Of mine?"

He nodded. "Just a few non-essentials."

"My cosmetics?"

"I put some of them back upstairs."

"Dang it, Bob! I needed them all down here. That's why I brought them."

"They were cluttering up my bathroom, Kayla. But," he whispered, pinning her against the mattress with his weight, "don't worry. When we're out shopping for baby furniture, we'll pick up a little vanity just for your cosmetics. A small one should fit between the sink and wall in that empty corner."

"Great! One that size won't be able to hold much."

"It will if it's tall enough. And one more thing."

She arched a brow, not bothering to hide how miffed she was, unable in the after-glow of sex to get angry now at the man who excited her more than any other.

"Our appointment with the lawyers is next Wednesday at two. You might want to start getting your clothes ready early so you won't be rushing around at the last minute."

"I'd forgotten all about going there."

"I knew it was coming up, but forgot the date. Fortunately their secretary called and reminded me."

"And half my cosmetics are upstairs. Wonderful!"

"It won't be a problem. You don't need that much make-up anyway."

"I'm not real happy about this, Bob."

"I know, babe, but we'll work it out. I promise."

"Famous last words."

"Trust me. Everything will work out." Before she could say another word, he kissed her, pinning her hard against the cool sheets, refusing to let her up until he felt her relax and wrap her arms around his neck, wanting more.

Chapter Nineteen

"Kayla!" Bob shouted, getting his keys and brief case, glancing at his watch again. "We don't want to be late. These attorneys are fussy old guys. When they make an appointment for two o'clock that means two on the dot, and not a minute after."

All week, Kayla had been worried about what to wear there, but finally settled on her light-weight amber knit sheath with the cowl collar and long sleeves. Bob had assured her continuously that her stomach still didn't pooch out too much to wear clothes that clung to her shape. But she fussed with her hair, deciding at the last minute to wear it in a bun instead of long and flowing. She'd changed from diamond stud earrings to plain gold hoops. Light brown suede pumps with a one inch heel and her light brown clutch bag completed her ensemble. This was so important to Bob she had to ensure she looked her very best. But Bob, characteristically, was impatient to just get on with it.

"I don't see why you're in such a hurry. It's not even one yet." Before she could do another thing, Bob put his arm around her shoulders quickly and ushered her outside. "The Lyric Center's clear downtown, and traffic's always bad on Fridays. By the time we get there and find a place to park, it'll be two easily. I don't want to keep these men waiting. I want to get in there and out, as quickly as I can."

Kayla sighed. It was going to be a very long trip. Bob was as nervous as she was, only he showed it differently.

"You remember what to say?" he asked, getting her tucked into her seat and the seat belt fastened for her as if she was a child. "We fell in love at first sight, surprising us both, and—"

"I remember. And knowing we couldn't live without each other," she finished for him,

"We got married as quickly as we could, because we don't believe in pre-marital sex." She forced a smile. "See, I know it by heart."

That stupid spiel Bob had written out for her and insisted she'd memorize while she was getting ready irritated her. But to placate him, she'd gone along with it.

What worried her most was having a face-to-face meeting with people she considered authority figures. "I just hope they like me."

"What's not to like?" he grinned. "Besides, their main concern is checking our marriage license and looking over the doctor's report confirming you're pregnant."

"Hope you're right."

"Of course, I am. I'm never wrong. You know that."

"Right!" she laughed. But knowing how uneasy, and talkative or quiet to the point of being sullen, she was when she was around those she considered to be authority figures, she was on edge. That was one of the reasons she didn't want to be a single mom. She saw teachers and principals as being pillars of the community who'd be sure to look down on her, especially if she didn't work at least part time or have another easily verifiable source of income other than just child support. Unfortunately Texas didn't have alimony like a lot of other states. Only if a person was on disability did the State allow for that, and even then, women had to fight so hard to get it, many gave up and tried to survive on income well below the poverty level.

***

"Are you sure I look okay?" she asked for the tenth time in the elevator. All the way here, she'd been fussing with her lipstick and her hair, making sure the ribbon was straight, her lipstick wasn't smudged, that she had on enough cologne without it being overpowering. She was getting on Bob's nerves.

"You look wonderful," he assured her, trying hard to hide his aggravation, careful to keep a neutral expression.

But Kayla wasn't so sure. She'd only seen the Lyric Center from the outside, with its expensive statues and courtyards around the building. She had read about it online, and was awed by it before she ever stepped inside. It was clear that all the marble and expensive art adorning the lobby, the mezzanine, the elevators; everywhere she looked, cost a fortune. Office space rental was known to be exorbitant here, and carried a lot of prestige, and now she knew why. It was like entering a new world where only the privileged few were allowed.

Sinking deep into the red and white Persian carpet as they entered the outer office of the Stewart & Partners Law Firm, Kayla got quiet, studying silently the expensive oils adorning the white silk-covered walls.

Looking directly into the blue eyes of the stylish blonde-haired receptionist who was dressed in an attractive blue and yellow silk dress, her shapely legs clearly showing underneath her high, white faux antique desk, Kayla glanced at Bob and was immediately aware of his change of demeanor. Not only did he not look at her, the way he quickly straightened his green silk tie and smoothed his hair as he stared at the receptionist annoyed the heck out of her. The leech! The girl couldn't have been more than nineteen, and he was preening…for her? He was nearly old enough to be her father.

Kayla cleared her throat, eying him stonily when Bob glanced instinctively at her. Watching him turn bright red, she was a little mollified as he immediately studied the carpet, looking sheepish.

Unfortunately though the young lady didn't seem offended by Bob's attention, and instead continued looking at him, trying to catch his eye again as she smoothed her own hair.

"Please be seated," she said, in a surprisingly deep voice, to Bob's request to see Mr. Stewart. "I'll see if he's in."

"Thanks," Kayla said in her frostiest voice, before Bob could say anything.

The girl's expression hardened immediately into an unreadable mask. Talking for a moment into the receiver, she buzzed them in. "He'll see you now," she said, her icy tone matching Kayla's. It's the last door on the left."

Taking her husband's hand, Kayla literally dragged him through the heavy wood door.

"I'm sorry," he whispered as they walked down the long, narrow hallway, carpeted in shades of dark blue, with expensive oil adorning the walls. "I didn't mean to flirt. I just…I don't know…maybe it's a habit."

But Kayla wasn't about to be so easily appeased. "We're supposed to be a happily married couple," she hissed. "It looks bad for the husband to be flirting."

She had a point. The problem was, he kept forgetting he was married now. It was still new to him, and flirting was just a habit. It didn't mean anything. "Kayla, I'm trying. I really am. I have no intention of being unfaithful to you. You know that."

"Then prove it by acting like a happily married man. Because if you don't, if I ever see you do it again, I'll call these lawyers and explain our little arrangement. I swear I will. You've either flown your last fling or I'll spill all. Your choice."

"That's blackmail!"

"So? You started it—"

"Oh, hello," she said, forcing a smile as a surprisingly tall, gray haired gentleman, dressed impeccably in a light blue Italian silk summer suit with a highly starched white shirt, stuck his head outside the last door. "You must be Mr. Stewart."

"I thought I heard someone out here," he said, running his alert brown eyes over first her then Bob. "I recognize Bob, of course," he nodded curtly to him then transferred his attention to her. "And you must be his new bride, Kayla."

She nodded, letting him take her hand and lead her inside the large corner office with a spectacular view of downtown Houston.

"You're from Odessa, aren't you?"

Again she nodded, impressed by his knowledge. She sat down on the gray leather sectional couch he indicated silently. "Originally, yes. But I've lived in Houston for the past several years."

"Yes. And during that time, you'd had, what? Three, or was it four, jobs?"

It was pointless to lie. He'd already checked her out, apparently.

"Four," she admitted, mortified, wishing there was a hole she could crawl into and hide.

Mr. Stewart walked to the window behind his huge desk that was cluttered with law books and various stacks of legal-looking documents, and looked out. "You were last employed as an administrative assistant, weren't you? For Entex?"

She nodded, thankful her job, or almost-job at the Merry Maidens Topless Maid Agency hadn't been noted. "I was laid off four months to the day after I was hired."

"You're very young yet. Sometimes it takes people a while to find out what their niche is in life," he murmured. Smiling thinly, he watched a sweet-looking elderly woman enter, carrying a silver tray on which there were assorted beverages. She sat it down on the large coffee table in front of them.

"Mr. Johnson, my partner, will be joining us shortly," smiled Mr.

Stewart, seating himself beside her. "Coffee, tea or a soda?"

"Coffee, please."

As the lawyer and Bob exchanged small talk, Kayla sat back and sipped her coffee. The cluttered desk and sweet looking woman was, she decided, window dressing to hide Mr. Stewart's sharp mind. He was nothing if not well-prepared for their visit, and had let them know it by zeroing in on her. But she wasn't offended. She found herself admiring the old guy.

"How do you feel about your new husband inheriting twenty million dollars, Kayla? Think your life will change much?"

Kayla choked on her coffee. *Twenty million? As in six zeroes at the end?*

"Oh, I see you didn't know," said Mr. Stewart, patting her heartily on the back. "I'd assumed you did. Most men, I believe, would be inclined to share the knowledge of their good fortune with their wives."

Did he suspect the true nature of their marriage? She was willing to bet he did, even if he didn't know the details. "I knew he was inhering something," she mumbled, trying to catch her breath, glancing at Bob who was studying his coffee as if it was the most fascinating thing in the world. "We…we just hadn't gotten around to discussing the details."

"You must have known it was a substantial amount. Isn't that why you married him?"

There was no way she was going to match wits this man. He'd win hands-down if she tried. The best course of action was for her to tell him the truth. "I married him because I love him, fortunately or unfortunately, as the case may be. To tell the truth, I'd forgotten about the bequest completely. We've, um, been busy cementing our conjugal relationship and planning for the birth of our twins."

Mr. Stewart coughed, looking momentarily flustered, glancing at Bob, who was studying the carpet. "I see," he said finally, laughing as if he'd just heard the funniest joke in the world. "No sense in asking you how you like it. You're expecting twins though? How interesting."

"We're very excited. Bob and I both."

"Well, congratulations. Looking forward to motherhood?"

"Oh, yes!" She sat up straighter, leaning toward him. "I just hope I can be as good a mother as my own. There's so much to think about and plan for. We're going to have to convert one of the extra three rooms we have. We haven't decided which one yet. But I'm in favor of the one downstairs. I'm going to breast feed and I want them close to our room.

I don't believe in letting babies cry unattended. I want them to know they're well loved and cared for. And I don't want to separate them either. I want them to get used to each other by sharing the same crib."

Mr. Stewart smiled at Bob. But Bob merely raised his brows, his expression blank.

"He'll be a good father," said Kayla, rushing to his defense. "He's still in shock. We never expected twins in our wildest dreams."

As Mr. Johnson, who was Mr. Stewart's partner, entered, the talk turned to routine details that had to be attended to, and what and how many of each document the lawyers needed. Kayla tuned them out. She was concerned about Bob's lack of interest in the twins. He was attentive now that the talk had turned to things directly connected with the money. But his emotional detachment concerning his impending fatherhood bothered her. Was he trying to be casual just for show? Or was that how he really felt...detached? As for the twenty million dollars, Kayla was stunned, but also angry.

Bob hadn't seen fit to share the amount with her. Did he think she'd start asking for more money than they'd agreed upon if she'd known? Actually, she might have. But then he could well afford it. Hell, maybe she still would. Why not? She was doing most of the work. Not only was he getting the one child he'd asked for, but he was getting two. It also looked like she'd be mostly on her own, raising them. Why else would he seem distant when she and Mr. Stewart had been discussing her feelings about being a parent?

Chapter Twenty

As the months passed, Kayla found herself more content than she'd ever thought possible. Bob had been home every night, and he'd introduced her to their two closest neighbors. The Hendersons, on the right, were an elderly couple who were empty-nesters and treated their tiny terrier, who barked shrilly all the time, like a spoiled child. They'd even taken to broiling meat for it every night because, they claimed, it couldn't tolerate plain old dog food.

But the Fergusons, on the left side, were very much like themselves. Jim was in his late thirties, and his wife, Sharon, was seven years younger, and had recently celebrated her thirtieth birthday. Although they didn't have children yet, they'd been trying for several years, and had just about decided on artificial insemination. Jim was an environmental engineer, while Sharon had recently become a temporary secretary; more to have something to do, than because they needed the money. Kayla had taken to having coffee with her some mornings when she didn't work

Sex, as always, was great, and he'd held to his promise of being faithful. But she knew something was up. While he hadn't flirted with the receptionist as they were leaving that day they'd met with the attorneys, he'd been just a little too congenial for comfort. Not only had he bought her an expensive wedding band set with diamonds the following month, on their third month anniversary, he'd also relented on using his exercise room as their nursery, at least temporarily. Taking advantage of his generosity, Kayla promptly filled it with baby furniture the following month, then rearranged it every other week.

But this month she was so tired, she didn't have the energy to do much of anything. Dr. Marsh had taken to having her in for sonograms every month, but couldn't find anything other than the twins, a boy and a girl, were growing at a phenomenal rate. As a precaution, she'd told Kayla to lay off having sex.

To perk up Kayla's spirits, Bob had taken to bringing home roses. This was the third bouquet this week.

"Of course I love them," she murmured, inhaling deeply their scent, as she put them in a cut crystal vase. "They're beautiful. I just don't want you spending too much money on me, that's all."

Bob almost laughed, considering he now had ten million dollars in his personal bank account in his name, with the remaining ten to be paid when Kayla delivered. He could well afford his little gifts. But he was on too much a guilt trip to be in a jovial mood.

Not only had Kayla not asked for more money, she was proving herself to be a damn good wife and an excellent homemaker. She'd learned to cook and had started getting up before him every morning, having a good-tasting pot of coffee and his breakfast ready when he woke up. She hadn't tried to clutter up his room either, leaving half of her things upstairs.

But Bob hadn't forgotten how furious she'd been when he'd had sex that one time with a woman whose face he still couldn't remember. And if she was put off about him going to bed with one woman, how would she react if she found out he was going to a stag party for an hour or so, where the opportunities for going to bed with strange young women hired expressly for that purpose would be endless? Not that he planned to take advantage of the situation, of course. It was just that he wasn't about to miss the festivities of his best friend's wedding. In fact, he was planning on taking Kayla to the wedding ceremony itself.

But it was best for her not to know about the party tonight. Thank God it wasn't being held anywhere around their house; it was clear on the other side of their sprawling city, the far southwest, close to forty miles away. So there was no way she'd spot him.

And he had been working hard, finally satisfying Collins, and even picking up a new client in the process. He deserved a break, a big one. So he'd let off a little steam while doing it, so what? It was harmless fun, and didn't detract from how he felt about her. More and more, he realized how much he relied on her, enjoying talking to her, seeing her smile and the way her eyes sparkled when she was happy. It was almost like, well, love.

But other men who were going to be at the party loved their wives.

That wasn't going to keep them from being there, so why should he stay home when his other friends weren't?

He'd just have to think of a suitable lie to cover his going, hoping she'd believe it. Pretending to be absorbed in his task of piling her plate high with the crisp, fresh veggies he insisted she eat every night along with her dinner, Bob avoided her eyes, feeling like the worst heel that had ever walked the face of the earth. He couldn't wait any longer. He had to give her a reason he wouldn't be home until late Friday night.

"I told you about Larry, right?" he asked conversationally as they sat down to eat.

"He's your best friend, isn't he? You've mentioned him. We're going to his wedding Saturday, aren't we?"

He took a deep breath. In a way, he wanted her to believe it. But if she did, he'd feel lousy for being such a cad. Still, he had no choice. He'd promised Larry he'd make an appearance, and a promise was a promise.

"Yeah, well, we are. But me and Joe, another friend who you'll meet at the wedding, have been debating about whether to take him out the night before for a few beers. It's not a party or anything like that," he added quickly, forcing a brittle laugh. "It's kind of a guy thing. You know, we'll talk sports, rib him a little, and give him pointers about what it takes to have a good marriage. Stuff like that."

She hid her surprise. He thought they had a good marriage? Maybe he'd really changed, after all. And here, she'd doubted him at times. "Sounds like fun," she agreed. "So you'll be home a little late then, on Friday?"

He nodded. "I might be. Larry gets off work around six, so Joe and I'll meet him at a local sports bar; I'm not sure which one yet, around seven. I should be home about ten. You don't have to wait up."

She clicked on the remote as they settled on the couch to watch the upcoming movie while they ate. "I understand," she smiled. "But it depends on how I feel if I wait up or not. I probably won't. Here lately, I've been a real party pooper, I know. I'm exhausted nearly all the time again. The doctor says it's natural, though."

"You don't mind if I go? You're sure?"

He was clearly up to something. She could tell by how he avoided looking at her. Instead of looking happy like he should've, his smile was too brittle, his joviality too forced. "I trust you," she purred sweetly, making sure he felt guilty as hell for deceiving her. "I really do."

But surely what he was up to wasn't serious? He'd just admitted he'd thought they had a good marriage.

Impulsively, he kissed her, pushing her deep into the couch cushions. "Have I told you lately how beautiful you are?"

"About an hour ago. And I love to hear it. But ...you'd tell me if there was something wrong, wouldn't you?"

"Sure," he lied, turning away quickly. Although he could feel her looking at him, she didn't say anything more, and started eating. He felt like a good-for-nothing rat, having to lie to her, and wondered for the umpteenth time what in the hell he'd done to get such a good woman? He was no saint; he'd never pretended to be. So shouldn't she be suspicious now?

His mother was always distrustful of his dad. And Kayla was more intelligent than she had been. But like now, she looked so sweet, her eyes shining with love, her smile so sympathetic. Dammit, what was wrong with her? Why couldn't she see he was up to something? Women were supposed to set limits for men, weren't they? That's why his parents had such a lousy marriage. His mother; as distrustful as she'd been, and as angry, hadn't been forceful enough.

Hadn't Kayla learned that from her own parents? It sounded like her mother was the boss in her marriage. But she was a steel magnolia who, instead of showing her strength, had camouflaged it under the guise of love and caring. Hell, she could've taught his mother a lot.

Why couldn't Kayla imitate her? If she was trying, she needed to try harder. She was much too subtle.

Then again, he was glad Kayla was the way she was because he wanted to go without being hassled. It wasn't like he was going to go hog wild and fuck everything in skirts. He was getting plenty of that kind of action right here. Chances were, he always would.

But despite his sermons to himself and his steadily building guilt, he was looking forward to losing himself for a while, having a little innocent fun, having a few stiff drinks, and hell, even engaging in little, harmless flirting with an attractive woman or two. He needed to let off steam, which was natural, considering how much stress he'd been under lately. In less than a year, he'd gotten married, turned his house upside down and inside out preparing for two new arrivals, and his architectural business had nearly doubled. Not only that, he was now a bona fide millionaire, and that created its own kind of stress, being propelled into a tax bracket he was still trying to figure out.

He was also trying to decide on his goals, now that he had the money to do whatever he wanted. He could've given up his business, but he loved it too much. He loved the challenges in getting a prospective client to go with his company, rather than another. He thrived on the competition, the interaction inherent in his business meetings and luncheons with people in power. He was one of few men who actually enjoyed dressing up in a suit and tie, and, now that he had an attractive little wife who'd make a great hostess, he was planning on giving some lavish parties in the future.

***

Bob felt good as he walked into the elegant lobby of the Hilton Hotel, his footsteps soft on the plush dark blue carpeting as he strode past the uniformed hotel clerks that were busy checking in guests, then on into the narrow hallway of three gold-tinted elevators. Through the windows at the end of the hall, he saw the bright sun setting, turning the cloudless sky shades of blue, purple and bright orange.

He was tempted to take off his wedding band. But the thought of Kayla waiting at home for him, stopped him. Pressing the elevator button, he looked at the slip of paper in the pocket of his white sports coat. The party was up on five, in a suite of four large rooms, with all the other rooms on the floor reserved for couples that wanted privacy. Getting in the elevator with several other men he vaguely recognized who were dressed pretty much like he was, he nodded. As the elevator stopped, he sank deep into the plush gold carpet of the hallway, then entered the dimly lit party room, which was large and opulent in a deliberately gaudy way. Pictures of scantily dressed nymphs and Bacchus, the Roman God of wine and revelry adorned the muted gold walls. It was furnished with numerous large and small couches in gold and white silk brocade, scattered close to the plate glass window in a large semi-circle. The couches were separated discretely by large marble statues and other fake objects d'art.

The groom-to-be was over in a far corner, oblivious to his guests, his attention devoted to the bevy of sweet young things who surrounded him; all clad stylishly in expensive after-five designer dresses, but clearly had nothing on underneath. Although they were attractive, they were a little young for Bob's taste. He wanted a mature, experienced woman to talk to, to pass the time with. He was only going to stay an hour or maybe two, then leave as soon as he could get Larry's attention so he'd know he had come. But right now, Larry was too engrossed in feeling up the little blonde closest to him.

Joe was off to the left, talking to an attractive brunette with long dark hair, clad similar to the younger women around Larry. She was more Bob's style, older by about ten years than the others, but since Joe seemed interested in her, Bob walked on by, nodding to his friend as he passed.

Entering another good-sized room through an archway which had a sunken hardwood floor, he headed toward the long polished bar. Getting a double scotch from the uniformed bartender with the Hilton logo, he stood there, looking around. The rooms were filling up quickly with well-dressed men and even better dressed young, attractive women. All the girls were wearing high, spiked heels and it looked like none was wearing hose.

"Got a light?" whispered the sultry, feminine voice of a striking brunette whose long dark hair hung halfway down her back, which was covered by a black knit sheath which left little to the imagination.

Flicking politely the lighter he took out of his coat pocket, Bob studied her as he lit her cigarette. Her eyes were magnificent; green, sexy, and knowledgeable, turned up slightly at the corners. She looked like she was in her early thirties; just the kind who could keep him verbally entertained for the short time he'd be here.

"Buy you a drink?"

She nodded. "Martini, very dry, with a twist."

Getting the cash, he nodded to the bartender, throwing some bills on the counter.

"Beautiful night," she sighed, holding his eyes over the rim of her glass as she took a sip of her drink, and edged close enough he could feel her breast on his arm. "It'd be a shame to waste it."

Amused by her open invitation, he ran his eyes slowly over her. She was built with long, lean, endless legs and firm, jutting breasts that he was sure was the work of a highly paid plastic surgeon. Too bad that he wanted just to talk. That beautiful body would indeed go to waste. Still, it didn't hurt to try to get her to stay with him while he was here. Maybe she needed a break. Taking her elbow as the bar rapidly filled up with boisterous revelers, he steered her to one of the blue brocade couches in a quiet corner where they could talk without shouting to be heard.

"Are you into sin?" she asked, surprising him; sitting close, crossing one shapely leg over the other.

"Excuse me?" he asked, glancing briefly at her bare thigh exposed by the short dress.

"I asked if you're into sin, baby," she purred seductively, as she ran her long red nails over his thigh. "I noticed the wedding band."

"I don't cheat on my wife, if that's what you're asking. All I want to do tonight is talk for a while."

"Too bad," she pouted prettily, lifting her hand off his leg as if it had turned into a red-hot poker. "I'm not much of a talker."

Before he could think of a suitably witty reply, she walked away, her little hips swaying seductively.

He should probably change his strategy, he decided, sipping his drink, looking around the room again. If he didn't, he'd be bored stiff sitting here by himself, and he couldn't go home just yet. It was only a little past seven. If he did manage to catch Larry's eye right away, he'd be home in an hour, which might make Kayla suspicious.

Studying his ring, he debated taking it off. Would it hurt if he did? He didn't want to stand out, being one of the very few men who had theirs on. He wasn't as old as Lester, standing close to the bar, engaged in what looked like serious conversation with old Harvey. Both men were in their fifties, and both had their wedding bands on.

"Penny for your thoughts," said a sweet looking blonde off to the side of him, wearing a sleeveless, white, virginal dress of muslin, with a full skirt and two big pockets about half-way down. Although the V-shaped neckline was a little low, showing just a little of the valley of her perfect breasts, it was far from indecent, and much more conservative than what the other women were wearing. Nor did she look the least bit aggressive. In fact, with very little make-up on and her hair stylishly short; just long enough to cover her ears, she looked so innocent she seemed out of place. And while she was holding a drink, the glass was full, looking like it hadn't been touched.

"Just thinking," he murmured noncommittally.

"About your wife?" she asked, edging closer, following the path of his eyes.

"Yeah. We're separated," he lied. *What the hell?* It wasn't like he going to do anything other than talk. But he wasn't about to advertise the fact now, thanks to the icy reception of the other woman when she'd heard the news. "I don't want to talk about her," he said honestly.

"I understand," she soothed, looking sympathetic. "Do you mind if I sit down?"

He stood quickly as she seated herself. He was mildly surprised at how short she was, only coming up to the middle of his chest. "Of course," he smiled, inhaling her cologne. Like the girl herself, it was understated. "To tell the truth, I'd like the company."

"It's hard to face the possibility of being single again, isn't it?" she continued. "If it's any consolation, I feel like you probably do. I just got divorced three months ago. This is the first time I've been out in the evening since then."

Was she telling the truth? He wondered, studying her big clear blue eyes and flawless, oval-shaped face with a sexy little mole close to her pink lips. She looked younger than most of the other women here, including those surrounding Larry.

"How old are you?" he asked, trying to hide his suspicion.

"Twenty-one," she whispered. "Got married right out of high school to my childhood sweetheart. It just didn't work out."

If she was lying, she was doing it perfectly. Not that her age really mattered, of course. All they were going to do was talk. But he didn't have anything in common with an underage teeny-bopper.

She leaned back and crossed her legs, showing just a hint of her silk covered knee. "It's tough to be on the rebound, isn't it?"

"Rebound?"

She nodded. "Maybe you're not at that point yet, but I am. I miss Jimmy a lot," she sighed. "I'm so lonely."

She looked so lost, he wanted to comfort her. But how to do it innocently?

"A pretty girl like you shouldn't have any trouble finding dates. I'm sure someone close to your age will turn up."

"Well, I wish they'd hurry. If I have to sit alone in my big, empty apartment much more I'm going to go stir-crazy."

"You live by yourself?"

"Yeah," she nodded. "I moved down here right after my divorce. I needed to get away, you know?"

How was she paying her bills? He wondered. Not that it was any of his concern.

"So what do you do for a living?" she asked. "Know anyone who could use a good secretary?"

"I'm an architect," he smiled. "My business is so small I don't need any help at this stage. But if you give me your number, I can ask around and pass your number on."

"Oh, would you?" she asked, straightening. "I'd be so grateful." Patting her pockets, she looked so helpless he wanted to comfort her again. "I don't have anything to write with though."

"No problem," he smiled, putting his drink on the table, taking out his business card and a pen. "Write your number on the back."

She wasn't even wearing any polish, he realized. She was so different from the others; so damned innocent and unsophisticated, what was she doing here?

"There." She handed his card and pen back to him. "That's my name, Lauren. And that's my cell. I can be reached any time." Bob's face remained impassive, but he wondered how in the hell she afforded an apartment, a cell phone and, while her outfit was simple, it wasn't cheap. "Are you afraid of me?" she asked, leaning back as he drained his drink. "Or just naturally shy?"

Feeling the warm scotch heat the inside of his chest as it rolled down, Bob forced a laugh, leaning back too. *Was he afraid?* He'd just thought he was being cautious. "If I was scared of you, honey, I'd be long gone."

"But you're so different from the other men here," she whispered, putting her head against his shoulder, craning her neck, looking up at him with her clear blue eyes. "You haven't once looked at me like you wanted to kiss me."

Bob's heart sped up as he automatically looked at her pretty pink lips, so soft and so close. *Should he? Hell, it was just a kiss.* It wasn't like he was actually cheating on Kayla. This girl was so damned innocent, so sweet; she wasn't like the others who were seeking sex.

Inclining his head, he bent to taste, intending to make it brief. But somehow, he wasn't sure how, the kiss deepened and his tongue started dueling with hers. Her breath was sweet tasting, with a hint of liquor on her breath. For such an innocent-looking thing, she kissed surprisingly well.

Coming up for air, he pulled her tightly to him, feeling her firm breasts sear his skin beneath his white shirt. She was so compliant, so willing to please, what harm was there in giving her what she wanted?

"You're the most knowledgeable man I've ever had," she whispered, running her hands down his arms then up again, squeezing. "So big. So strong. You feel so good."

Dammit! Should he give her what she really wanted? He loved Kayla. But…there was something about this girl that drew him like a magnet. Then again… Abruptly, he loosened his hold as he pictured Kayla in his mind. He couldn't hurt her.

"Please, baby," Lauren begged, keeping her arms around his neck, holding him tighter. "I'm so lonely. I haven't had a man in months. I've been chaste ever since my husband moved out six months before we got the divorce. It's been nearly a year since I've, well…since I've been close to a man."

Looking down at those pretty pink lips, deeply inhaling her subtle perfume, feeling her pert breasts pressed against his chest, he wanted her so badly; his erect penis was straining against his pants so hard it hurt. "I…um…" He felt like he was drowning in those clear blue eyes of hers as she tightened her hold, wiggling slightly as she adjusted her hold, slowly rubbing her breasts against his chest. "I…oh, dammit," he hissed, crushing her lips with his, exploring her sweet mouth with the force of his pent-up hunger. She was so willing to please, she surrendered instantly to his sensual assault, meeting his tongue with hers, engaging in a frantic duel borne of need.

He hadn't wanted to do this. Hadn't planned on it. Had tried to avoid it. But the way the girl stretched against him, fitting her body to his, entwining her fingers in his hair felt so damn good, fueling his desire, he couldn't have stopped himself if someone had put a gun to his head.

"Oh, baby," she purred as he scooped her up, and headed for one of the private rooms. "You turn me on like no one's ever done before."

Looking down at those breasts of hers within inches of his lips, he no longer cared about anything but getting her under him and screwing her senseless, giving into his sexual need to possess her firm little body in a male ritual as old as time.

***

Kayla was nervous. Lying on the couch, feeling like a beached whale, she absently watched a re-run of an old movie she'd seen many times before. She tried to relax. But she couldn't. Bob had been in a strange mood lately and that worried her. Uncharacteristically, he'd merely picked at his oatmeal this morning, leaving half of it and bypassing altogether the homemade coffee cake she'd struggled to stay awake last night to make. She knew it tasted good. She herself had eaten three slices of it this morning.

Restless, she turned awkwardly on her side, feeling edgy. He hadn't come home for lunch after his meeting with his new client, which he sometimes did, not only for food, but to indulge his passion for her. Unfortunately, that was out of the question now, thanks to doctor's orders. Although he still seemed contented and satisfied with their relationship, he hadn't ever told her he loved her. Not once. Instead, he'd complimented her looks, her cooking, and sometimes showered her with gifts.

She knew some of his attentiveness and consideration, though, was because she was carrying his babies. Although she knew he'd never been around children, he'd try hard, she sensed, to be a thoughtful and devoted father. He'd already created a trust fund for them, and had signed over his life insurance policy to her, and had made a will. What the terms of that will were, she didn't know, but she didn't doubt she and the twins would be well taken care of in the event of his untimely demise.

She yawned as she glanced at her watch. Eight thirty. She'd hoped he'd give her a quick call to at least say good night. Maybe she should just go on to bed. Chances were she was concerned about nothing. She'd read pregnant women were sometimes more emotional than usual, especially with their first pregnancy. But try as she might to assure herself everything was fine, she still felt something was very wrong.

Surely he wasn't having a relationship with another woman? Or was he? She knew he missed having sex. She did too. But if she could forgo it for a while, why couldn't he? She was sure, on some level, he loved her. And she was beginning to suspect he knew it as well. Yet, he still hadn't admitted his love, damn him.

Getting up, she got another small glass of red wine, which her doctor had told her was perfectly acceptable. Maybe she was just jittery from being in the house alone at night for the first time in ages, even though she knew it was safe with the burglar alarm and Bob's gun in the drawer of the bedside table in case she noticed strange noises. Maybe they should get a dog eventually. Dogs were attentive to threatening sounds, and some burglars were even frightened of them.

The thing was she wasn't as scared by the thought of an intruder, as she was concerned about her husband. Something was wrong. She *knew* it was. But *what?*

***

Bob realized his mistake from the moment he threw the girl on the bed, following her as he jerked off his tie and tore off his sports jacket.

In spite of his desire to get her alone, his penis went limp as a picture of Kayla, pregnant with his babies, surfaced in his mind. With her love for him shining clearly in her eyes, she'd kissed him good-bye with feeling, telling him to have a good time. And what was he doing to repay her?

She'd be so much better off if he killed himself and let her find a decent man.

But as grandiose as that idea was, it did nothing to ignite his libido. Dispassionately, he watched as the girl struggled up and eased her dress down, revealing her low-cut, French style, pristine white bra with her abundant breasts spilling out of the lace cups. As attractive as she was, he desired his wife more. Maybe he was sick or crazy, or hell, just getting old, but that was the way he felt. Quickly, Bob draped his tie around his neck and hooked his sports coat with his thumb. "I'm sorry, honey," he said, extracting a hundred dollar bill and putting it on the bed. "I'm just not in the mood right now."

Although she hurriedly grabbed the money, Lauren had the good grace to at least look disappointed. "In case you're wondering, I am, um, what the other girls are. We all work for the same agency."

Bob nodded as he opened the door, disgusted by her admission, but not surprised. He waved to Larry vigorously enough to catch his eye. Then he left, feeling foolishly virtuous, but damn good.

Breezing down Westheimer, he opened all the windows, letting the wind blow his hair. Spotting a chili dog drive-through place, he stopped impulsively and got a half dozen. Kayla loved these things, and there was nothing he'd rather do than pig out in front of the boob tube with her by his side.

***

"Bob?" asked Kayla, waking up, confused, struggling to sit up on the couch. Had she fallen asleep? *Again?* This was beginning to be an annoying habit.

"I'm home, honey," he said, dropping his sacks of food on the coffee table and sitting quickly down beside her, kissing her with all the passion he felt.

"Oohh," she murmured, snuggling close, leaning her head against his chest, surprised by his sensual hunger. "I'm glad to see you too."

Holding her tight, Bob felt like he'd truly come home, not only physically, but emotionally as well. This was where he belonged. For the first time ever, a woman truly loved him, not for what he had or could do for her, but because she loved him. Maybe she just had bad taste, but he was going to do everything he could to keep her love and prove himself worthy of it.

Kayla sniffed the air. "I smell food." She inhaled deeply. "Chili dogs?"

He grinned as he extracted the flimsy paper containers stuffed with hot dogs, chili, chopped onions, and overflowing with melted cheddar cheese. "I feel like pigging out. Thought you might, too."

"You know I do!" With gusto, she put a mound of the paper napkins from the sack on top of her rounded lap and dug into the best hot dog she'd ever tasted.

"Anything good on TV?" he asked, kicking off his shoes, grabbing a hot dog.

"The usual. Re-runs. But I don't care what's on as long as you're with me." She took another bite of her hot dog.

Putting his arm around Kayla's shoulders, he hugged her to him and tenderly wiped some chili off her chin.

Chapter Twenty-One

Kayla sat up awkwardly in the pitch black room and glanced at the digital clock, wincing as yet another contraction assaulted her. It was just half past two and only five minutes since she'd had the last one. Did three contractions coming every five minutes mean labor? *Now?* At this ungodly hour?

Feeling something wet rush out of her, she scooted gingerly over to where Bob was snoring loudly. His being so peaceful when she was in agony infuriated her.

"Bob! My waters have broken. It's time." She punched him hard. "Wake up. I'm in labor!"

Bob opened one eye. "You're dreaming," he mumbled, turning over. "Go back to sleep."

Kayla punched him again with all the strength she had. "Something's coming out of me, and I've been having steady contractions for the past half hour. I wish I was dreaming. But I'm not. I need to get to the hospital."

With a sinking feeling, Bob opened both eyes. Then he realized what she'd said. "Are you sure?" he asked, popping straight up. "There's no mistake? Get your suitcase and I'll call the doctor and tell her we're on our way."

"There's no time," she screeched, breathing hard as yet another contraction took her breath away. "I tell you I'm in labor. Get me to the hospital. Now!"

Rushing out to the den, he picked up the phone and dialed the doctor's emergency number. "You aren't a trained physician, so you can't be sure. Just relax, babe. Trust me. You getting nervous like that won't do you any good."

"Oh, my God," she shuddered, interrupting him as she started shaking hard, as the strongest contraction she'd had yet slammed against her so hard she nearly saw stars. "Something's wrong! I know it is!" Slamming the phone down, Bob raced back in the bedroom and felt her forehead. She was warm. Too warm. Was she running a fever?

Racing back out, he grabbed the phone again, only this time he dialed nine-one-one with his hands shaking so bad, he misdialed three times. "Don't worry, babe," he called out to her. "I'm calling an ambulance. That'll get us there faster." *And get you some professional help, just in case, God forbid, something's gone wrong.*

Absently, Kayla listened to Bob on the phone. She felt so light-headed, so weak. It was probably better this way, she decided. As rattled as Bob was, they'd be lucky not to get into an accident if he drove. "Please God," she mumbled with ragged breath, bending over, holding her head in her hands. "Don't let me lose the twins. I'll start going to church. I'll do anything you want, only please let my babies live."

"They'll be here shortly," he shouted, rushing to the front door to open it so if he didn't hear them knock, they could come in. Then, heading into the bedroom, he turned on a light in his closet, and grabbed a pair of pants. Catching sight of the soaked bed with pink slimy things in what looked like congealed jell from the light spilling into the bedroom, his heart sped up. He quickened his pace, jerking out the first shirt he touched and putting it on.

Knowing that personnel at nine-one-one always made whoever was calling stay on the line, Kayla was skeptical as she laid back. But she was too dizzy now to summon the energy to question him.

"Can you sit up?" he asked, taking hold of her shoulders, bending down. "Or is it too painful?"

But just as she opened her mouth, another contraction shook her body. With sweat continuing to pour off her, the force catapulted her towards him, her head resting against his stomach, her hands clutching his waist.

Sagging against him, she blinked her eyes, trying to will back the darkness that threatened to overpower her. She was still furious at him which fueled her anger at Fate, too mad to meekly give into it.

"You don't care about me or the twins," she railed weakly. "All you cared about are the damn millions you'll gain if I deliver even one healthy child. As long as I satisfy the terms of that stupid will, you'll be happy. As if money can take the place of two precious little lives."

Having read some women get hostile in labor, Bob let her talk. In a way, it was good that she did. It showed she was still lucid and able to fight hopefully for her life.

"Don't give up, babe," he said, sounding far away from her, as she felt him steady her as he eased down beside her, cushioning her against his chest, bending with her as he eased her forward so she wouldn't pass out. "You've always had spunk. You need to get some blood to your head so you won't faint. Don't fight me on this, please. Just let me guide you."

If she'd had the strength, she'd have slapped him. Was he being condescending now?

"It's okay to hate me," he continued. "I know you do. But there's only one way to get your revenge. You have to make it through this, and I'm going to be right here, going through it with you every step of the way."

He was trying psychology on her now? How dare he?

"Paramedics," shouted a male voice coming through the door Bob had opened earlier. Male footsteps clattered down the entrance hall, into the den, and on through the open door of the bedroom. "Is this our patient?" he asked, coming immediately to Kayla.

She's in the end of her seventh month and is carrying twins. I think labor's started. She's having steady contractions." Edging up close to him, he lowered his voice. "We had chili dogs last night, and she ate four. Could that have anything to do with this?"

The man shrugged. "We'll know later."

He turned to Kayla. "Hi there, ma'am. My name's Sam and my partner's name is Jerry. Don't worry about a thing. We're going to take real good care of you."

"Jerry!" he shouted toward the direction of another man's footsteps. "We've got a premie mom in here. Get the stretcher, IVs, and breathing mask"

"Just take it easy, ma'am," he said, turning his attention toward her again. "I know you're scared, but try to breathe through your nose. It'll help, believe me. Me and my partner here have been doing this for ten years now, and have seen a lot of premie moms. You're going to be just fine."

Bob frowned. If that was the case, he wondered, why did the man look so worried?

"We're going to start you on some Magnesium Sulfate to control any nausea you may have," continued Sam, lifting her up with his partner, easing her onto the stretcher. "Then, as we make you all comfy in our luxurious bed some people call a stretcher, we'll give you some air to help your breathing, along with what your doctor tells us is okay for you to take to ease your contractions."

Spotting the microphone on Sam's shoulder with an earplug looking thing in his ear, Bob realized they were keeping in constant contact with someone, probably a doctor at the hospital who'd consult with Kayla's doctor.

Kayla tried hard to keep her eyes open, fighting against the constant tug of darkness threatening to overtake her. It was so lulling she was strongly tempted to give into it. There didn't seem to be any harm in it.

But then she didn't know if it'd hurt her babies or not, and she couldn't summon the energy to ask.

"Kayla!" shouted Bob, causing Kayla to come to with a jolt. "Please, honey, don't pass out on us. Not now. You've got so much to live for. Please hang on just a little longer."

"Breathe deeply through this, ma'am," Sam instructed, as he slapped an oxygen mask on her nose and mouth. "It'll make you feel better."

Feeling numb, Kayla felt the slight prick of the needle on the back of her hand, which was probably an IV, at the same time as a hard piece of plastic was placed over her mouth with two tubes going up her nose. She wanted to ask how much longer before her babies could come. She wanted to make sure they were okay, even if it meant delivering them right now. But her upper lip refused to move underneath the stiff plastic of the oxygen mask, and she couldn't summon the energy it would take to remove it.

"Let's get going," said Jerry, jumping in beside his patient as the ambulance turned on its blaring siren and screeched out the drive. "Let's get this show on the road."

Bob held onto Kayla's hand as the ambulance bumped and skidded along the streets, and then onto the freeway that was partially under construction. Looking at her pale face, which was soaked with sweat that continued to pour off her as she opened her eyes, staring at him with a vacant expression, Bob felt his heart break. He loved her so damn much!

"Kayla," he whispered, bringing her hand up to his lips, wanting to keep her alert, afraid she'd slip into a coma. "You've got to make it through this. I know you can, if you'll just try. Please, honey. If not for me, then for the twins. I know I told you to name them, but I've been thinking about their names too." he lied. "What about, um, Roscoe and Regina? Or Richard and Rochelle? I don't want a Robert, Junior." He squeezed her tiny fingers, kissing them. "What do you think about those names, honey? Do you like those, or are there other names you like better?" But Kayla didn't answer. She heard him. But her lips refused to move to form the words. Instead, she looked helplessly into his eyes.

Bob swallowed his tears. His world would collapse without her. She was the cornerstone around which his life revolved.

As the ambulance slammed to a halt in front of the hospital, Bob felt his heart slam into his stomach as the medical team went into action, with doctors jumping in and shouting orders, following Kayla out of the ambulance and into the emergency room, as nurses filled syringes and poked needles into her and slapped monitors on every bare patch of skin. Before he realized what was happening, he was sitting alone in the empty ambulance. Unable to hold back his tears any longer, he wept.

***

Bob paced back and forth in the tiny waiting room, feeling heartbreak. God was going to punish him for the way he'd treated Kayla and was going to take her away from him. He knew he was. He'd never been a religious man before, not ever, but he'd noticed the power of positive and negative energy. Surely there was a higher being who controlled the ebb and flow of such things, whether he be called God, Allah, or whoever.

Kayla believed in God. Maybe he should, too. Why not try praying? Maybe it'd help. "Dear God," he muttered, "I know you hate me, and that's okay. Just get Kayla through this, help her to give birth to our babies, and I promise I'll reform. I won't go near another woman ever again. I know what a terrible husband I've made her. But if you'll let her live, I promise we'll join a church and go every single Sunday."

He had no idea if God had heard him or not. He hadn't felt the sense of peace he'd somehow expected. But maybe God would look in on Kayla and see for himself the condition she was in, and help her.

He glanced at his watch again. Kayla had been in surgery for over an hour now. What in the name of God was taking so long? It was nearly five in the morning, and not a peep from anyone in the operating room with her. No one had entered the surgical area just a few feet away after the initial influx, and no one had come out.

Of course, he wanted them to take their time, to give Kayla the best of care. But surely someone, anyone, could have poked their nose through the double doors to tell him they'd stabilized her, or she was giving birth to fine healthy kids, or something.

He wanted a cigarette bad. But he didn't dare leave to go in search of a store to get some. Taking a swig of tepid coffee he'd bought from a nearby machine, he grimaced as he forced it down. His stomach was in knots and his head pounded violently. But he knew it was nothing compared to what Kayla was going through. Damn him! Why did he always think about himself? *She* was the one who was in jeopardy and the odds were stacked against her. Could she overcome them? He didn't know. He'd never seen her like this before, under this much stress.

What could he do to help her? Surely there was something. There had to be! Pacing faster, trying to think, he jumped when he saw, out of the corner of his eye, a large man in a pale green surgical cap and gown striding toward him. The middle-aged man's eyes were tired and red-rimmed with large bags under them. As he removed his mask, Bob's heart sank. The man wasn't smiling.

"You Mr. McKnight?"

Bob nodded, searching the doctor's troubled blue eyes

"I'm Doctor Skinner. I work with Doctor Marsh on her more serious cases." He sighed as he put his hand on Bob's shoulder. "I wish I could tell you everything's all right. Unfortunately, I can't."

Feeling his knees go weak, Bob fought the dizziness and nausea, and leaned back against the wall.

"We had to take the twins by Cesarean Section. So far, they seem to be holding their own, but it's too soon to know if they'll make it or not. They both weigh only four pounds. One, your son, has a tiny hole in his heart. It may heal on its own in time, and he'll be left with a functional heart murmur. But we don't know yet. They're both in incubators in the Neo-Natal ICU and we're feeding them intravenously. I think it would be a good time for you to look at them"

Bob felt the blood drain from his face. *In case they aren't there later?* "And my wife?" he asked, his voice shaking.

"She's holding on, but just barely. We have her in ICU, down a floor from the Neo-Natal unit. Her labor stopped before we got to her, so the Cesarean was unplanned. She lost two pints of blood and we had to transfuse her. She's very weak and is running a fever now, too. She goes in and out of consciousness. We've got her on oxygen and some IV drips to help stabilize her. But it's too early to tell if she'll make it or not."

Bob's heart stopped and he doubled over, as everything around him dimmed as a small patch of the gray linoleum floor rose to meet him.

"Get a grip, man!" scolded the doctor, sounding far away, as he put his strong hands on Bob's shoulders and yanked him upright. "This is no time to chicken out. You've got to be strong now for your family. They're going to need every ounce of strength you can give."

"Can I see her?" Bob asked, his voice so thin and reedy he barely recognized it. "Can I talk to her? I promise I won't stay long. But I have let her know I'm here."

Doctor Skinner looked him over with his brows furrowed.

"Please!" Bob implored. "I'm her husband!"

The doctor continued to vacillate, searching his eyes with a worried expression.

"Please! I've got to see her!"

"Well…considering she's asleep, I guess it won't hurt for you to stay a few minutes. But if you talk to her, whisper. She can still hear you, if only subconsciously. And I know how upset you are, but please don't tell her. She needs to be confident about her outcome. She's young, and if she thinks she can make it, she probably will." "I understand," Bob said, following after him.

"Take the elevator at the nurse's desk and go up to floor three. You'll see a sign directing you from there.

In a daze, Bob nodded, doing meekly as instructed. He couldn't lose her now. He wouldn't. Somehow, he had to make her understand she had to live. She was young, and, before her ordeal, she'd been in pretty good health. She had good doctors too, the best money could buy. And St. Luke's Hospital was one of the best in the world, so the physical resources were there.

Seeing the signs ahead directing people to the ICU, he started hyperventilating, trying hard to breathe, but unable. Falling against the wall, he tried to get himself under control, doubling over, bracing his hands against his knees. He didn't know what he should do. For the first time in his life, he felt totally out of control, as dizziness assaulted him. He'd never been this scared in his life. If she died, he didn't know what the hell he'd do.

"Can I help you, sir?" asked an elderly nurse who started to pass him by, then stopped with a concerned look. "Are you ill? Do you need to see a doctor?"

Bob shook his head, not voicing his thoughts. "I'm okay…I'm just… my wife's in ICU. The doctor said I could see her. But I'm afraid I'll just upset her by showing her how afraid I am about her condition."

"If you don't want to go inside the unit, you can see her through the window from the hall," she persisted. "It's an option we offer. All of our patients there are visible from the hall."

"Can she see me through the window, too?"

"If she opens her eyes, of course," she smiled, taking hold of his arm, walking with him. "There's nothing to be afraid of, sir."

"Do you think she'll want to see me?" he gasped, his steps faltering. "When she went into labor earlier, she blamed me for getting her pregnant." Although he'd dismissed it earlier, he started to worry about it. Had she meant it?

She laughed merrily. "This will be your first child, right?"

He shook his head. "We're, I mean she's, having twins. So we'll have two. But this is the first time she's been pregnant."

Locking his arm in hers with a vise-like grip, the nurse tapped her cheek with her forefinger, clearly thinking as they walked down the hall.

"Ah, yes. I remember her. She's our newest arrival."

He nodded, unable to speak.

"Ah, here we are," said the nurse with a complacent expression, taking hold of his shoulders, pushing him toward the window. "Look over to the right, there, the third bed down. See her?"

"She has her eyes closed. Is she asleep?"

"There's one way to find out."

Bob swallowed nervously, wiping his sweaty hands on his pants. "By going in, right?"

She nodded. "It's not that hard to do, sir. Just put one foot in front of the other, then ask her a question. If she answers, that means she's awake."

Unprepared for the bright lights inside the room, he shielded his eyes as he slowly walked into the long, oblong room with ten beds; five on each side. Each bed was separated by a long, light green curtain on rounded poles, open at the front. Except for the rhythmic bleeps of all the hooked up monitors, the room was as still as death.

Stopping at the bed the nurse had indicated, Bob started trembling as he studied her. He'd never seen her so pale. She was as white as the sheet she was laying on. Hooked up to three IVs and two monitors, her lower face was covered by a thick plastic oxygen mask With her eyes closed, and her damp blonde hair pushed straight back, she looked vaguely familiar. But … he looked down at the chart on the foot of the metal bed. This wasn't Kayla. It couldn't be! Had there been a mistake? Had the wrong name been written on the chart?

"This isn't Kayla. It can't be!" he whispered at the nurse who had come inside the room, and was standing behind him. "You don't recognize your own wife, sir?"

"Not looking like this, I don't." *But…but it was, God help her.* "Kayla?" he whispered, advancing toward her. "It's me, Bob. Can you hear me, honey?"

But Kayla didn't answer. Her eyes remained closed, her face was impassive.

Sitting down gently beside her, he took hold of her hand. He'd never been around sick people before, and it unnerved him. Especially since the person now lying there motionless in that sterile bed, and in that damned sterile room, was the woman he adored. "You're going to be fine," he whispered, hearing the squeaky soles of the nurse's shoes as she walked out. "The doctor said you sailed through the operation. And you should see our babies, Kayla. They're beautiful." While he didn't like the idea of lying to her, he felt he had to. Besides, they were small lies. "They both have your beautiful eyes. And…and my nose."

He looked her over carefully, trying to see any reaction, no matter how small. Was she unconscious? Or merely sleeping?

Lulled by the bleeping of so many machines, he closed his eyes in the motionless room, bowing his head down on the bed beside her legs. He wouldn't fall asleep, he decided. He just needed to be with her, giving her what little strength he had.

But what seemed like moments later, he was grabbed by the scruff of his neck, pulled up bodily, and shoved rougly out into the hall.

"What in the hell are you trying to pull by staying an entire half hour, and falling asleep on her bed, for God's sake?" hissed Doctor Skinner.

"That's a very sick woman in there. Have you taken leave of your senses?"

"A half hour?" asked Bob groggily, wiping his eyes with his fingers, trying to shake off the feeling of unreality of being woken up so abruptly.

"I'm sorry. I didn't plan on falling asleep. The last thing I remember was talking to my wife."

Opening his mouth, looking like he was going to say something, the doctor sighed instead, as a passing nurse handed him a stack of charts. "Why don't you go home and get some sleep?" he suggested, putting his arm around Bob's shoulder, steering him down the hall toward the elevator. "We have your number, I'm sure. We'll call you if your wife wakes up, or if there's any change in her condition."

Bob hesitated. He didn't want to leave Kayla, and the drive to his house would take an hour, maybe more. And how could he get to his house without his car?

"What're you waiting for?" asked the doctor. "I told you to go home!"

Great! He could risk a confrontation with the doctor who could, if he wanted, bar him from seeing Kayla for as long as she was in the hospital. Or he could just get out of there like the doctor wanted.

Bob twisted out of his grasp. "Can I at least tell her goodbye?" he asked. "I don't want her to wake up expecting to see me, then see I'm gone."

The doctor cocked a brow. "If you do, do you promise you'll cut it short like a good little boy?"

Starting to mutter something under his breath, he caught himself, and instead made an X over his heart and nodded. "Scout's honor."

Looking pleased, the doctor stepped aside. "Then be my guest. But I'll only give you two minutes. She needs her rest."

"I understand," Bob said over his shoulder, wasting no time as he headed quickly back to the ICU. "I'll be in and out fast."

"Why do I doubt that?" muttered the doctor. But as another nurse handed him a new stack of charts to look over, he headed wearily toward the nurses' station, with Bob already forgotten.

"Honey," whispered Bob as he neared Kayla's bed, taking gentle hold of her hand again. "The doctor thinks you could do better if I took a break right now. I don't want to leave you, but ..." his voice trailed off as he felt the subtle, but distinct pressure of her fingertips against his.

"Honey? Are you okay? Kayla? Oh, baby, are you awake?"

As he edged closer, examining her eyelids, he swore her eyes were moving underneath. It wasn't a lot. But he saw them tense and then start to flutter. Before he could make sure, however, he was pushed rudely aside by the starched flying white coat of the doctor.

"You were right, Sarah," whispered the doctor, addressing the nurse behind him. "She *is* waking up."

"I can't take the credit, Doctor. It was Mary who saw the change on her monitor. "Thank goodness. All her systems are beginning to stabilize too."

Feeling so relieved he nearly collapsed on the spot, Bob braced himself against the wall. "She squeezed my hand," he whispered. "It was faint, but I felt the pressure."

"Maybe you were right in paying her a visit," said the doctor. "She seems to have improved."

Taking hold of Kayla's hand again, Bob's eyes zeroed in on her beautiful brown eyes as she opened them, then closed them, then opened them again and stared directly into his. Dear God! He loved her so damn much! She was the most beautiful woman in the world. How could he have ever succumbed to the allure of the other women? Continuing to gaze into Bob's eyes, Kayla tried hard to focus and think. Where was she? Why did Bob look so worried, so concerned? The last thing she remembered was terrible pain and being wheeled out of their house. She recalled seeing the outside of their brick house pass by in a blur, as she was whisked into the waiting ambulance. Then nothing, except bits and pieces of passing scenery, the face of an older doctor looking at her with a worried look, and seeing an occasional nurse.

"I think we can remove the oxygen mask," said the doctor. "She's coming to. Let's see how she's able to breathe on her own."

Bob felt his heart break. Without the mask around the lower half of her pretty face, her lips were caked and dried. Very gently, he sat down beside her and dipped a tissue from the tray beside her bed into a plastic glass of lukewarm water and softly moistened her lips. "Oh, babe, I love you so much. I was so worried about you."

"My…my babies," she hoarsely croaked.

"They're fine, honey," he said, raising his brows, glancing at the hovering nurse for confirmation. "A beautiful girl, and a boy who looks just like you." The last thing she needed was bad news.

"Can…I see… them?"

The doctor came forward. "As soon as you're strong enough. Your job now is to rest. As soon as you're able," he continued hurriedly as she furrowed her brows and opened her mouth, "I promise we'll bring them both and let you hold them when I think you're ready."

Feeling guilty that he'd forgotten all about them, Bob made a mental note to go up there to check on them before he left the hospital.

Hopefully by the time Kayla saw them, their son's heart would be mended.

Quickly, the nurse eased her arm under her head to help her suck on a tiny ice chip the nurse's aide gave her from a Styrofoam bucket.

Bob searched her face, seeing a renewed determination to regain her strength in her beautiful brown eyes as she held her little head up to do obediently what the nurse wanted. Eager to help, he put his hand under Kayla's head as the nurse relinquished her hold.

Kayla was a lot stronger than him. Underneath her gentle exterior was a spine of stainless steel. How could he have missed it? Why hadn't he seen it before? He'd taken her so much for granted. And he'd nearly lost her!

Blinking back tears, he squeezed her hand. She was here now beside him, feeling his resolve to become the best husband in the world. This was where he belonged, where she belonged, until 'death do us part.'

Never had he thought of their wedding vows, even when he'd absently repeated them at their marriage ceremony.

Which reminded him; she'd wanted a church wedding. It was a little late, but why not? Couples renewed their vows all the time, sometimes going through the ceremony again. But he'd wait until she regained her strength to bring it up. The last thing she needed was to plan a wedding.

"She's doing very well," smiled the nurse, beaming at Bob as she took Kayla's pulse, watching her thirstily suck the ice, without trying to take the whole thing into her mouth. "If you keep up at this rate, Mrs. McKnight, you'll be out of here in a few days."

"You're in the ICU," Bob explained to her, getting another cube of ice out of the bucket.

"It's routine for new moms who've had a C-section," the nurse lied with a bland expression, as she removed two of the three needles in the back of her hand.

"I had a C-section?" croaked Kayla, tensing immediately.

"Just as a precaution," smiled the nurse, giving Bob a warning look not to say anything. "We wanted to make sure we got your babies out safe and sound."

"And they are, right?" Kayla asked, starting to relax and lean back against the pillows the nurse plumped up behind her.

"Oh, yes. Beautiful, they are too. I've never seen more attractive babies."

A wistful smile touched Kayla's lips as she wearily closed her eyes. "I...can't wait to...see them," she murmured softly, her eyes fluttering closed as she drifted off to sleep.

The nurse turned to Bob, touching his shoulder, motioning him to follow her into the hall. "She needs to sleep," she whispered. "But if she keeps doing this well for the next few hours, we'll be moving her to a private room this evening. She's making a remarkable recovery."

Going back quickly into the ICU before the nurse could stop him, Bob hugged his wife and kissed her cheek. "I'll be near," he whispered. "I promise you I'll always be, if you'll let me. But they want me to leave for a short while now, so you can get the rest you need."

Hearing the squeaky soles of the nurse head toward him, he kissed his wife again, then left without protest.

Epilogue

Smoothing down the floor-length skirt of her white satin gown, overlaid with tiny seed pearls, Kayla studied her pregnant silhouette in the large gilt framed mirror as Janna fussed with her veil and adjusted the glittering rhinestone tiara.

"Almost time," Sharon beamed, walking into the red and gold dressing room of the church? "How's the bride-to-be?"

"I feel ridiculous," Kayla laughed. "Here I am, three months pregnant with our second set of twins, and I'm getting remarried in a white dress to a man I've been married to for seven years now."

"You look lovely," Sharon insisted.

"You don't think I show too much?"

"No," she shook her head, averting her eyes. "Besides, it's not your fault you got pregnant after you'd reserved the church and Rockefeller's. If their waiting list to get these places weren't so long, you could've changed the date."

Taking out her lipstick from her tiny white beaded bag, Kayla started fussing with her lipstick, putting on another coat of baby blush pink, as Janna took two bobby pins out of Kayla's hair and replaced them with a rhinestone clasp. "I honestly didn't think I could get pregnant again. Bob and I've been trying three years now. And, wouldn't you know it, just as we got everything planned and the deposits paid, boom! I find out I've conceived."

"Well, I think it's very romantic to get remarried and have the wedding of your dreams," sighed Sharon. "I wish Jim would propose to me again."

"Hate to interrupt this, girl," grinned Dottie, sticking her head in the door. "But your groom's pacing."

Kayla took a deep breath and picked up her bridal bouquet. "Show time," she whispered, as Janna lowered her veil and the organist started playing the wedding march.

***

Looking at his bride as she prepared to walk down the aisle on the arm of George, through whom they'd met, Bob found himself falling in love with Kayla all over again. Her sweet, shy smile as she looked at their guests was so endearing he felt tears sting his eyes. He'd remained faithful to her, but then why shouldn't he have? She was the best thing which had ever happened to him in his wretched life. She instilled him with hope for their future together, and a steely determination to steer them in the right direction. He thanked God every day she'd come into his life.

"With this ring, I thee wed," he whispered solemnly, looking down at his bride with the love he felt showing in his eyes. "To have and to hold. In sickness and in health. From this day forward. 'Till death us do part."

Kayla's heart swelled with love, as he slipped the diamond wedding band onto her finger. As she repeated the vows and slipped his wedding band on him, their eyes met and held with silent love and understanding that caused her heart to soar. She'd never before believed in soul mates. But she knew without a doubt she'd found the love of her life that fateful day seven years ago, when she hadn't thought things could get much worse.

The end

About the author

Born in Houston and raised all over, Ayn wrote her first novel, "The Stormy Sea of Life" when she was eleven. It was never published, but it whetted her appetite for writing. To further her goal, she took journalism courses throughout high school and talked her way into writing for two school newspapers

Settling in Houston during her junior year in college, she soon met a man at church and married him in 1972. During the first ten years of her marriage, she started writing again and perfected her style. Then in the early 1980s, she sent out novel after novel, only to get rejected. Realizing something was amiss, she then pulled back and started on a smaller scale, freelancing for various newspapers and getting published consistently. But she never gave up her love for writing novels. Ayn has published four novels.

Latest titles from Black Velvet Seductions

Their Lady Gloriana by Starla Kaye
Cowboys in Charge by Starla Kaye
Holly's Big Bad Santa by Starla Kaye
Her Cowboy's Way by Starla Kaye
The Love She Wants by Mila Winters
Punished by Richard Savage, Nadia Nautalia & Starla Kaye
Accidental Affair by Leslie McKelvey
Right Place, Right Time by Leslie McKelvey
Her Sister's Keeper by Leslie McKelvey
Playing for Keeps by Glenda Horsfall
Playing By His Rules by Glenda Horsfall
Sympathy Dance by Sue McConnell
The White Spider of Savignac by V. L. Smith
The Stir of Echo by Susan Gabriel
Rally Fever by Crea Jones
Only the Lonly by Susan Gabriel

See more of our titles at
www.blackvelvetseductions.com

Our titles are available from:
Amazon
Smashwords
LuLu
Nook
and other retailers

Find Black Velvet Seductions on Facebook
And follow BVS Books on Twitter

www.ingramcontent.com/pod-product-compliance
Lightning Source LLC
Chambersburg PA
CBHW032143020726
47496CB00003B/687